# CARIBBEAN HARVEST

SHADOW TIER
BOOK 4

STEVE STRATTON

PRATTON MEDIA

# ALSO BY STEVE STRATTON

**A Warrior's Path** - The Lance Bear Wolf Origin Story
https://www.stevenstrattonusa.com/warriorspath
Finalist in the 2024 Storytrade Book Awards "Military" category

**Shadow Tier** - Book 2 in the series
https://www.stevenstrattonusa.com/shadow-tier
A 2023 MWSA Bronze Award Winner

**Shadow Sanction** - Book 3 in the series
https://www.stevenstrattonusa.com/shadow-sanction
A 2024 Killer Nashville Silver Falchion Top Pick and a 2024 MWSA Bronze Award
  Winner

# COPYRIGHT



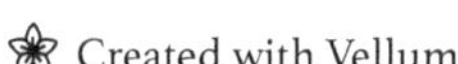 Created with Vellum

*For Elle who lit the fire.*

"Think of yourself as dead. You have lived your life. Now, take what's left and live it properly."
— Marcus Aurelius, Meditations

# PROLOGUE

2010 - Peruvian Naval Headquarters, Callao Naval Base

"Mister Cortez" stood on the pier inside the submarine pen. The flood lights consumed by the SONAR absorbent skin of the German Type 209 submarine.

It brought together the two key elements necessary to accomplish his goals: stealth and range. Its sleek waterline hinted at its hunter-killer capabilities.

Not a whisper of a thought six months ago, the Peruvian Navy's need for cash had collided with his hunt for a new means of secure transportation.

"Cortez" took in the enormity of his purchase. *I will take care of you*, he thought. It was like when he had found his wife; everyone had said he married up.

Admiral Xavier broke his reverie. "I apologize, Mister Cortez. We did not expect you to close the deal so quickly. We still have an additional two months of repairs and updates to complete."

"This is not a problem," Cortez said. "You have the secure space ready for me?"

"Yes. Do you require medical attention? My intel cell reported that the recent attack on your headquarters was a serious firefight."

"I am fine—it was a through and through," Cortez said, wincing at the involuntary movement of his shoulder.

"Good. I have received all necessary clearances so you can operate as you wish. When the updates are completed, we will perform sea trials, fix any issues, then deliver the boat to your base."

"As agreed, now, I need that room. My business never takes time off."

"Yes, sir. follow me," the admiral said.

Cortez followed to a conference room inside the submarine command headquarters. The placard on the door indicated the room had been assigned to Deep Water Engineering Services.

He expected there to be listening devices. His trust of the Admiral went as far as the eighteen percent commission he'd been paid to set up the purchase.

The other end picked up. "It's done. They will deliver the product in ten weeks," Cortez said.

"The support team?"

"Thoroughly vetted. They are taking part in the repairs, updates, and delivery of the product. The third party is thrilled and is giving us two defensive devices at no cost."

"Torpedoes... That could change everything."

Cortez cringed. *If that gets out, we could be sunk before we sail.*

# 1

Shadow Tier Headquarters MacDill Air Force Base Tampa Florida

It's 0600 and I'm standing in our headquarters parking lot with Elle Parker, the Deputy Director for Intelligence.

Elle also happens to be my wife.

Before heading into the office, we stop in front of our truck to discuss the ongoing shift in drug demand.

"The report I was reading on the way in was from DEA with CDC input," she says.

"They report users moving away from marijuana and cocaine to heroin laced with all kinds of stuff, including fentanyl. It's killing users."

"I bet it's a profit-driven decision," I say. "There will always be a marijuana market, but the big money is in the new hybrid forms of heroin. I can get lost if I stare into the enormity of the problem too long."

"Agreed," she says. "Let's get after it."

As we head to our offices, I focus on El Chapo. Some of my teammates who have been with me since the start refer to that focus as an obsession.

The Sinaloa Cartel's violence has been escalating, creating a cry for action, and the Mexican government is finally pushing back for real this time.

My friend—and blooded brother of the fight—General Carlos Gonzalez, leads the Mexican special mission units.

He has taken away Mexico as a safe haven for the cartel's leader.

The government's illegal crops eradication program is also having an effect and El Chapo appears to be looking for new locations to grow his products.

All I have is rumor and hearsay, but I believe there is something to the idea that he would look at Venezuela or Cuba to continue his expansion and market domination.

I drop my backpack off in my office and do a quick email check. There's nothing that can't wait, so I head to the Secure Compartmented Information Facility, or SCIF. We pronounce it skiff—like the word for a small boat.

*Time for the morning update.*

Across the table from me sits Thadeus, aka "Gus," Morgan, my number two. Since he's been working undercover, transporting drugs for the Sinaloa Cartel, I don't see him too often.

"Am I happy to see you, Gus?"

"Yeah, brother. All good. Kid has the details."

He's on Elle's left. To her right is Kid, his real name is John Wayne. He hates the ribbing he gets.

Kid is our Chief Technology Officer and manages our signals intelligence, cyber offense, and big data analytics systems.

He's also in charge of the analyst team we call the Wizkids.

They care for and feed Providence, the analytic and machine-learning based engine we use to sift through petabytes of data.

"What yah got?" I ask.

"We've got an NSA intercept, and a sighting of El Chapo at Aeropuerto Internacional Santiago de Cuba. He flew in late with his intelligence lieutenant, Ignacio Aguila," Kid says.

"He's a former Cuban army intel colonel," Elle says. "He transferred to G2; the Cuban version of the Agency combined with the

FBI. Two years ago, he retired and went to work for El Chapo. According to the Agency, he's well connected."

"Any insight on who they are meeting with?" I ask.

"Not yet," Kid says.

"What's the intercept say?"

"It's not what it says, but that it provides the location of our priority HVI," Kid says referring to High Value Individual.

"How is that possible?"

"Two ways," Kid says. "The first is someone placed a tracker on Aguila or something he carries. The second, and more likely, is Cyber Command or the Agency has hacked the Chinese Huawei cell phone he carries."

*I wonder if it's the Agency's new dust technology.*

When I raise my head, they're all looking at me. "Sorry… working the possibilities."

Morgan smirks.

"What?" I ask.

"Cuba takes a harsh stance on drug trafficking—to include the death penalty. We could save the taxpayers a lot of time and money if we sold him out in Cuba," Gus says.

"I like it. In Cuba, El Chapo doesn't have the people or infrastructure to slip away at the last second like he does in Mexico. I need to find out what's going on."

**2**

______

S hadow Tier Headquarters, MacDill AFB

Elle doesn't wait a beat. "Are you crazy? It's like saying you're going to operate in the Soviet Union. Or even worse, East Germany during the Cold War. It's a police state. G2 has infiltrated all parts of Cuban life."

"The Agency's assets are operating there 24 x 365. If they can, I can," I say. "The opportunity is too good to ignore."

Elle gives me stink eye. "Let the Agency work this one, Wolf. I do not want to live by myself while you're rotting in one of their hell-hole prisons."

I turn to get Morgan's input. His hands are skyward, indicating his surrender.

"Look, we can't provide effective support from here, even if the Agency takes on the mission. And no one else knows El Chapo like I do," I say taking a long pull from my coffee.

"I understand it's a non-permissive environment and the risk is higher than normal. But it's an opportunity to put him in a prison he can't escape. I'm going."

Elle surprises me: "You go; I go."

"Aren't you guys worried Russian intelligence has shared your dossier with the Cubans?" Kid asks.

"No. My last dust up with the Russians was over biological weapons, not drugs. China is their go to partner now." I say.

"Are you willing to bet your lives on it?" Morgan asks.

"We'll use a Venezuelan couple cover story," Elle says.

"How cute," Morgan says. "Come on, Kid, we've got work to do."

A chill runs along my spine as a lump forms in my throat.

I want to say no to Elle joining me, but going as a couple means less risk than my going it alone.

In the intelligence world, they call it profile softening.

Couples ping internal security radar with a lower signature than a steely-eyed singleton hunter.

My first stop would normally be our commander, General Erik Davidson, but I'm operating on the *'better to beg forgiveness than ask permission'* model.

I end the meeting and head back to my office, where I call a former special forces buddy, Price Kamis.

He's with the Agency's ground branch, and he's got connections to their maritime section—which, in my mind, is the safest way to infiltrate Cuba.

I always prefer free fall, but we can't get close enough to the island to drop in or execute a high-opening parachute insertion.

Inserting by plane or helicopter is too risky, and I place those modes in the emergency exfiltration bucket.

I'm also not a fan of the hot and slow "special compartment in a shipping container" idea, so that leaves only one other method.

And I'm not a big fan of it, either.

Since he got hurt on a mission, Price is working at the Agency's headquarters.

While recovering, he's been assigned to work with Matt Quinn, the lead scientist in the Science and Technology division.

Of course, Matt's nickname is Q. I hear he doesn't like it, but it stuck.

I walk back to my office, where I can access my Top Secret email account and pull his last email to get his number and make the call.

The encryption syncs, and the phone rings twice before it's answered.

"Quinn."

"It's Wolf, sir. Is Kamis around?"

"Wolf, how are you? You should visit. I've got some new tech that will interest you."

Quinn knows I'm a tech nerd. "I bet you do, sir. Does tomorrow morning work?"

"Must be important. I'll make it work. Stand by, I'll get him."

A couple of seconds later, Kamis comes on the line. "Wolf, what's happening, brother?"

"Got something in the planning stages and need a secure way to get across the Straits of Yucatán for an island vacation."

"Are you crazy? Why in the heck would you want to go there? It's like a police state."

"I must be... I'm hearing that a lot lately. My priority HVI is in Cuba, and I need to find out what he's up to and stop it."

"Okay, I know how stubborn you can be. I'll get the maritime section chief to email you a contact on the high side. You're not thinking submarine infiltration, are you? I hate those things."

"Not my favorite either, but I'll have to wait and hear what they offer. Tell them it's for Elle and me. We'll see you tomorrow."

"Cool. I'll work with Q to put together a selection of tech."

"Sweet. Out here," I say, and end the call.

Means of infiltration in process, I stroll over to Elle's office to tell her we are headed to Langley.

"Do you mind if Kid joins us? He can meet with his counterparts," Elle says.

"Good idea." I go back to my office to send the flight request to our aviation section.

While completing it, a new message icon appears. I finish the request and open an email with the title 'Dive Tours International.'

The message states that I can engage the operator directly at her website, and she has everything we'll need for mission success.

As is the norm for classified mail, there is a URL but no link, so I memorize it, grab my burner phone from the locker, and walk outside.

I enter the Internet address and access the website for the scuba diving and sport fishing business belonging to Captain Samantha "Sam" Williams in Cancun, Mexico.

The website features her boat: a large, sleek-looking Cabo 45 express, with dual, upgraded fifteen-hundred horsepower motors.

From the pictures and descriptions, it appears she has all the gear needed for transiting the strait between Mexico and Cuba.

Now all I need to do is pick a date and time.

Out of the accumulated hatred I've locked away over the years, a voice says, *The sooner the better. Avenge the death of your parents.*

I close my eyes, and an image of the black wolf stares at me, his yellow eyes venomous—and all-consuming if I stare back too long.

*Soon, my friend. Soon.*

I head back into my office and send an email request through the office of Elizabeth Harding, the Agency's Deputy Director for Operations.

I request a country brief and a sit-down with the team handling their Cuban assets.

Task completed; I head to our operations center.

Elle and Gus are poring over a map on the multi-screen wall display.

Built to project on a four-by-six grid of high-definition screens, the National Geospatial Intelligence Agency Map can be zoomed in to the foot level.

It is way more fidelity than we need to determine suitable landing sites.

"How did you know I'm thinking water infiltration?"

"Only thing that makes sense," Gus says.

Then Elle states what we all understand but dislike, "The Cuban-side asset will tell us the place and time."

"I know. But it's good to have a sense of the area and conditions we'll experience when we infiltrate. These maps have layers for everything. Gus, turn on the currents layer."

Like the winds aloft layer I use for parachute insertions, this one has arrows showing the current.

He adjusts the time forward and the tidal numbers in a metadata box change. We take turns gaming the infiltration, that is until Elle decides we are done.

"Boys and their toys. I'm hungry. Let's get lunch," she says.

With his famous pearly-white smile, Gus, my Hollywood-good-looking friend, holds up his keys. "I'm driving. The Longtab Pub has great wings and Cubans. Just what we need to get in the mood."

# 3

Tampa, Florida

Lunch is good, plus Elle and I get to watch "the man, the myth, the legend" in action with the waitress.

We tip well for her trouble.

The rest of my day is in my office, slammed with the administrative workload I despise.

As the years have gone by, I have been dragged, just short of kicking and screaming like a petulant child, into administrative and quasi-political roles.

I advocate for continued funding while fighting against the goal of some in our leadership chain to increase our mission scope into counterterrorism and weapons of mass destruction.

We've got more than enough on our plate fighting the drug war.

I hate that I must take time away from doing my job to respond to requests that would have Shadow Tier prosecuting non-drug related missions.

I'm in the grind of filling out yet another badly coded online form when my secure line rings. I recognize General Davidson's number.

"Wolf, when can you be in my office?"

Davidson's office is in the US Special Operations Command headquarters. "In the time it takes to log off and drive over, sir."

"Good, see you in fifteen."

"Yes, sir."

The US Special Operations Command, SOCOM is a short four-and-a-half-mile drive from our facility at the southwest end of the primary MacDill AFB runway.

I park and enter through the front door, scanning my badge and handing the guard my backpack.

Cleared to enter, I head up to his office on the third deck and knock then enter.

I find him perched on the front of his desk, relaxed. *It's unusual for my by the book Commander.*

"How long has it been, Wolf?"

I'm surprised by the question.

It was his idea to create Shadow Tier. He was there with the leadership at the meeting.

The same one where I was told I wasn't going to the stockade at Leavenworth, Kansas and instead starting a new unit to fight the drug war.

I can feel it in the air. It's like a whiff of smoke before being assaulted by the fire.

As I say the words, I'm dreading what's coming next. "Twelve years, sir...and please don't. We need you. I need you."

"Wolf, it's time. I'm twenty-eight years in, and it's time to give back to my family. My last day is thirty days from today."

I get it. He's a good man who recognizes the sacrifices his family has made for his career.

But for me, it likely means another step away from my teammates and operating.

I'll be caught in a cycle of meetings and trips to Fort Bragg, the Pentagon, and the White House; there will be little to no time for missions.

But he's not going to suggest anyone else take his place. "I understand sir, and I'm sorry if I sounded self-serving."

"It's okay, Wolf. Everyone has an operational end date… especially leaders like yourself. I've put forward your name as my replacement to the Secretary of Defense and the Agency Director. Both concur and have put your name forward to President Fairbanks and his transition team. You need to take the unit into the future."

"Thirty days and counting. It doesn't seem like enough time."

"It is. And now you know why I have been pushing more of the administrative load your way. You are about to become the notional CEO of a multi-national, multi-million-dollar business. I think you're ready, and I need you to start working by my side tomorrow. Together, we will make sure you have a smooth transition."

"Thank you. I appreciate it, sir. But we've got intel placing El Chapo in Cuba and I want to help the Cubans put him in prison. My team and I are headed to Langley to get a tech overview and briefing on their in-country assets before we complete our planning."

"Are you planning to go to Cuba solo?"

"No, sir. Elle and I are going as a couple. We can catch El Chapo outside his normal protection and support infrastructure."

"Crazy, or smart like a fox, I'm not sure which. I approve the operation, but whatever you do, don't let your emotions around El Chapo take over. If they do, you and Elle will likely spend the rest of your lives in a Cuban prison. I'm giving you nine days. One to visit Q, and eight to prosecute the mission. Then I want you both back in Tampa. That's an order, understood?"

"Yes, sir. Nine days."

# 4

-------

D<sup>AY 9</sup>

Joint Base Andrews Prince George's County, Maryland

To save a nickel, Elle and I, along with Kid, catch an early morning plane ride north with the Commander of Special Operations Command.

He's headed to the Pentagon for the day, so we take seats in the back.

It's not the luxury ride our Gulfstream is. The commander's aircraft is a converted tanker, configured for war fighting as an airborne command post.

But I'm an old soldier, happy with decent coffee and a plan for a Cuban vacation.

The only inconvenience is that we're landing at Andrews Air Force Base, twenty-nine miles from Langley.

After we land we grab an Air Force sedan and head south.

I jump on the DC beltway and turn on the radio to WTOP news.

We listen to the national and local events: Elle comments on the simplicity of living in Tampa versus the nation's capital. Kid is in the back, sitting quietly, taking it all in.

After we check in through perimeter security I head to our assigned visitor slot.

It's up front and unexpected. Q is outside and waves as we exit the car.

Elle and I head toward him, and Kid goes off to his meetings.

Elle hugs Quinn. "I'm so happy to finally meet you, Missus Wolf."

I laugh. "Elle Parker, say hello to Matt Quinn."

"Wait, what? You're not married?"

It's Elle's turn to laugh, and she takes his arm, walking toward the building. "No, no. You're right we are, but it's not always good to be associated with him, if you know what I mean."

Quinn's eyes dart between Elle and myself. *Good play, my wife.*

When we get to the building Price Kamis holds the door open. "I know what you mean," he says.

"Nice. I used to think of you as a friend," I say before man hugging and back slapping Price.

"Are you always like this?" Q asks.

I respond for the three of us: "Yes. Until it's time to get serious."

Inside Q's division, there is a low hum of activity.

Scientists, engineers, and techs are building, testing, and attempting to break all kinds of technology used by Agency personnel around the world.

There is a coffee bar with doughnuts, bagels, and yogurt. I pour a cup of coffee, doctor it with honey and half and half, then grab a cinnamon twist. "Elle, you want the usual?"

She's already moving to a different table—one loaded with tech. "Yep."

I join her at the table and give her a bottle of water.

"What's that?" I ask, pointing at a model reminding me of a shark.

"Good place to start," Quinn says. "It's our suggested method of infiltration. It is a mini sub designed to look like a shark. You sit in it like a kayak and its automated system will place you within one meter of your preset landing site."

Price jumps in: "It's built primarily for rebreather use cases in one atmosphere. When you get out, it swims home to the mothership—in your case, Captain Sam's boat. I've tested it and it's easy to operate. Not nearly as complex or creepy as a normal mini sub."

"But is it private proof? Remember who you're talking to. We're a couple of dirt soldiers, not Navy SEALs," Elle says.

"Yes, private proof and fully automated," Q says.

"What are the specs on depth, speed, and endurance?" I ask.

"It will operate at a depth of thirty meters, but you would need more air and to decompress. A Draeger rebreather is the best option for your mission profile, no bubbles," Q says.

Price puts his hand on the model. "Good news is, Captain Sam and her crew have deployed this system four times, and each one resulted in a successful infiltration."

"Okay, what do you have for us when we're dry?"

"You're headed into a signals intelligence dense environment," Q says referring to systems that can find and intercept all forms of communication with the exception of smoke signals.

"G2 and their new Chinese partners listen to everything."

He points to little cylinders that remind me of the salt and pepper shakers you used to get with an airline meal.

"These devices are communications simulators, Quinn says. "The pale gray units emulate cell phones. The black transmits continuously on radio frequencies. Squeeze to activate, then toss them into a river or the back of a car, or attach one to an animal. The bad guys will be chasing them for as long as three hours."

Elle picks one up. I know she loves this stuff too.

"You can have six of each," Q says.

No one outside our little group is in hearing range, so I ask quietly. "Have you gotten any further with your tagging dust?"

"How do you… no, never mind," Q says. "The answer is yes."

"What's that?" Elle asks.

"It's not dust, it's micro-reflective tags made up of fine particles," Q says.

"Apply it to someone or something, and we can track it from above, or…" Price picks up another device on the table, "…you can use this monocular to see the tagged individual a mile away."

"What are you thinking, Wolf? Using the tags as a backup in case Aguila isn't carrying his phone?" Elle asks.

"Yeah."

"That's a good idea, Price says. "I have experience with Russian trained Cubans—not leaving an electronic footprint is something they pay attention to."

The rest of the briefing is tech I am familiar with, so my mind wanders off to the elephant missing from the table.

There isn't a single item I can use to end El Chapo.

I guess I can beat him to death with the monocular, but my bare hands would be easier.

I suspect the DDO has her hand in this.

Elizabeth Harding is the type to worry that someone not under her control might assassinate the wrong person at an inconvenient time or place, like Cuba.

But, it's okay.

Unlike 007, I'm not licensed to kill; I only drop bad guys when they're a threat to my life or my teammates.

The beast I keep at bay roars at the thought of capturing versus killing El Chapo.

When the moment comes, I'll have to remind myself I am not an assassin, our policy and standard operating procedure is to capture first.

The briefing ends, and we thank Quinn and Kamis.

We amble to the cafeteria for a bite, and afterwards to the analyst briefing.

Good folks with lots of interesting profiles on Cuban leadership.

I get them thinking how El Chapo will attempt to subvert Cuban leadership with money—in my mind, it's his biggest motivator.

Elle and the analysts spend a good forty minutes talking about the counterintelligence forces and technology we'll be facing.

She's rightly worried we have an intelligence gap concerning Cuba and their new best friends: China's Ministry of State Security, MSS.

It's their national level intelligence services that, like ours, has a division in charge of foreign operations.

"When the Russians departed, they left behind all their technology. So, the Cuban's have the latest Russian SIGINT capability and now the next generation Chinese tech. We've seen it used very effectively in Africa," an analyst named Deron says.

"How do we beat it?" Elle asks.

The discussion dies with responses that are not uplifting: "We do not have enough data," and "Not sure. You could try that."

Then the analysts pile on, adding to the list of people, and now entire agencies, who think we are crazy for going.

As they say, knowing is half the battle.

I'm ready to fight the other half.

We say our thanks, collect Kid, and head to Andrews to catch the flight home.

I'm thinking the time for talk is done.

*Now it's time for El Chapo to have a bad day.*

**5**

D AY 8
Straits of Yucatan, between Mexico and Cuba
It's a no moon early morning, but the sky is dominated by the Milky Way.

The starlight makes it easy for me to see.

The water is warm as I slip over the side of Captain Sam's SAMMY II and join Elle in the high-tech shark we'll use for infiltration.

It's technology heavy and reminds me of one of those got-a-tool-for-everything Swiss army knives.

My hands tremble uncharacteristically.

I struggle to get my gear-laden five-foot eleven-inch frame comfortable in the seat.

A voice in my head is saying, *Slow and steady.*

I'm sweating and my stomach is churning at the prospect of this trip.

I'm not a Navy SEAL. I'm a dirt soldier. US Army Ranger and Special Forces. I prefer a parachute or helicopter insertion.

Two hours later, the automated systems have us headed toward our landing site, and I'm trying to identify the root of my agitation.

My rebreather works as it should, the shark is on course, and we have plenty of battery capacity.

So, it's not the infiltration itself.

Elle is sitting to my front, and I realize I'm second guessing myself.

*Was it a good decision?*

She's been with me since the start.

She's not only my wife, confidante, and best friend, she's also one heck of an operator.

A heartbeat later, I'm second-guessing our cover story.

*Will it meet the test?*

It has me doubting the wisdom of forcing this mission.

"GPS shows the current is pushing us south," Elle says, the full-face mask and communications system giving a tinny ring to her voice.

"Roger that." I check my console; the automated system has already adjusted for the current. "The system adjusted for it."

I fall back into my rumination's, taking some consolation that Morgan is ready to assist from his Key Largo base of operation.

He's less than an hour away if we need to bug out.

He always has my back—he's saved my life three times. He thinks the count is higher.

Morgan has been living the drug transportation cover story since he was contracted by a former El Chapo lieutenant that we took out of play.

The former insider is now in witness protection like her brother.

Morgan's penetration of the Sinaloa Cartel is the deepest we have ever managed.

"Four more miles."

I access the navigation guidance system and it flickers then settles into a part of the coastline that does not resemble the area we planned for.

We are south of the pre-set course, so I override the system to increase our speed and set a north-northeast heading.

*Is the GPS malfunctioning or being jammed?*

"Something is wrong with the guidance system," I say over the intercom. "I've gone to manual and headed north."

"Okay, but is it better to do a restart of the navigation computer and let it get us back on track?" Elle asked.

"Maybe, but as flaky as it is acting we could lose it."

"Roger that."

Elle's primary role during infiltration is to monitor the automated passive SONAR system.

It's not long after I set the new course, my console alerts me that there is a contact.

"SONAR classifies it as an OSA II patrol boat." Elle says, her voice tense. "Speed twenty-six knots. It's on an intercept course."

"Roger that. They don't know we are here or they'd be pinging their SONAR."

As the Cubans continue to close on our position, I use the intercom to ask, "You ready?"

"Yep." She peeks over her shoulder; she's getting nervous.

I hear the boat through the water now.

We have not planned for this, but the pre-mission intelligence briefing on Cuban coastal patrol boats identified the depth of keel and the propeller at six feet, and we are running at fifteen.

*Is nine feet of clearance deep enough?*

An image of President John F. Kennedy's boat, PT-109, getting cut in half by a Japanese destroyer flashes in my mind's eye.

I take a breath to calm down and stop my hand from shaking and squeeze Elle's shoulder.

She squeezes my hand in response.

I check my watch and think about going deeper just when the Cubans roar overhead.

We are slammed one way, then the other by the propeller wash.

My rebreather is ripped from my mouth, and I scramble to find the hose.

As I struggle to take a breath, my dry bag comes out of nowhere and the double carabiners that we use to connect them to mini-sub strikes me over the left eye.

Dazed, my brain is screaming, trying to tell me something.
I'm confused, struggling to put the pieces together.
Then it registers; Elle is no longer in front of me.

**6**

———

traits of Yucatan, two miles off Cuba

Cursing at myself, I take a breath from the rebreather before I push myself free of the mini-sub and head down into the darkness.

*Darn it, Wolf! Think.*

I turn on my dive light and kick as hard as I can.

The Kevlar line I set up to keep us connected rubs across my arm. It's taut.

I shine the light on it and want to shout.

I pull hard and Elle appears out of the darkness.

She is unconscious.

With my vision graying, I grab her vest and kick with everything I have for the surface.

When we reach the surface, I find the buoyancy button on my dive vest and release a long shot of air to keep me on top where I scan the ocean around us.

The patrol boat is motoring away, so I make myself a floating island and bring Elle onto my chest, turning her onto her side.

She's not responsive.

Her pulse is weak.

I open her mouth to drain out the seawater, then roll her on her back, inflating her vest to the max.

I focus on getting her to breath.

After four rounds of five breaths, Elle vomits seawater and starts breathing on her own in short raspy inhales and gurgling exhales.

My hands scrabble across her gear and I grab her spare air bottle.

*It's not oxygen but will it work?*

*I have no idea.*

I ask my spirit guide for help.

Several blasts of air and I'm hoping the extra pressure will bring her around.

I roll her back on her side, and she purges more seawater and coughs, the rales deep and wet.

She grabs my arm and squeezes so hard the pain is exquisite.

*She's my fighter.*

It takes another ten plus minutes before she's functional.

She's still coughing, but the vomiting has stopped. Elle whispers, "My head hurts over my left ear, what happened?"

"Our dry bags attacked us." I joke. "This blood is from a carabiner mutiny." I say pointing to the cut on my forehead. I get nothing in return; she's too weak to laugh at my bad humor.

"I didn't get us deep enough," I say.

"Did I… uh, drown?"

"Yeah. It's why it's hard to breathe."

The best thing I can do for her now is get her ashore and rested.

I'm not sure where the Shark is, so I locate the Big Dipper low on the horizon.

The two stars at the end of the cup point to Polaris, the North Star.

Now that I know where it is, I get my east-west bearings.

I start swimming a north-north-east heading, pulling Elle behind me as she rests on her back.

I scissor kick to rise and scan the ocean one more time. In the distance, the patrol boat is continuing south.

"You rest. I've got this," I say.

A short time later, I can make out the coastline in my night vision monocular.

The one thing I remember from scout swimmer school training, besides the cold, is the idea of flood current; we are being helped by the incoming tide.

I switch my monocular to infrared and use the reticle to estimate the infrared chem lights are four hundred meters to our southeast.

My joy at being this close is shattered when I get a better view at the top of a swell.

I see the markers are set in the abort pattern, two x's.

Elle surprises me. "Why are we slowing, Wolf?"

"The lights at our landing site are showing 'abort.'"

"We can't risk going back." Elle tries to catch her breath. "It's two hours until sunrise...what are we going to do?"

*We're out of time and energy. I'm not at one hundred percent, and she isn't even close.*

I check my impulsive thoughts.

*I nearly got my wife killed. I can't afford to make a rash decision.*

I close my eyes and picture the variables.

I see no alternative.

*We must go forward; we don't have a choice.*

"I'm skipping the infiltration sites and heading to the emergency exfiltration location. From there, we'll move inland and make contact."

"You go, I go," Elle says, coughing, then falling silent.

My heart stutters.

I would do anything to protect my wife, and I have a feeling I'll be doing it again before this mission is over.

I am not sure anyone has done what I'm about to do, but it will get us noticed.

The question is, who will see it first; our team, or the goons from Cuban intelligence?

7

Parque Nacional la Mensura, Cuba

Retired Cuban intelligence colonel Ignacio Aguila watched as El Chapo shaded his eyes. The test plots of opium are to their southeast and partially into the rising sun, making them both squint.

The platform they stand upon was built into the side of La Mensura mountain solely for this visit by the head of the Sinaloa Cartel. "Why so many plots, Aguila?"

"This is part of our cover story. You are looking at a pharmaceutical test plot. It is designed for the approved production of opium, which will provide much needed medicines."

"If the Cubans have control of this sector, why do we need to hide anything?"

*He still doesn't understand the threat,* Aguila thought.

"As your head of intelligence, it is my job to defend us against all threats, including American drones and satellites. They have no reason to be looking at this part of Cuba, but that does not protect you if the Americans reposition a satellite and it flies over this area. Their computers analyze everything now, not just the target."

El Chapo stared at Aguila. "You think like a Russian... it's overkill.

If we lose some, so be it. Our partners have tasted the profit potential and are acting like addicts, already demanding more money. I have them hooked, so I will take advantage while I can. The tests can continue, but you've got thirty days to get four-hundred additional hectares of poppies in the dirt."

Aguila followed El Chapo to his jeep and security team who were waiting to take him back to the safe house near Santiago de Cuba airport.

He stared into the middle-distance as he drove away.

*It always goes badly when El Chapo thinks he's invincible.*

Their G2 liaison, newly promoted Major Luis Ochoa walked out from behind a militarized version of a Chinese Geely SUV. They shook hands and the major spoke in Latin. "Mentor, it's been too long."

Eight years ago, Aguila picked Ochoa out of the streets and got him into a military prep school where he excelled. He had continued to mentor the young man and had brought him and his street instincts into G2.

At six foot plus, with a wrestler's two-hundred-pound body, he looked all business. His longer than regulation black hair and bright green eyes, a striking combination.

Aguila suspected Ochoa's recent experience during a nine-month mission to the Democratic Republic of Congo would serve him well.

Attacked almost daily, Ochoa coerced a young woman into spying for him. He had stopped the attacks by slaughtering the rebels and burning their villages.

Ochoa checked over his shoulder to ensure no one else was within earshot. "He is satisfied with the testing?"

Aguila related El Chapo's demand. "The boss said the Cuban leadership we have subverted is demanding more money."

"My asset said the G2 director has plans to bring the president's inner circle to the partnership and have them hook the president," Ochoa said.

"When he is done, Cuba's metamorphosis to the Russia of the Caribbean will be complete. They will be richer than they can imagine, and we can both retire, never to worry about money again."

"Interesting analysis and possibly true. But one day at a time, my friend. We have not set the conditions to guarantee success. I take it all the security preparations are complete. The park is off-limits?"

"Yes, sir. The Black Wasps teams are actively patrolling the perimeter. Their cover story is training for counter-drug operations."

The Black Wasps were the elite of the former mobile brigade.

Composed of men—and sometimes women—who operated in small teams of four or five personnel, they had undergone training by Russian Spetsnaz, and now train with Chinese special forces.

"Perfect," Aguila said. "Let's go to Lourdes. I want to talk with our Chinese counterparts about what the Americans have overflying Cuba. While Cuba itself is not a target, the facility is. And our new friends may yet prove helpful."

#

As they bumped off the steep and narrow dirt road onto pavement, Aguila released his grip on the front dash bar and exhaled. "What have you learned about our primary threat?"

"I have spent hours getting to know Lance Bear Wolf—his life, his time in the military, and his family. He is obsessed with Mister Guzman. He is a target that Wolf cannot refuse, and he will not care that we are Cuba."

"Exactly, how will you defend against him?"

"Defense, no. Once we fix his location, I will be the hunter and he the prey."

**8**

———————

Straits of Yucatan, one mile off Cuba

I swim parallel to the Cuban shoreline, headed for the emergency exfiltration site.

Even if the asset is captured and forced to talk, we are still good; the asset only knows the infiltration locations.

An hour later, with help from the strong current, I recognize the area from the digital map.

The surf increases as we near the beach and the line goes slack. I roll over on my back to check on Elle. "You ready for this?"

"Yeah," she says and coughs again.

A single thought pushes me forward.

*I need to get her to dry land where she can rest.*

I roll over and kick as hard as I can through the surf.

My line to Elle alternates between slack and taut.

*There must be an undertow.*

I realize I'm not headed straight in, so I swim at an angle to fight the current pulling us south.

We ride the last three-foot wave to the shore.

On my hands and knees, I scurry up the beach, pulling her beside me.

She flops next to me, wheezing and coughing. I hug her close.

I whisper, "This isn't what I expected after reading the travel brochure."

Elle coughs hard, her head slamming my chest. "Get dry."

I get my head back in the game and open my dry bag to retrieve my Lone Star Armory TX4 Duty Carbine. I had them made for those of us operating in Mexico and South America.

Its 7.62x39mm AK configuration makes it hard for the Sicarios to identify us in a gunfight.

I attach my suppressor then combo night vision and infrared monocular to scan the area.

Elle is doing the same. When I turn away, there is the sound of a wetsuit zipper being pulled.

I steal a peek over my shoulder; she looks like a native Venezuelan. Beautiful as always.

Quinn said the pills she took are an advanced version of the original pigmentation-darkening capsules developed for Studies and Observation Group in Vietnam.

"What are you staring at?" she says.

"You. Your skin is…"

"Darker?" she croaks out.

"That is the idea, right?"

In between coughs: "Do I pass?"

"With the pocket litter and your back story, you'll survive a spot check."

"Your turn," she says.

I dive into Mystery Ranch backpack and change into my dry clothes.

My satellite phone is in a mil-spec Ziplock bag in the top pouch.

I turn it on and hide the screen to block the light.

Once it's connected to the satellite constellation, I key in 2031, our code for dry feet, hit send, and stow it back in the Ziplock.

With our wetsuits and gear in our dry bags, I find a place to dig a hole.

I use my hands to set aside the top sand, then dig through the wetter sand until I can hide both bags.

I fill the hole and cover it with top sand.

Next, I grab some old grass fronds and sweep them back and forth behind me.

I do it from the tide line to Elle, who is now just below the crest of the final dune.

Footsteps erased; I crawl up the dune beside her.

There is an irrigation ditch fifty meters to our front.

On the other side, sugar cane at least twelve feet tall.

I lean over to Elle and whisper. "I'm nervous the saltwater has effected our earbuds. Let's replace them and check comms before we move."

She nods and we pull new ones from a side pouch on our packs. I whisper. "Radio check."

"Good copy," she responds. "How about me?"

"Good to go. Let's head south along the dike until we find a spot to turn east. The final checkpoint is five kilometers southeast of here. I'll take point. Let me know if I need to slow the pace."

"I can do anything for five klicks. Just go." she says, checking her watch. "Sunrise is in thirty-seven minutes."

I know she's tough, but I'm worried about post drowning edema if she pushes too hard.

Four minutes later, we are patrolling east on a track not wide enough for a vehicle.

*Are donkeys and carts still used to harvest sugar cane after the burn?* I wonder.

On my right is a wall of stalks much taller than those on the left.

I check my watch, thirty minutes have passed, and the sun is rising, but it's dark on this trail, and will be for some time with the height of the sugar cane.

I shoulder my rifle to scan ahead with night vision.

Three men are facing the north side crop.

I motion to my wife, and we slip into the dense plot.

I want these guys to move by sooner than later; we still have two and a half kilometers to go.

They're taking their time. Finally, after several long minutes, they pass us.

When I estimate they are 150 meters to our west, we leave the sugar cane and start walking with a purpose.

I'm focused on the intersection ahead when Elle comes over my earbud. "Do you smell it?"

I keep moving, but pay attention to the air.

The odor registers a second or two before the crackling sound.

I stop and we watch the flames grow.

The area we are headed to—between us and the checkpoint—is being burned prior to harvesting.

I point to the crossroads. "Let's pick up the pace."

She takes off jogging.

I follow and hear her rales and coughing, so I run past her and stop at the intersection.

It's clear ahead, but the roar of the fire drowns all other sounds, so I need to check the crossing road.

I peak out past the cane.

To the north there is an Army truck with men pouring out the back. In the opposite direction, there is a six-man patrol whose leader is pointing my way.

*Rookie mistake, Wolf.*

I spin to Elle. "Turn off your comms. We've got company. I'll lead them away like we did on the reservation."

"Okay, I'll hide in this field, and won't move until twenty-two hundred. Then I'll head to the next checkpoint." Elle says.

"Forever plus two."

"Don't be a hero, Wolf. Forever plus two."

Forever plus two is our code, for I love you forever plus two weeks.

Our version of "I love you... I love you more."

She leaps into the sugar cane, and I take off back the way we've just come.

Knees high, I sprint away, hoping this is not the last time I see my wife.

*Why did I push so hard for this mission?*

My plan is to run the escape and evasion corridor in reverse, so Elle heading to the next checkpoint inland on the route is the right move.

*Are our transmissions giving us away?*

I run back toward the fire and smoke, when it crosses my mind that the Chinese might be supporting the Cuban Army now.

Bullets zip by and I lose those thoughts, running for my life.

# 9

Southern Coast, Cuba

Forced to the north side of the track between the sugar cane fields, I sprint by the wall of flames.

My face reddens as my eyes water from the smoke. It hurts to breathe through my nose.

Still burning sugar cane leaves float on the air, their dance mesmerizing if not for the soldiers trying their best to kill me.

I slide as if heading into third base in the middle of the track and rotate onto my stomach, the torrent of bullets filling the air overhead.

I empty my magazine, shooting on full auto, sweeping my barrel back-and-forth knee high across the road.

There are screams and the gunfire drops.

I scramble to my feet and run.

At the first intersection, I go north.

The E&E corridor included a tidal canal on its north side, which the map software estimated at sixteen feet wide.

Like my SEAL teammates, I see salvation in getting wet.

Effective gunfire starts closing in.

I run the last thirty meters zigzag, then spin my TX4 behind me and do my best Tarzan into the canal.

I swim under water into some reeds where I surface and find a floating chunk of tree branch sailing by and grab it.

*The tide is going out.*

I grab a black micro transmitter from my cargo pocket, squeeze it, jam it into a notch in the branch, then send it on its way.

I pull myself deeper into the muck and bring my rifle to my left, in case this plan goes sideways.

In the reeds, I surface just enough to bring my eyes and nose out of the water.

Through the stalks, I see trucks arriving and men piling out.

A Chinese officer in a blue beret is giving orders when another man steps from the cab.

He speaks into a handheld radio while looking toward the sky.

His shoulder patch indicates he's with the People's Liberation Army Ground Forces, PLAGF a unit like our 75th Ranger Regiment.

I don't understand what he's saying, but seconds later a drone buzzes overhead, following the canal toward the sea.

*Maybe Q's tech worked.*

I'm relieved for a second... until the officer yells and waves his hand along the canal.

I submerge and shrug off my backpack, holding it in front of my torso.

It's got a built-in, level IIIA bulletproof soft insert, which, with the water just might save my life.

I pull my emergency air bottle from a side pocket and inhale a shot, my brain enjoying the effect.

Suddenly, the shooting starts, and the muted sounds increase as the bullets get nearer.

The reeds are falling around me and I'm thumped as two rounds hit the backpack.

One penetrates the vest and hits the container I'm holding, nearly ripping it from my hand.

It's spewing air, so I put my hand over the jagged tear and pray the soldiers don't see the bubbles.

The shooting stops and I take another breath from the bottle, which gets cut short as the oxygen runs out.

There are muted voices, then the trucks rev their engines.

I'm at the edge of my breath-holding ability, but afraid to surface.

I accept the discomfort as the noise and vibrations from the trucks wane.

Cracking, the surface with my nose, I take in some water-tinged goodness, then start moving the opposite way of the soldiers.

I want to get two more intersections to the east.

*Away from where I got discovered.*

At 2 kilometers in, I clear away the scum to use my Sawyer filter and sip the cool water.

*It's fresh.*

*Good; check saltwater crocodiles off the list.*

*Now it's just snakes and alligators.*

I scold myself for even thinking about water lizards.

As sure as my name is Wolf, eyes and part of a head appear to my left.

Luckily, his or her eyes are only the width of three fingers apart.

The closer the eyes, the younger the animal—and less likely they are to attack someone of my size.

When the eyes disappear beneath the surface, my hand instinctively goes to my Randall knife.

Just a reassuring touch to make sure it's where I expect it to be.

I realize I've been holding my breath and exhale, then continue my combination mud-walk and swim east.

By the time I get to the intersection I want, the sun is overhead and the humidity is thick.

The slightest wisp of smoke hangs in the air, the light breeze doing little to move it out.

I listen for two minutes, then drag my sorry self out of the canal.

I cross over into a field of sugar cane that doesn't look ready to burn, and get as deep as I can, pulling the canes closed behind me.

When I find a tiny open spot where the seeds must have failed, I pull my camo netting from my pack and tie it overhead.

I stop and listen again; the faintest of vehicle sounds seem distant, so I take the vest out of my pack.

One bullet slowed enough that the insert stopped it, the other penetrated the insert and my backpack too.

The air bottle was the only thing keeping me from being gut shot in a slimy canal.

*I'm good with being lucky, but never plan on it.*

Now I need to get this mission back on track.

# 10

---

El Chapo Safe House South of Santiago de Cuba Airport

Ochoa stormed into El Chapo's safe house.

Less than a mile from the airport, it also provided easy access to the Transcargo Cuba facility, which would serve as the warehouse before product shipment to America.

"Your radio transmission was clipped. Did any of your men get a look at him?" Aguila asked, peering over his computer.

"Yes, but from a distance, through smoke and fire. They described him as six foot tall and dark hair."

Aguila recognized his agitation. "Come. I need coffee." He walked into the kitchen and poured a cup for his "wrecking ball," then poured one for himself.

"Our coast watchers put us in the right area," Ochoa continued. "But the farmers are doing their pre-harvest sugar cane burn... he used it to his advantage. They say he runs like a gazelle. The Chinese lost him at a canal but traced his signal to the beach, where it disappeared."

Aguila stared out the window beyond the MI-2 helicopter his protégée had arrived in. He scanned the seagrass and short beach beyond. A seagull, bright white against the blue-green water, floated on the air.

Aguila suppressed a smile, the tranquility of the moment disarming.

"He is by himself?"

"Correct."

"Thoughts?"

"It's Wolf. It's in his nature to work alone. And... informants say he still harbors deep hate for El Chapo."

"Interesting," Aguila said. "I look at his past and see him always as part of a team. Rangers. Special Forces. Even pre-Shadow Tier, he fought Sinaloa with teammates. I do not believe he is alone."

"Yes, I'm sure he has a team backing him. The file you provided says Shadow Tier has all the sections we have—intelligence, communications, transportation, logistics. But I believe they are in Mexico or Florida. Wolf is the only one here, and the only one we must focus on stopping."

"I have my doubts, but we will work the problem your way for now."

"Excellent. The Chinese advisors are motivated to find Wolf as a gesture of good will," Ochoa said, pulling an envelope from his cargo pocket and handing it to Aguila.

"What's this?"

"I do not know. On the way here, G2 vectored me to a landing zone where an officer handed it to me with instructions to deliver it to you."

Aguila read the letter, dropped it in the sink and used his lighter to set it on fire. "We haven't yet harvested one crop," he said in a growl. "The illustrious director of G2, General Ruben Zaragoza, is demanding more for himself."

"Greed is a powerful addiction," Ochoa said.

"Yes. Socrates said, '*He who is not contented with what he has, would not be contented with what he would like to have.*' El Chapo does not respond well to these kinds of demands," Aguila said glancing out the window.

"You and I need to have a face-to-face with Zaragoza so I can explain how things work. That is, if he wishes to live long enough to spend what he has already been paid."

"El Jefe would threaten Cuba's intelligence director?" Ochoa asked. "Is it wise?"

"Is it wise? No, but it is how the Mexican drug lords rule their business. I will communicate on his behalf. The deal has been set. There is no negotiation in El Chapo's mind, " Aguila said pausing for effect to let the truth sink in.

"Once a deal is reached, you keep your word, do your part, and no one dies. For now, we will play along with Zaragoza's reckless game, so we can take advantage of his and the Chinese's resources. With them, we can capture Wolf in twenty-four hours or less."

# 11

Southern Coast, Cuba

In the past, Elle and Wolf had taken different routes to confuse hitmen sent to kill them—but it had been minutes, not hours, and she had been able to communicate with him.

The thought of Cuban and Chinese technology that could find and track them scared her.

Laying down, she put her face in the crook of her arm and took some deep breaths to center herself.

The smoke wasn't so bad with her face near the dirt.

Gunfire roared in the distance then stopped as fast as it had started.

Later, trucks drove by and she was left with the dying sound of the burning sugar cane.

Elle spent the rest of the day improving her space.

She put her camo net overhead and made sure her rifle was clear of sand and dirt.

Between tasks, she ate, drank, and remembered the first time she met Wolf.

It was at USSOCOM headquarters, the day after he had been deported from Mexico.

Wolf had fought his way through a gun battle that cost him his stepfather and wounded his mother.

The following day, his mother was assassinated in the hospital.

In response, he captured the an intelligence chief and interrogated him.

The cartel lieutenant was killed by his own people in a rescue attempt, at least that was Wolf's story.

She let him know she understood the need for revenge.

Her best friend was killed by a mafia assassin in Bosnia.

After Wolf confided in her, their friendship started to grow.

Three years later, they married, with one ceremony in Tampa and another on the Crow reservation with the last of Wolf's extended family.

They'd been through a lot compared to the average couple, but she considered it a blessing.

For all the good, there was one thing that caused her to lose sleep. Wolf's obsession with Joaquín Archivaldo Guzmán Loera.

*He lives rent free in Wolf's head.*

Wolf claimed it was because El Chapo was still priority one with leadership.

It was true, but it was also based on a foundation of loss.

His parents and close friends had died at the hands of the cartel.

They had talked on the flight to Cancun and agreed they didn't need to kill El Chapo to be successful.

"All we need is the Cuban president or one of his inner circle advisors to see evidence of drug trafficking," Wolf had said.

*How do I keep him focused?*

*Play the role of shrink?*

*I'm the one seeing the psychologist?*

Elle rolled over on her back and watched the last light fade as darkness filled the sky and stars popped into view.

She took down her netting and prepared to move out by listening and becoming one with the night.

When she scanned the sky, the Milky Way did its best to be the center of attention.

She slowly worked a different route out of the cane field using her monocular on infrared setting to scan the road.

Nothing in range, she started east toward the next escape and evasion waypoint.

She increased her pace and at the intersection she turned south, expecting to find another road or track off the beaten path.

The plantations in the area oriented their fields, roads, and irrigation in a perfect square pattern aligned with the cardinal directions, making travel easy.

In the groove, burning through the kilometers, she sensed movement to her left.

She slinked into an irrigation ditch and quietly laid on her back.

*Just walk by.*

The noise continued, then stopped.

Her heart raced and sweat trickled along her back.

A snort from her front.

With a shaking hand she flicked the selector on her rifle to full auto. Elle peered over the berm with her night vision and sighed.

*Stupid pigs.*

A rock hit her leg.

She rolled onto her back, bringing her TX4 to bear, then stopped as she recognized the whispering voice.

"Hunters following the hogs." Wolf said.

Elle relaxed her head into the dirt, happy to have him next to her again.

Seconds later, she detected the hunter's footsteps, then voices.

They followed the path the pigs took and continued out of hearing range.

Wolf crawled to her side, wrapping his arm around her. "How youuu doing?" He asked failing at his new york accent.

"I'm good, you smell foul. Is that burnt hair?"

"Yeah, I had a hot date, but it got hairy, and I had to leave... No? Okay, let's go. I want to get to the checkpoint before sunrise."

He knelt and scanned the area using IR then stood extending his hand toward her.

She slapped Wolf's hand away and stood on her own then moved out without a word.

*Can't believe I'm in Cuba illegally with my bad jokes husband.*

*Lord save me.*

Elle checked her watch; ninety minutes since they left the ditch.

Now they were side by side separated by a row of healthy corn.

They checked their sectors around the waypoint.

A six-foot long by five-foot wide pump house.

Not impressed, Elle whispered. "What the heck Wolf. One way in and one way out?"

"Not according to the Agency.

Plus, it's supposed to be a temporary stop, not a long term hide site. I'll go check it out."

She cleared the road and tapped Wolf on the leg.

He scuttled across, opened the door, and rushed inside where he flashed his IR beacon twice in the corner of the window.

Elle checked the road one more time before crossing the dirt track.

On her way across, large drops of rain splattered on her head.

By the time she entered the pump house, the rain fell in earnest.

The storm intensified, pummeling the tin roof, making it hard to talk.

Elle grabbed Wolf and spun him around, forcing him against the wall.

She pushed into his lips, hugging him tight to her.

Her voice trembled. "I was scared I'd lost you."

"Not happening. I'm yours forever, plus two."

"Forever plus two," she said after a cough.

"I understand this is stressful, being here without the support of our teammates. I remember what you must be experiencing from my first singleton mission. But it will change when the asset comes for us."

Elle stifled a cough and nodded.

Wolf handed her his monocular. "See the hatch next to the pipes? It's our second exit, and it leads right into the cane field behind us.

I'm going to use it to see if I can sync with our satellite constellation and get a message out."

The rain grew harder.

It was so loud on the tin roof she resorted to shouting to hear her own voice.

"Okay. But I don't like it here. If we get discovered, we're done."

## 12

———

Pump House, Southern Coast of Cuba

I sent the burst message, trusting our low-probability-of-detection satellite phones will work as advertised.

The Shadow Tier satellite constellation is a low earth orbit network that, as it grows, will ensure uninterrupted communications via micro-satellites.

Small and short-lived, the satellites can be launched from a specially configured F-15 Strike Eagle fighter plane.

I question if the signal can push through the rain, but I'll get a confirmation text—or not—at the top of the hour.

I'm schooled on the Russian signals intelligence, SIGINT equipment used at the Lourdes facility.

They are a well-known component of a risk matrix when operating in Russian influenced countries.

But now we are facing a Chinese advanced systems threat—some of which are direct copies of ours and other NATO countries—and I'm concerned.

As we hide out in this pump house, it hits me full force: Elle and I have stepped into a big boy fight.

At the Joint Special Operations University, I read about fighting an adversary with similar capabilities; they called it "near-peer." I haven't seen it since that paper, but it's stuck with me.

While Cuba's military is second-or third-rate, the introduction of Chinese advanced collection systems can't be overlooked.

As the Caribbean equivalent of East Germany back in the day, we need to keep our operational security tight while limiting all electronic emissions to the bare minimum.

My stomach growls and I pull a protein bar from my pack.

It's a bit of a mess, but I cut around the entry wound and hand the larger part to Elle.

Between coughs, she points to the holes in my pack. "How'd you get shot but not hit?"

Her eyes widen as I tell the story. I'm laughing at my luck, but I can tell it's not helping. "Not my day," I conclude, then, before she can respond, I switch topics.

"Might need to resend the message after the rain stops. The low power of the transmitter keeps us from being detected but it has problems in dense foliage or heavy precipitation."

"I know. I got the training too, remember?" She says and tries to take a deep breath.

The result is coughing.

It takes a minute before she can talk again. "We're using LPD satellite communications—if needed we can tunnel through the cell network to get to the Internet."

She pauses and breathes slowly. "I remember what Harris said, so what's got you worried?"

I don't want to add to her stress level, so I deflect. "Will the team understand what we've done? Moving inland against the asset's abort signal?"

Elle whispers, her delivery broken by gasps for air. "Of course, they will. They're smart and crafty like you... but that's not it. You mentioned a Chinese soldier possibly talking to a drone operator. It's them isn't it... the Russians are good, but their intelligence units aren't here anymore... Now it's the Chinese who are investing in Cuba... and therefore, MSS must be partnered with G2."

"I don't understand how you see through me, but yeah, you're right. Where are the Cubans and their new partner when it comes to SIGINT integration and military drones? Are they integrated? Or are they kept separate and operated by the Chinese—which I think is the case.

"Why does it matter?" Elle asks. "It's the same result—the Cubans get access to advanced technology."

"Yes, but if it's not integrated, it means the Chinese operators are in a different chain of command. They will share, but only when they consider it in their best interest," I say and pause as it comes to me.

"In the seam between the two chains of command with differing missions and goals is where we will operate."

"So, continuing the mission... and its ultimate success... hinge on the support of the Agency assets... there's no chance we can do this without them?"

"You know the answer is yes, but there's way more danger and time needed to develop the situation. We need to know they are on our side and can provide the access we need to get inside what El Chapo and Aguila are working."

Elle takes a shallow breath and exhales. "Hinges flex both ways. I don't like depending on people I don't know."

I sense the concern in her voice and give her the truth.

"I understand, you've had an asset turn and your best friend died as a result. Trust must be proven, and even then, we keep it tight. As you've experienced, the world of spies is a dangerous place, where alliances can change with the wind. During this operation we need to be mindful of its ebbs and flows."

*Ebbs and flows, cute words for the danger I've put my wife in.*

*We're not secure and she needs time to recover.*

*How much help can she be?*

*Should I get her out of here now and go solo?*

*She'd hate me but she'd be alive.*

# 13

TransCargo Santiago de Cuba

After lunch, Aguila asked Ochoa to drive him to Trans-Cargo. "I want to see this building that El Chapo spent his money on."

Situated at the top of the bay, in the shipping and cruise line district, the builders had completed the new ship maintenance and repair facility two years earlier.

Aguila had just joined the cartel and overseen the project himself in preparation for their buyout from El Chapo.

Built to accommodate vessels much larger than the currently docked sixty-four-meter-long boat, it provided top-of-the-line-security.

Like the secure hangars built for America's B-2 bombers, the building limited electrical emissions to a maximum of twenty meters and even at that distance, you would need cutting edge systems from America or China to make sense of the weak signals.

They passed through security and into the building.

"The corporate signature of the guard force, cameras, and countermeasures are impressive," Aguila said.

"Not normal for Sinaloa operations."

"What is normal?" Ochoa asked.

"Lots of cheaply acquired mean-looking men strolling around with AK's. All with a 'come near us and we will shoot you' attitude."

*This must be an improvement,* Ochoa thought.

They stopped at the reception desk, and a man hurried from the back. "Welcome, gentlemen. I am the general manager, Carlos Sanchez, at your service. Please, please, come this way." He turned and strode along a hallway.

When they entered the maintenance and repair area, Aguila shielded his eyes from a welding torch mere feet away.

Past the welder, he stopped, mouth agape. Ochoa stepped to his side and whispered.

"This is why El Chapo is at the top—he does the unthinkable."

Before them sat a vessel the Cuban Navy had attempted to procure before US sanctions blocked the sale.

*How did they keep this from me,* Aguila thought.

The general manager babbled on, but Aguila paid him no attention, instead walking across the gang plank to the vessel.

He put his hand on the sail, needing to touch the former Venezuelan Navy Type 209 submarine.

*It's not a dream.*

The general manager tugged at Aguila's arm. "Built in 1976, this boat was upgraded in 2004 and again just weeks ago. With her new navigation and battery systems she is a very capable when operating in areas such as the Gulf of Mexico."

"Aguila," someone yelled.

He spun, then smiled when he saw it was his peer in the Sinaloa organization: Diego Resendiz, who managed transportation.

A former Mexican Marine transportation officer, he had taken over after Lance Bear Wolf killed his predecessor at a Sonoran desert distribution center.

Diego crossed the gang plank and shook hands with Aguila. "You must be Ochoa," he said.

"Yes, sir," Ochoa said.

"Good. It's time for our intelligence cell to see the rest of the operation."

The retired colonel gnawed on his tongue, a nervous habit he started at a young age.

*Why did El Chapo keep this a secret from me?*

*How am I supposed to execute a counterintelligence plan when I don't know the full operation?*

Resendiz led them back to the office area and a room with no windows.

The far wall held large-screen displays, and a map zoomed out to show Cuba and the Gulf of Mexico.

Different colored icons littered the map, marking ships at sea.

"The crew is professional, but coin operated," Resendiz said. "They are Venezuelan navy mercenaries. El Chapo paid one hundred and sixty-five million for the submarine. He also hired two senior engineers to manage the maintenance of the boat over its expected ten-year life span."

A young lady in tight black pants and a V-neck white blouse advanced and asked if they wanted coffee or something stronger.

"We'll have coffee," Aguila said, observing her respond to Ochoa's smile.

Resendiz broke the spell. "Welcome to our ops center. I have modeled it after intelligence you supplied on the US Navy. We are pulling in feeds from a dozen collector systems of Cuban and American origin, and others from Central American and Caribbean countries."

"Does it include coast guards and navies?" Ochoa asked.

"Good question. The answer is yes— if they have their transponder activated."

"How much will the submarine hold?" Aguila asked.

"We are repurposing crew space as we speak. My estimate is two to three times the traditional narco-sub tonnage."

"Thirty tons is a lot of ballast. How do you propose to test your theory?"

"Slowly my friend," Resendiz said inside a chuckle.

"Where is the other end of the pipeline? Thirty tons is a lot to unload and get ashore," Ochoa asked.

"Ha! I like him, Aguila. We are the owners of three decommissioned oil rigs off the Texas and Louisiana coast." Resendiz then turned to speak to an operator.

"Zoom into the New Orleans location."

"The platform has been renovated," Resendiz continued. "Just enough to store product until it can be forwarded by boat or helicopter. Like Walmart, the sites will become our offshore logistics centers."

"What's their distance to land?" Aguila asked.

"Forty-two miles off Louisiana," Resendiz said. "And forty-eight and thirty-five off Texas. All of them are over the horizon when viewing from shore."

"Do Customs and Border Patrol or the Coast Guard overfly the rigs?"

"Seldom. And if they do, it's on the way to a problem at a working rig. When we acquired these platforms, we chose them based on their relative isolation."

The young lady returned with steaming cups of dark liquid and highball glasses filled with a brown liquid.

The bottle of Havana Club Union rum hinting at Cuba Libres.

She rolled the cart to them and smiled. "Coffee as requested. And something more appropriate for a toast."

Resendiz handed each of them a glass. "A toast—to the new silent service!"

**14**

———————

Farm Pump House, Cuba

The rain has stopped, which I'm thankful for.

*It sucked trying to stay awake.*

I spent all night sitting next to Elle on the cold concrete floor with my back to a cinder block wall.

Her restless sleep bounced between sweats and chills.

The continued rales and labored breathing are not the indications of recovery I'm expecting.

She seemed strong when we reconnected, but now I'm worried she overdid it.

There is a buzz , and I retrieve my satellite phone that I have next to the dirty little window.

They received my text and the asset is on the way.

I position the antenna at the dirty little window and acknowledge the message.

I return to my wife and touch her forehead.

She looks like we've just completed an August mid-day run back at MacDill.

I'm hoping the fever will break, but it's gripping her tight.

*Have I taken her on a mission she isn't ready for?*

"Elle, wake up hun." I should let her sleep but linking up with local assets is the most dangerous part of any mission in a denied country.

The Agency's bravest have paved the way, but like those shifting winds, we must be ready to fight in case allegiances have changed.

She stirs and groans. "Did you get the license plate off the truck that hit me?" Her eyes flutter open, and she sits, scooting back against the wall.

"Feeling any better?"

"No. Now that the adrenaline…" she gasps for air, "…has worn off, everything hurts. I've got mud in my veins. No energy."

"I hear you, but I need you to fight through. At least, until we can get you some meds and more rest. The asset is on the way. Can you do that for me?"

"Do I have a choice?"

"Ahh, no. Unless you want around the clock interrogation, no food or water, and battery powered stimulation sessions."

Elle closes her eyes and shakes her head, letting me know it's not funny.

#

Ninety minutes later, I hear a vehicle approaching so I chance a look out the window.

There's a woman in a flatbed Ford slowing down to scan the area.

She stops and jumps out, spins to check 360, then runs to the door.

Two knocks. "Long day."

I'm at the door, suppressed SIG P320 pistol in hand. "Longer night."

"We must go. Now!" she says.

Bona fides out of the way, I open the door and find a petite, young-looking girl. Or woman. I'm not sure.

I drop the pistol to my side and extend a hand to help Elle stand.

"Is she okay?" the woman asks.

Elle groans. "I've felt better. Let's go."

I grab my pack and jog to catch them as my wife follows the asset to the truck.

The asset pulls bench seat forward.

She points to a gas tank, which has clam-shelled open. "Stuff your packs and weapons in here."

We do, then she looks me in the eye. "I meant all weapons. If we get stopped and you're searched, it won't end well. Trust me now or I drive away."

I take the P365 pistol from the small of my back, stuff it in my pack, and close the gas tank. "What should we call you?"

"Call me, Lisa. Your first stop is a safe house outside Havana. We'll change vehicles once we're closer to the city."

"How long?" Elle asks.

"Two hours. Get some sleep. We'll have a doctor waiting for you."

We are thirty minutes inland when I see flashing lights in the distance.

Our asset doesn't seem worried. "Should we take a side road?" I ask.

"This far out, it's probably an accident."

Elle wakes and rises. "Problem?"

Lisa stares out the window for several seconds. "Maybe. You're my workers, and she is sick. What are the names on your passports?"

I'm trying to judge Lisa's fear level; she's giving off a routine business vibe. "We are Rosa and Hector Zarate."

We slow to a stop and inch forward in the line of mostly farm vehicles like ours.

When we get to the front of the line, I hold my wife in my arms and hope my concerned husband look is convincing.

Elle's fever has come back, so she closes her eyes and lets her coughing and mumbling in Spanish tell the story.

Police officers jump on the running boards and stare at us.

The one on Lisa's side asks for her license, then asks what she's doing and where she is headed.

I keep my eyes on Elle and comfort her while Lisa talks with the police.

Elle coughs out phlegm, and the officer on our side leaps off the running board.

Lisa uses Elle's coughing to suggest a lung issue needing testing to confirm she is not contagious.

She mentions bird flu, Middle East Respiratory Syndrome, and something else I don't catch.

The policeman's eyes grow wide, and he hands her back her license then waves us through.

When we're clear, Lisa laughs. "Evidently, he's heard of MERS and SARS."

Thirty plus minutes later, we pull into a cement plant. The rock crusher is banging away like an off-kilter dryer.

In the background there is the ubiquitous beeping sound of heavy trucks backing to dump rocks and gravel into the hopper.

The landscape, buildings, and equipment are gray.

The air is filled with dust, reminding me of the 'moon dust,' as we call it, in Afghanistan.

We drive along the fence for 30 meters and pull into a garage attached to an old house.

Lisa exits the truck. "Grab your stuff and come inside."

**15**

——————

gency Safe House, Cement Plant Southwest of Havana

We follow Lisa into the safe house, I take point, pistol in hand.

I sweep in, moving to clear the living room while Elle takes the bathroom.

I don't like clearing rooms by myself, but it has to be done. I call, clear.

Elle calls clear and we meet in the hallway and listen at the bottom of the stairs for a couple of beats before entering the kitchen.

I find Lisa, coffee in hand, starting another pot.

I lower my pistol and sense Elle sliding next to me.

"Sorry if I seem a little skittish, it's my first time," Elle says.

"Me too. We're not spies, we hunt cartels."

Lisa continues making coffee.

"I can see it. Knuckle draggers. That's what you Americans call yourselves, right?"

I pull out a chair for my wife and she flops into it

I place my pistol on the table to observe the assets reaction and sit next to her.

"Not exactly. We have experience operating undercover but more in a police kind of way."

"Then you're not rookies. It's the environment. Cuba is my home, so I don't feel the pressure of operating while under constant surveillance like you do. But trust me when I say a mistake can be fatal. Let us help you—it will ensure we all see tomorrow."

"I appreciate it and we will. No arrogance here."

"When do we head to the Havana safe house?" Elle asks.

"Our ride should be here before eleven. Get some rest."

Elle leans into me.

"You're safe here," Lisa says.

Elle looks at me and I nod; she heads for the couch.

Lisa gets my wife a blanket.

When she returns to the kitchen, she pours each of us a cup of coffee, then sits across the table from me.

"You've got a strong woman there," Lisa whispers. "But she's on the ragged edge of total exhaustion. What happened?"

"She drowned during the infil."

"Are you trying to be funny?"

"Not at all. I didn't have us deep enough when a patrol boat ran over us. She got knocked out in the prop wash. It's sea water in her lungs. She needs diuretics, a doctor, and more rest."

"Okay. I'll make a call and see if we can't get to Havana sooner." She pulled out a cell phone and texted. "No guarantee they can change the pickup, but they will if they can."

#

We've been going over the route into the city and our switch to a different vehicle.

Lisa also provides an overview of the safe house, letting me know we'll get a walkthrough later today.

She stands, pushing back her chair.

It scrapes across the linoleum floor, reminding me of our tiny house on the reservation.

Lisa's cell buzzes. "They will be here in five minutes."

Elle is shivering in her sleep. I shake her shoulder and step back. She sits up and asks, "Time to go?"

"Yeah. How are you feeling?"

"Cold, but better," she says through a shiver.

My eyes move to the motion as a van arrives.

The logo and writing on its side proclaim it's the number one parts supplier to heavy equipment companies in Cuba.

Lisa calls out and we catch up with her at the back door.

"He's pulled next to the garage. We'll go around the back of the house and side of the garage to enter the van," Lisa says.

We follow her into the van.

The floor is littered with milk crates of brake parts; there are transmissions strapped against the walls.

"Store your packs under the toolbox behind the driver," Lisa says, "There's a latch that will open the compartment."

She points to the latch, and I feel around until I find it, and we stash our gear.

"Okay, now get dirty," she says. "If we're stopped, you are apprentice mechanics just arrived from Venezuela."

I grab the dirtiest old part I can find and rub the grease and dirt into my hands.

Elle does the same and wipes her nose with the back of her hand for effect.

Lisa hands us some overalls. "Put these on."

The closer to Havana we get, the more police I see from my limited view out the windshield.

*Almost every intersection.*

*How many am I not seeing?*

I keep my police-state thoughts to myself.

Forty minutes pass and we pull into a business maintenance bay.

"There's the bathroom," Lisa says. "Leave the coveralls here and get clean. I'll get your packs. The next ride is a lot nicer."

We clean off the oil and grease.

Lisa is waiting outside the bathroom.

A devious grin flashes across her face before she clears it.

I don't trust her as much as I appear to.

My flight or fight response is activated.

I reach into my pack for my pistol and stuff it under my belt in the small of my back.

Lisa leads us out the back to a waiting SUV.

It's a large Chinese Geely, like a Chevrolet Suburban.

The rear hatch is open, so I toss my pack in.

Elle does the same. As we start to walk around to the passenger side, Lisa says, "Sorry, I'll take the packs. You take their place."

Elle hands her gear to our asset and is crawling in, but I stop. "I thought you said this ride would be nicer."

She laughs. "It is. I bought this SUV two days ago."

I give her my version of the not funny look, then feel my wife tugging at my shirt.

I toss Lisa my pack and smile at my wife.

When I climb in, she wraps her arm around me as the cover is pulled over us.

*This isn't so bad;* I think as the SUV starts and we take a right out of the business.

It isn't long before I've stopped counting the turns and tracking the time.

Eventually, we come to a stop, and I hear a garage door opening.

After it closes, the hatch pops open.

We follow Lisa out of the garage into a hallway.

Its combination of Spanish Baroque and subtle neoclassic touches speak to an era of a free Cuba.

She walks to the bottom of a stairwell.

An older man stands at the top.

"Rosa and Hector, this is our cell leader, George," she says.

George looks more like an accountant than a spy master. "Welcome to Cuba. You are our first visitors. I'll introduce you to the team. If they seem skittish, please understand."

Elle is not hiding what's she's thinking; I assume it's the same thought I have.

"Excuse me, George. We understand that we are far from the first."

He descends the steps and looks me in the eye. "While I have no knowledge of other Agency activities in Cuba, up until today we have been an intelligence collection cell. The breadth of my businesses permits us unrestricted access across Cuba, and we are prepared to support you. Do you wish to continue?"

"I apologize. I meant no disrespect and yes, we wish to continue," I say, squeezing Elle's hand to signal my concern.

*Great, we're getting support from a cell that is good at reporting secrets but has never executed kinetic operations.*

George gives us a slight smile and moves a cart of cleaning materials out of the way so he can slide into the alcove.

He presses a panel under the stairs; it moves back, and he enters with Lisa following.

Elle releases my hand and I draw the pistol, holding it behind my hip.

I follow her through a tunnel around to the right, where I see George opening a steel door.

We enter to find two women and one man standing around a large table.

"Here is your support team. Fernan and Novia, a husband-and-wife team, and Ilena, our medic and armorer," George says.

My wife drops into a chair and Ilena rushes to her side, putting a hand on her forehead, she bends over and listens to Elle breathe.

She gives George a nod.

"We will help you put El Chapo in a Cuban prison," George says. "But first she needs help."

*I don't have time for this.*

I chastise myself when I raise my head and see everyone is looking at me.My mission focus obscured the real priority one, getting my wife healthy

*I'm letting the president's timeline impact my thinking.*

"Yes. Doctor first!"

**16**

———————

gency Safe House, Havana Cuba

"Have her take one every four hours… it's a diuretic," the doctor says, handing me the pills. "And she needs more rest."

Overcome with fatigue, Elle is in an upstairs bedroom fast asleep. I thank the doctor one more time before he goes.

Then I pour myself a coffee, adding honey for the sugar boost and cream to tame my stomach acid.

I've been trained that great leaders utilize a process of continuous assessment combined with the agility to adapt to changing conditions; right now I need to adapt.

*I've got a sick wife.*

*This cell has never supported a mission like this.*

*I'm drinking coffee in Havana, burning time and need to get to Santiago de Cuba as soon as possible.*

George strolls into the kitchen and pours himself a cup of coffee. "Follow me, and bring your packs."

I amble downstairs with him to the team room.

He stops at a storage cabinet, reaches around it, then slides the cabinet left, exposing a doorway.

I duck through, and immediately recognize a smell reminding me of Hoppe's number nine-gun oil.

It's their armory of sorts; as a weapons guy, it breaks me out of my fugue.

Ilena looks up from a pistol she has in pieces before her.

"Let me run you through your weapons choices. We have standard Cuban military models and a few specialty weapons. There are two Russian AS Val 9mm suppressed submachine guns, and two suppressed Makarov PB pistols. A half dozen Russian MP-443 Grach pistols at the end of the workbench round out the choices."

I take the LSA TX4 rifles from my pack and Elle's and hand them to Ilena.

She admires them.

"I've heard this is possible, but your two are the only rifles of this type in Cuba. So, for now, you must use one of these, she said pointing at the Val. We will transfer your TX4's to our safe house in Santiago de Cuba."

She tosses me a Russian Val.

I function check while suppressing a smirk. "Does it malfunction often?" I ask.

She grins. "Now and again."

"Where can I try this out?"

"Right here," Ilena says pushing the side of a cabinet.

*Another hidden passage behind a cabinet.*

*What other patterns have they fallen into?*

"This tunnel leads to the necropolis across the street. It's twenty-five feet below the road. No one will hear us." She says leading the way. At the bottom, she hands me ear protection. "The red circle in the cutout is your target."

I test fire a short burst; it's on target.

The weapon functions and shoots where it's pointed.

*That's good enough if we need to break contact.*

George is waiting when I get back to the work area. "Come. I want to familiarize you with a few things."

Turns out it's the locations of the alternate safe houses in Havana's suburbs, escape routes, and communications protocols.

I'm focused on memorizing the details and before I realize it someone is cooking and it's my favorite two ingredients, onions and garlic.

"It's dinnertime. Let's wash and go upstairs," George says. "I'll show you around the rest of the house."

The floor above the garage is also the living area with a living room, a library, the kitchen, and dining room.

Off the kitchen is a small breakfast nook.

The old Cuban architecture combined with the hand-built furniture and cabinetry give the home a stately but comfortable feel.

*I appreciate getting the layout of this home, I now have a clearer idea of how to bug out if the brown stuff hits the rotating oscillator.*

I trot upstairs and wake Elle.

She seems better for the rest.

I hand her another pill. "Take this with your meal. The sooner you rid yourself of the excess fluid, the better you'll breathe."

Elle stands and groans while stretching. "That smells good. What time is it?"

"Dinner time. Let's go… they're waiting."

In the dining room, Ilena helps George bring in the food.

"My wife sends her apologies at not welcoming you to our home. She and our daughter are attending to her mother at her home in the west of Cuba," George says.

The table fills with beef picadillo, rice, fried plantains, and a salad of lime, pickled tomatoes, and onions.

Ilena says grace. As soon as she says "Amen", Fernan and Novia start gabbing and laughing while passing the food around.

I glance at Elle and see her eyes moisten, as mine do too.

We're grateful for these people and what they risk by having us here.

When everyone's plate is full, our host stands, wine glass in hand. "I propose a toast. To our guests and our quest. As Doctor King said, 'when evil men plot, good men must plan. When evil men burn and bomb, good men must build and bind..."

Elle steps into the pause. "And he finished by saying, 'when evil men shout ugly words of hatred, good men must commit themselves to the glories of love.' I think what he meant is, we can't let ourselves become what we hate."

**17**

---

Cuba Intelligence Headquarters, Havana

The beauty of the former Direccion General de Inteligencia—now known simply as G2 headquarters—belied its dark secrets.

An odd combination of architecture stolen from Moscow's Lubyanka prison on the outside, and vestiges of the Saint Petersburg Hermitage inside.

A classic example of Cuba's former love for everything Russian. Aguila noted the missing banners and patriotic posters from his time in service. The shift toward China was not so subtle.

Aguila and Ochoa had escorted El Chapo on the midday flight from Santiago de Cuba to Jose Marti airport south of Havana.

Thirty minutes prior to landing, a young lady had come from the back of the plane and applied Shorty's disguise.

The shoes added two inches to his height, and the foam piece and new slacks six inches to his girth. The beard and glasses presented a professorial look.

He inspected the image in the mirror for several seconds and grunted. The young lady retreated to her seat in the back of the plane.

The drive to headquarters proved uneventful in the G2-secured motorcade.

The silence inside the armored SUV was permeated with what Aguila recognized as El Chapo's anger, just short of rage, at having to make the trip.

The motorcade had swept around the back of the building and into the underground entrance the former colonel had heard of but never seen; it was the director's private entrance.

As they exited the SUV, he glanced at his boss, a man he'd come to know since joining the cartel.

*General Zaragoza has made a deadly mistake. He assumes he has leverage,* Aguila thought.

Ochoa stayed a respectful distance behind both men as they strode up the replica of the Hermitage's Jordan staircase—grand beyond the reality of the corrupt organization they were about to engage.

Aguila steeled himself for what would come next. Not the meeting, but the removal of an impediment to his boss's business plan.

And it was certain he had a plan—which no one was fully read in on given his recent penchant for compartmentalization of operations.

At the top of the stairs, they were first met by a stern-looking woman who escorted them to the end of the hallway and the director's suite.

They were met by General Zaragoza, who immediately closed the doors behind them.

Thin and hawkish in appearance, the general looked pained as he smiled. "Mister Guzman... Colonel Aguila. Welcome to Direccion General de Inteligencia."

The general pointed to some chairs in front of his desk and walked around to his on the other side. "Please sit. Coffee, or something stronger?"

El Chapo grunted as he sat. "No. Why are we here?"

The director fidgeted and glanced at Aguila, who gave nothing back. "Good. Straight to the point."

El Chapo stared impassively at the general, letting the silence carry.

Zaragoza took a halting breath. "Well, ahh, the reason I ordered your visit is to, ah... renegotiate our percentage of the profits from our partnership."

During the early meetings leading to their deal, Aguila had spent considerable time explaining what partnering with the Sinaloa Cartel would entail, both the positive and negative aspects.

He had focused on how rich the leadership could become. To be honest, he may have minimized how El Chapo would look badly upon someone trying to cheat him or extort him for more money.

But that was in the past.

Now he sat in disbelief that General Zaragoza had the audacity, or rather greed and stupidity, to try to change what his boss considered a settled contract.

"It's a simple matter. A minor adjustment to increase our share of the profits as they grow," Zaragoza said as he pushed a printout across the desk.

"Here is the schedule showing the increase at various values after costs are accounted for. At its core, this adjustment motivates us to help you grow. A win-win for both of us, don't you think Mister Guzman?"

El Chapo's eyes flitted to Aguila who sighed his understanding and stood leaning across the desk.

"Director, we have discussed this before. We have a contract with you. One in which your profit grows in line with ours. As previously agreed, you are already motivated to help us. And we have provided generous pre-payments as part of our multi-million-dollar investment in time, materials, and personnel here in Cuba. *Do not* let greed blind you to the riches you will gain."

The director bolted from his seat, his pathetic smile turning to a growl as he pointed a finger at Aguila.

"You cannot talk to me like that! I am still your superior, and you would do well to remember it. Or I'll have you both thrown in one of the cells below, where you trained with the Russians."

*The idiot is going to blow my cover,* Aguila thought.

El Chapo grabbed intelligence chiefs arm and pulled him back into his chair.

"Stop. Your anger is wasting time. Time we could all spend making money, no?" He folded the printout and stuffed it into his jacket. "I will have my accountant review the increase, and if we can make it work, we will. But maybe it's only possible after several successful harvests. Such is the way for crops versus synthetic drugs. You will have my confirmation in twenty-four hours. Agreed?"

Aguila struggled to keep his face impassive. *What's El Jefe thinking?*

Zaragoza ceased giving his one-time friend a you disgust me look and turned to his boss with a smile. "Yes, of course."

"Good. We go back to work," El Chapo stood and Aguila followed him to the door.

He was surprised at the empty reception area but knew the conversation had been recorded.

*Zaragoza is dangerous, and we need to tread lightly.* At least, that would be his recommendation.

It all changed in an instant when they were back in the SUV.

"Who does this hombre estupido think he is?" El Chapo asked.

Aguila realized the statement was rhetorical and waited for his boss to continue.

"We haven't sold the first harvest, and he tells us to increase his share. He thinks he has leverage."

"El Jefe, Zaragoza is powerful. He disappears people every day. He's used to getting what he wants here in Cuba."

"We may be in Cuba, but he's in my world now. My rules."

"Yes, El Jefe. Your rules."

"Send Ochoa. Tell him to do it ugly."

# 18

———

José Martí International Airport

Ochoa and the security team followed the colonel and El Chapo to Hangar 7.

When they stopped near the plane, Aguila exited the car and strode back to where Ochoa sat in the follow-up vehicle.

"El Chapo wants the director dead. Make a spectacle."

After they departed, Ochoa went inside the terminal to rent a car, then headed back into Havana and the safe house he had rented.

Set in central Havana at the intersection of Calle 4 and Calle 35, it backed to the necropolis on its west side.

The Plaza de Revolucion was less than a mile to its east. The capitol buildings were three and a half miles northeast, toward the harbor.

The two-story cement block building provided three routes of ingress and egress. Plus, the ability to cross a two-lane road and be in a grove of trees on the edge of the necropolis and a large group of crypts.

Ochoa had covertly broken into two of the crypts, creating hide sites with water and food for five days, two pistols, and two AK-47s.

Aguila thought it overkill, and had kidded him about the crypts—while nodding his approval.

The house was plain from the outside, but had air conditioning, a landline, and internet.

One of the cartel's computer techs had configured two laptops.

They were large and bulky, but supposedly military grade, blocking all external emissions.

The Cubans had provided an encrypted link to Venezuela through the undersea cable. From there, a VPN tunnel into Ecuador provided internet and access to the cartel's systems.

"Slow, but workable while secure" was what Ochoa was accustomed to from his time as a Black Wasp.

He expected the same from the cartel, security trumping access and speed. Ochoa fished a cold beer from the refrigerator and was at the kitchen table when his cell phone buzzed.

It was Aguila; the text was labeled "Zaragoza girlfriend," and included the address and pictures of the house and the girl.

The second text was labeled Zaragoza home and wife, and included a location and pictures. The third text, a phone number, would signal General Zaragoza's departure from G2 headquarters.

Ochoa realized the concept he visualized would work: make a statement, but be non-attributable.

He drank the last of his beer and moved to the garage in search of tools for the night's "exercise in pain" as payment for bad judgement.

His plan included the flexibility to strike at either location, creating a story with the wife or the mistress at the center of the tragedy.

Miss Zaragoza killing the general and his mistress would tell a classic tale of a scorned wife who had spent many years at the general's side, blah, blah, blah.

*Too boring. But if the mistress is the victim* AND *the perpetrator...*

The basis of Ochoa's reputation for successfully completing assignments was largely built on his adaptability. His ability to process all the variables in the moment and make, at least as his superiors had seen, good choices.

But he lived by the American version of Murphy's Law: "No operation plan survives initial contact."

Ochoa secured his knock out kit, tools, tape, and a roll of five-millimeter plastic sheeting in his backpack and waited. He passed the time in his front room, reviewing the information he had been sent. When he was done, the only thing that remained was to control the pace of the mission.

*It's what has kept me alive.*

A text buzzed his cell phone with the code; General Zaragoza was on the move to his mistress.

Ochoa checked his watch; it had been the dozen minutes he wanted.

He jumped in the rental car and headed out. His map indicated it was just over 10 kilometers from his safe house around the Port of Havana to the mistress's.

Once there, he observed that the house was a step above the other houses in the area. It was enclosed by a nine-foot-high wall with the obligatory broken glass glued to the top.

There was an electronically controlled solid gate, with a pedestal mounted intercom, and cameras at the corners of the property and the gate.

All, no doubt, paid for and installed by the government.

Ochoa also expected a security system and internal cameras—both of which would be turned off for the duration of General Zaragoza's visit.

From his position across the street in Parque Guaicanamar, he watched as a short silhouette passed in front of the second-floor bedroom, followed by a larger one.

The sky was overcast and beginning to deepen its shade of gray, as the sun set behind the clouds. He checked his watch; *another forty-five minutes and the general will head home.*

It was two hours later when Zaragoza left. Surprised at his stamina, he scanned the house and surrounding area one more time. He found no other indications of surveillance.

No one would dare to physically track the general's movements.

*They must be tracking his phone or car.*

Ochoa strode across the street. Increasing his speed, he ran two steps up a tree and vaulted off, grabbing a nearby branch then climbed above the wall.

There he inched out on a bifurcated section of trunk. There were no tracks for guard dogs inside the wall and no sounds.

On a previous mission, he'd learned the hard way that not all guard dogs are vocal. Some are virtually silent until they try to rip off your arm or leg.

Confident the video and security systems were her only protection, he dropped and rolled into the camera dead zone. He stopped for a beat and scanned for motion sensor lights.

Finding none, he scurried around the house to the back.

He placed a small, circular microphone on the sliding glass door and listened. The mistress was thanking her maid for dinner and giving her the rest of the night off.

Ochoa backed into a shadow and slipped on surgical gloves as he waited for the maid to leave. Once she was gone, he picked the lock at the servant's door. He slid inside and held position.

When he heard the TV come on, he moved through the servant's quarters into the kitchen where he stopped with a view of the target.

He was behind her as she sat on a couch watching TV.

She laughed at the comedian and was reaching for a glass of wine when Ochoa knocked her out with a blow to her temple.

# 19

General Zaragoza's Mistress's House

Ochoa found the remote on the floor and switched the TV to the Blu-Ray player.

He searched her library of disks and inserted a movie from Columbia; a cheesy story line about love, betrayal, and death.

He stared at the twenty-something woman, cataloging her classic Cuban features and supple body. As a courtesan to Cuban elite, the choices she had made to get ahead disgusted him.

He pushed the thoughts aside and looked through her purse, taking her cell phone and stuffing it into his cargo pocket. To prepare her for transport, he dosed her with a lethal shot of propofol.

Ochoa took the full fifteen minutes he'd set aside for the task to make the house look like she had stormed around angry before heading to Zaragoza's home.

*The glass of wine flung at the TV was a nice touch.*

After a quick search, he snatched the driveway gate and garage openers, and hustled across the street to his car. He drove through the gate and around the circular drive to where he could back into the garage and stuff the mistress in the truck.

*This will take a while, the general's house is in the opposite direction, outside of town.*

It took over an hour to get to Zaragoza's house. The home was built plantation style and included thirty plus acres of working farm and cattle.

Ochoa cruised by the entrance to the farm and turned down a dirt track leading into a wooded area about a hundred meters further on.

He parked and stood outside the car to listen. He pulled the pistol from his waistband holster and spun the suppressor on to the Russian PB—a variant of the Makarov.

Hearing no human activity, he took off for the house.

Squeezing into a hedgerow facing the back of the house some fifteen meters away, Ochoa jumped back at a snarling sound. The sky had cleared, and the quarter moon provided enough light to make out the form of a small animal.

It lunged for his leg; before he could think, he shot it. Suppressing a curse, he scanned the house and its surroundings.

A minute passed with no lights turned on and no one coming to investigate, so he took a knee and inspected what turned out to be a dead fox.

He checked the ground around him and retrieved the spent brass shell casing.

Ochoa took several deep breaths to center himself and sprinted across the open area to a door on the side of the garage. He tested the handle, and it moved.

*Unlocked. He thinks he's safe here.*

Ochoa entered the dark garage and used the red light on his headlamp to scan for the door. He didn't expect it, but he also looked for any venting he might use to listen to the activity in the house.

The garage turned out to be a simple add-on, with no access to other parts of the house besides the door. He leaned into the door and listened to someone on the other side.

Their words unintelligible as the water ran, presumably at the sink. When the running water stopped, a female voice said, "I'm going to bed."

He heard the shuffling of feet and the voice of Zaragoza. "I have reports to read, then I'll join you."

After his targets had left what must be the kitchen, Ochoa waited for two minutes, then tried the doorknob. It turned, but the door didn't open, so he started working on the deadbolt with his pick kit.

It took a full five minutes to unlock it. He cracked the door and listened for a second, then entered.

The kitchen was classic Cuban, with colorful and decorative tiles adorning the walls.

In the low light of the single-bulb lamp next to the landline, the kitchen appeared to be for show rather than actual cooking.

But there was an empty bottle of wine and another half full. Next to it was a bottle of rum and an empty bottle of tuKola.

*Good! One's drunk and the other is relaxed.*

Room by room, Ochoa cleared the house. His expectation was that the general's office would be near an outer wall of the house, probably with a window to a nice view.

To minimize noise, he stayed against the walls when crossing areas with wooden floors. He stopped at an elaborate archway and listened to someone slurping a drink and rustling papers.

He stepped back, fell into a shooter's stance, and slowly stepped into the archway until he had a clear sight picture of his target's forehead.

The pistol popped and the back of the general's head blew into his chair and sprayed a fan of blood across the walls in a Pollock style painting of death.

From upstairs, he heard the wife call out. "What was that? Is everything okay Paco?"

Seconds after her husband did not respond, Ochoa heard heavy steps on the stairs. He placed the pistol in the small of his back; the heat radiating off the suppressor made him squirm.

He opened his backpack and drew the box cutter, sliding to the inside of the door. The wife cursed Zaragoza's lack of response, then froze with a gasp when she turned the corner.

He sliced the box cutter across her jugular, her hands going to her throat. Again he sliced, this time through her nightgown across her belly.

The blade was deep enough to expose her intestines, and she instinctively grabbed for them, releasing the pressure on her jugular. Ochoa stepped in front of her as the life left her pleading eyes and she crumpled to the floor.

Like testing a downed deer or wild hog, he drew the pistol and touched her open eye with the suppressor. Getting no reaction, he went out the way he had come in.

Back in his car, he glanced at his watch. He had all the time he needed to stage the scene.

Ochoa would record the details; if anyone else tried to extort more money from El Chapo, they would know the consequences.

Ochoa's skin prickled and a chill ran the length of his spine. Adrenaline coursed through his body. The power of the moment was not lost on him.

"Break a contract with the Sinaloa Cartel and pay the price," he said. "Now I can focus on Wolf."

**20**

———

DAY 7

Agency Safe House Havana, Cuba

It's 0530 and I'm in the hidden room that sits behind the garage.

The walls and ceiling are painted a tan color that limits the harshness of the workshop lighting.

Elle sits next to me, with George and Lisa across the table.

I inhale deeply through my nose; I'm surprised that there's a distinct lack of dampness or musty smell.

"Two days gone, and we're no better off than when we started," I say.

"Did you think we'd have to fight our way in? I didn't," Elle says.

*Davidson told me not to let my emotions get in the way.*

"Yeah okay, okay, you're right. Let me reset. Phase one, infiltration and contact with assets complete. Time to start phase two, gathering evidence of El Chapo's partnership."

"This is where we think we can help you," George says. "For years we have been tracking the Russians and G2. We know where their safe houses and warehouses are, and have a growing, though less comprehensive, list of the same for Chinese intelligence."

"The database also includes G2 leadership and many of their homes," Lisa says.

"Great, but El Chapo will not use any of the sites in your database. His number one priority is escape. In Mexico, it's often a tunnel. He's so paranoid, he even has a lieutenant he calls his master of tunnels. But I don't expect that here."

"My opinion is that he's somewhere near the airport and the water," Elle says. "Somewhere with quick access to an airplane or boat, and defensible. His mode of operation back in Mexico is in and out. If they have planted opium fields, he will visit and return to his safe location."

"I agree with Elle," I say. "Let's not forget, he still has a billion-dollar cartel to run, so he needs clandestine and secure communications. Our support team is focused on finding his location."

"So, beyond looking for indicators of a secured facility or safe house around the airport," Elle says. "There's another thread to pull. Retired Colonel Ignacio Aguila. I believe he's the key to finding El Chapo. I'm confident he's played an important role in creating the partnership, and more than likely is El Chapo's link to General Zaragoza."

*This is going to be a grind.*

I catch George winking at Lisa as she suppresses a smile. "If we start with the premise Zaragoza is the point of contact for Aguila, we have a way forward," he says.

"You have someone with access?" I ask.

"Not directly, but we can make it happen." George's chuckle carries a devious tone. "Let's say our asset is in the dugout waiting to get in the game."

Cubans love their baseball, so I carry it forward. "How do we get this player in the game?"

"We create an opening on the team," Lisa says.

"Okay. So, your person works for G2, somewhere close but not in direct contact with General Zaragoza. But you can change that. Seems to me you've had this idea in place but have held back."

"Only because we were waiting for it to occur naturally," George says. "It's time to help the process along."

"Good," Elle says. "Do it. Does the player have the technical kit to get us voice and video of a meeting?"

"Audio, yes. And more if the opportunity presents itself," Lisa says.

My curiosity meter spikes. "What is more?"

"Give us the magic dust we were told you have, and we will have the asset attempt to mark your target," she said.

I look away to hide my rising anger and take a deep breath to calm myself.

*What else were they told?*

Lisa and George's faces—the spy's faces—hold no clues, so I hold my thoughts.

"How long will it take to task the asset and get surveillance started?"

"We can task the asset tonight and bring her into the game tomorrow morning—if everything goes as planned," George says.

*I don't like the sound of that.*

"What's the cornerstone of your plan?"

"Clostridium botulinum. General Zaragoza's assistant is going to be very sick."

Elle voice squeaks. "You do know too much toxin and she dies, right?"

"We do," Lisa says. "A micro dose is all she'll deliver. Just enough to have her stay home for five or six days."

*So, the asset is a woman.*

"Okay, it's settled," I say. "You guys get your designated hitter in motion. Elle and I will check in with our team."

I grab some fresh coffee for me and a glass of water for Elle, then sit in front of the computer.

It's connected to the Internet and I insert a thumb drive that starts a double encrypted VPN and accesses an IP address on the dark web.

From there, I enter an agency-built application.

It harnesses microprocessors across an ever-changing number of desktop computers owned by Joe and June average.

The processing amounts to noise on a single computer, but together they give us the power to look like a desktop that's authenticating credentials to a travel booking site.

It may be slow, but Quinn assures us it's unbreakable; even the NSA tried.

My report to ops is short and to the point: we're good. Pulling threads.

My intelligence request is simple: a targeted signals intelligence and cyber search for El Chapo around the Santiago de Cuba airport and west to the mouth of the bay.

Elle and I laugh at the response we know comes from Kennedy.

"Like a fine wine whose full flavors and richness of bouquet are only experienced after thoughtful decanting, you too will uncover the truth of the vintage."

It's Kennedy's goofy way of saying the real work is just starting.

**21**

———————

G2 Headquarters, Havana, Cuba

"Yes sir! Right away," Captain Isabel Lambarri said. She had just been told to report to the director's office. His office manager and personal assistant was out sick.

*I have to get this right, so George's friends will take Lisa and I to America.*

She left her desk and entered the lady's restroom, where she stood in front a full-length mirror and straightened her uniform. She checked her hair and makeup, then nodded and headed upstairs.

The staff stairs were full of people scurrying about and talking in whispers as they did their duty for Cuba.

She entered the reception area through the side door, stopping in front of the director's chief of staff and snapping to attention before saluting. "Captain Lambarri reporting as requested, sir."

"At ease Captain. That was your first and last salute in this area or the director's office. Am I clear?"

"Yes, sir."

"Good. We focus on efficiency—making sure the director has what he needs to protect the people of Cuba. The director usually arrives promptly at 0900 for his staff briefing, which normally lasts an hour. The rest of the day is meetings," he said taking a sip of his coffee.

"Three times a week he is driven to Havana to brief the president. And similarly, he meets with the heads of military intelligence... although that happens here as much as at the joint command center."

He handed her a piece of folded paper. "Here is your username and password for the assistant's computer. Are you familiar with the scheduling program?"

"Yes sir. From my work for the director of counterintelligence."

"Good. You come highly regarded. Get this right, and there could be a promotion, Captain."

*There it is. The carrot. I'll just settle for not getting caught.*

Lambarri took a seat behind the utilitarian, but substantial wooden desk. It's rich hue reminded her of the teakwood furniture she had seen in her father's office before his death.

He had died on a flight with a general officer; one, who rumor said, was on the outs with Castro.

The plane had never been found; their bodies never recovered. The rumors only furthered the mystery—and made her ripe for recruitment by the Agency.

Once their mother was gone, she had brought her sister into the work, too.

She accessed the computer and went straight to the scheduling program to see what the day entailed. There was the director's staff meeting, then the army head of intelligence, then a break at 1130 for lunch out.

At 1300 a finance review, followed by a check in at 1400 with his "Chinese mission liaison," which was G2 shorthand for their Ministry of State Security.

At 0900, the heads of the G2 directorates assembled in the reception area, whispering amongst themselves as they waited. At 0930 the chief of staff told them the meeting was canceled and would be rescheduled for later in the day.

Lambarri was sure she was not the only one to notice the strained look on the chief of staff's face, or the beads of sweat on his brow.

Another thirty minutes passed before the rumor mill started. The director was sick. The director's mistress had kept him busy all night. He was in conference at the president's relocation site.

As time wore on, the rumors got more complex and outrageous. Lambarri called a friend in security who cut through it all. "He's dead. His wife and mistress, too."

She hung up as General Eduardo Delgado, the deputy director, stormed into the reception area followed by the chief of staff. "Reschedule the staff meeting for noon," Delgado said. "Cancel all other meetings today. And bring me some coffee!"

"Yes, sir."

Delgado and the chief of staff entered the director's office and closed the doors behind them. Lambarri locked her computer and scampered to the small kitchen off the reception area to prepare a tray.

Her mind reeling, she quickly assembled the service, then stopped. She spun and opened the liquor cabinet. Grabbing some rum and two tall glasses, she filled them with ice and cola before adding a stiff amount of rum.

Before rolling the loaded service cart out, she hesitated for a moment to collect herself. *I must show them calm and effectiveness. I have to keep this job.*

Resolute, Lambarri rolled the cart to the door and knocked before entering. The two men stopped talking and the general came forward to meet her. Delgado was not shy about checking her out.

"Your coffee sir... and something stronger as the situation warrants," she said.

"See? I told you she's smart. Just finished top of her class at the advanced officer's course," the chief of staff said.

"Good," Delgado said. "Consider yourself my permanent assistant, Major Lambarri."

Lambarri came to attention. "If there is nothing else sir, I will adjust your schedule. Would you like the noon meeting to be a working lunch?"

"Yes. Good idea."

She left the room, closing the door behind her. Outside, she sighed with relief and took her seat. Logging back in, she sent a form email to the cafeteria to prepare lunch for the director, chief of staff, and the ten directorate leaders and their staff.

After she rescheduled the staff meeting, she made sure the other assistants replied to the update.

It was near 1300 when she canceled the last meeting of the day via a call to the Chinese mission office.

Expecting it to be a long day, Lambarri went back to the kitchen and poured herself a coffee. She was taking a sip when it hit her.

She had been promoted, and she apparently had the eye of the new director for G2. A quote from Sun Tzu came to her: "In the midst of chaos, there is also opportunity."

**22**

―――――――

El Chapo Safe House Santiago De Cuba

After the news broke about the scandalous death of the director, El Chapo ordered Aguila to call his friend General Delgado to schedule a meeting. He had told Aguila he was too busy to meet, but the colonel had insisted, telling him Zaragoza had worked on an opportunity that he should at least hear out.

An opportunity of immense value to whomever inherited it. At the hint of money, Delgado summoned his assistant, and the meeting was immediately scheduled for nineteen hundred at G2 headquarters.

\#

Ochoa picked them up at the airport and provided security as El Chapo and Aguila were escorted to a private entrance in the G2 headquarters. They were met by a female assistant who took them to the third floor.

Guzman admired the officer's beauty and grace as she first knocked, then opened the door, letting them into Delgado's office. Once inside, he ordered Ochoa to wait in the reception area.

When the doors closed, Aguila, the former peer and friend, stepped forward and man-hugged Delgado. They slapped backs and laughed.

"It's been a long time," Aguila said.

The general held on to his arm. "Too long, my friend."

The colonel was about to introduce his boss when Delgado interrupted him. He held out his hand. "It is a pleasure to meet you El Patron—and let me ensure you the partnership continues with no changes or new stipulations. Please sit."

El Chapo watched as the general winced, his grip weak. *They are not the hands of someone who leaves the office.*

"Good," he said. "You know Zaragoza attempted to extort more money from me before we even harvested the first crop?"

There was a knock at the door and the assistant entered with her service cart. "You may leave the cart," Delgado said.

After the doors were again closed, the general made Cuba Libre drinks for all. "Yes, I know... I advised against it. You will find me a man of my word. And one willing to invest more to make the partnership profitable. I believe we must focus on growing and securing the business, then the profits will take care of themselves."

When El Chapo did not respond he added, "Tell me what you need. If it is within my power, it's yours."

El Chapo glanced at Aguila who nodded.

"We can do business," El Chapo said. "But there is one thing I need from you—there is a man with the American government. Aguila will send his details. If he is in Cuba, you must kill him immediately. Do not capture him or detain him. Understood?"

"Si. I will lead the hunt myself."

**23**

---

Lambarri Apartment, Havana Cuba

Later that evening, Isabel sat at the kitchen table pondering the missed opportunity. For security's sake, she had left the recording device and dust at home. She chided herself for the miss, but knew there would be additional chances to record and mark the former G2 colonel.

*How could I know I'd be so trusted on my first day—or any day when working for the director.*

After the director and the visitors had left, she had completed her security sweep of reception and the director's office. Lights off, she set the security system for the director's office, then accessed her computer.

Lambarri had inserted a thumb drive her Agency contact had given her. It opened a virtual desktop where she entered one of the username and password combinations she'd found earlier in the day, inside the safe behind her desk.

She had whispered her thanks to the hospitalized former assistant and was surprised when she was logged in with what appeared to be super user access. She accessed the personnel database and searched for retired senior officers.

*Super user access, really?*

She found retired Colonel Ignacio Aguila, but not the bodyguard or the short man. She ran another search in the active personnel database, but after a few minutes she got nervous and logged off. When she accessed the directory where the logs were kept, she was surprised at the limited entries. The personnel database was the same, few entries.

Lambarri was well versed in the computers, networks, and databases used at G2. They were nineties vintage and easy to navigate, especially with her elevated access status. But what encouraged her was the lack of access logging.

She realized if she only went in when it matched the director's schedule, she would stay under the radar of the security team. For once, she appreciated their lack of sophistication. She cleared the logs, signed off, and headed home.

#

Lambarri's spying had been passive to date, but that was about to change, and so was the risk to her and her sister. A chill ran down her spine. She rubbed her arms as she left the kitchen and headed to her personal computer.

Plopping into the chair, she glanced at the photo of her parents and happier times. She had been five, and her sister, who shared a birthday, was a precocious one-year-old. She sighed. A trace of a smile was quickly replaced by determination to change their lives.

She logged into her computer and opened the steganography program the Agency had hidden in the network buffer memory. After selecting an image of her new rank, one star on her shoulder board, she entered her report to her handler.

Moving to her email account, Lambarri crafted an excited message to her uncle in Venezuela, telling him about her promotion and how much the jump to the senior officer ranks meant. She closed the message, wishing him continued safety in his oil rig job.

*Complexity equals risk,* she thought as she sat back and contemplated her situation.

Her thoughts were interrupted when the "new mail" icon flashed. Her uncle never responded this quickly. She opened it: "Congratulations on the promotion and good wishes. You are my lucky charm. I am okay, but one of my co-workers got hurt and had to be flown out by helicopter. Love you, your proud uncle, Javiero."

Lambarri opened the hidden program, selected the attachment, and after the program did its magic, read the message. She read it a second time, and pushed back from the table, knocking over her chair.

She wanted to scream but couldn't. Like in Russia, Cuba's leaders were getting rich on the back of the working people.

But now her handler had indicated her position was more important than stopping the world's largest drug cartel from poisoning Cuba from within.

*Complexity.*

She did four cycles of deep breathing to calm herself, then smiled, mind made up. George would be her new contact, not the faceless bureaucrat back in Virginia who didn't care for Cuba. She would talk with her sister in the morning.

While she still drew a breath, she would fight for a better Cuba. And it included one not eaten from inside by greedy men hooked on the profits from producing and selling drugs.

#

DAY 6

The following morning, Isabel met Lisa at a noisy coffee shop next to the University of Havana. Coffee and pastries in hand, they wormed their way toward a table in the back made noisier by the overwhelmed dishwasher hustling for all he was worth.

They drank and ate, making small talk for a few minutes, taking stock of the surrounding people. Like the East Germany of the Cold War, Cuba was, in many respects, a police state.

Not as bad, some would say, but you could never be sure who was on G2's payroll. Isabel leaned in and whispered. "I'm done with Uncle Javiero. I want to report to George."

Isabel watched Lisa's face, not seeing any tell that she questioned her sister's sudden demand.

Lisa sat quietly for a minute, then leaned in and whispered. "It may hurt our chances at a new life, but if you feel it best for us, I will let him know."

Isabel gave a tight-lipped smile of appreciation. "New life or not, we cannot let the Sinaloa Cartel do what it has done to Mexico, here in Cuba."

**24**

———

**D**AY 6

El Chapo Safe House, Santiago de Cuba

First coffee of the day in hand, El Chapo stared out the sliding glass doors to the ocean. Not one for a lot of reflection, his mantra was, "Take action. Always move forward."

But this morning was different. He was not in his beloved Sinaloa, or even in the mountains of Chihuahua. He had been forced out, made to run. He growled, letting it turn into a sigh.

*One more week and I go home. Let them come for me. I will make them pay in blood.*

In his quest to produce drugs suited to the appetites of the increasing number of wealthy addicts in America, El Chapo had changed course many times. He had brought innovation into the market in the form of synthetic additives to primary drugs like marijuana and hash.

But while synthetics held great promise, opiates still ruled the current market. Thus, the move to opium and the farming of more poppies. And doing so in the one place no one would suspect: Cuba.

He'd learned a lesson or two along the way, and number one was the diversification of his cartel business into legal business and services like money laundering.

Number two was the value of moving from Mexico into South America, Europe, and Asia. Right behind that was number three: employing scientists focused on making his drugs more addictive.

He also thought that like big pharma, having them all in one place to collaborate was the way to go. And it was—until Wolf and Gonzalez had teamed up to destroy the lab and all its research in one attack.

So now, like his bank accounts. everything he did—or contracted someone to do—was compartmentalized.

And like Wolf's team, he operated a spy-agency-cell type of organization, with many isolated cells orchestrated to achieve one outcome. The result was that the penetration or destruction of any one cell had a limited effect on the overall business.

He was simultaneously working to grow his cartel, while waging war with the Mexican and US governments. His latest bet was the production and shipment of opium, morphine paste, and high-grade heroin to the United States.

When hired, Aguila had delivered on his promise to take care of a leak and push the Sinaloa intelligence unit to a higher level of performance.

So confident was El Chapo in Aguila's unit, he had them start to penetrate his own organization at the cell level to weed out incompetence and poor threat detection.

This morning, he would personally vet the cell-based system put in place for this high-risk, high-reward project. He'd summoned Aguila and his security team, then headed to the mountains. It was not long before the cool morning air filled his open window.

As they climbed the switchbacks to the first site, El Chapo broke the silence. "Today we test the protection of the processing sites. When Wolf gets to Cuba, I want to insure uninterrupted processing. The submarine must be full to maximize my investment, and I want it to sail in three days."

"Yes, sir. We are working under the assumption that Wolf is in

Cuba, hunting us at this very moment. I suggest we take a play from the computer security team and present the potential attacker with something to find. The staff call them honeypots—targets the attacker cannot resist," Aguila said.

"He is very smart. You will have to act as if you are the workers and not security. He does not attack the workers—just the security and the processing facility," El Chapo said.

"To draw him in, the fake location must be slightly less well hidden and less secure than the real labs—but without it seeming too obvious." Aguila said. "Even if he locates the real labs, we need him to choose the fake."

"I will ensure it looks and smells like it's a real lab," Ochoa said.

Due to their co-location with the poppy fields in the south-facing valleys, the processing labs visit took some time. At one of the sites, they found the senior worker slumped on the floor, injection kit by his side, the tourniquet still on his arm.

Ochoa disappeared the man and a new leader was chosen. At another location, they found the men and women working through wreckage after what appeared to be an explosion and fire. The grisly remains of the former site leader and an associate were burnt to a char, their skulls locked in a rictus of death.

Aguila and Ochoa rode together in the follow up vehicle on the way back. Guzman had his driver stop at TransCargo, his pre-shipment warehouse, so he could check in with Resendiz. Once there, he ordered the submarine to sail in three days.

It was well after lunch when the convoy pulled back through the gate of the oceanside house. As they walked through the entrance, Aguila's cell rang. When he answered, they all stopped and waited to see what the call was about.

"What do you mean crashed? Yes. Yes. Okay, I will send someone to take care of it."

Aguila seemed to consider his words.

"El Jefe," Aguila said. "One of the trucks transporting product has crashed coming down the mountain. With your permission, I will send Ochoa to take care of the problem and get the product back on the road to the warehouse."

"Agreed. Ochoa, get them back to work. Inspect each driver for drugs and alcohol and fire anyone you find using. We can't have screwups like this... not now," Aguila took a package from his backpack. "Here is ten thousand to compensate the driver's family. Extend our condolences and remind them to stay quiet."

"This is too much, El Jefe," Aguila said. "Three is better, five is generous. These people are used to having much of what they need provided by the state."

Guzman waved a hand. "Five then."

"Si, El Jefe."

Unknown to the boss, five thousand dollars was like hitting the lottery when compared to the eight dollars a day most Cubans made. It would create a furor in the local community.

## 25

———

Mensura Park, Cuba

Ochoa jumped from his SUV. "Who are you?" He asked pointing at a young man who was directing the gaggle blocking the road.

"I'm Leto Vega, one of the drivers. Who are you?"

Ochoa bored into Leto with his dead eyes. *No fear, and demonstrating some leadership. I might be able to use him.* "You can call me Max. I work for the people paying you. Who are these men. Have you recovered the product?"

"They are from the nearby lab and have recovered some. I told the men to load it into the remaining trucks. Getting the driver out of the mangled cab took some time."

"Any idea what caused the accident? Was he drinking or using?"

"No, he drank a little, but not at work. I think it was his brakes. I heard a screeching sound, like metal on metal before he left the road."

"Okay. Get the rest of the product in the trucks. You'll find a tarp you can wrap him with in the back of my SUV. "Do you know…"

Leto interrupted Ochoa. "Yes, I knew Chepe. He was my sister's husband."

"Is there someone else who can drive your truck?"

"No. There is only the four... ahh... three of us now."

"Okay, here's what we'll do. We'll deliver the product. You and I will take the body to a mortuary where he can be taken care of and we'll go to your sister's house so I can pay my respects."

Leto gathered the men, adjusting their assignments, then grabbed the tarp. Ochoa followed him to the body and watched as they gently wrapped him and took him to the SUV.

Other than a few lacerations, he looked as if he was sleeping. His chin touching his shoulder was the giveaway his neck was broken.

*Not a bad way to go. Quick and painless.* Ochoa huffed. *Not likely in my line of work.*

It took another hour to recover the rest of the product and cross-load it into the trucks. Before they left, Ochoa gave each man one hundred Cuban dollars, letting them know the teamwork was appreciated.

He sent the processing lab workers back, and had Leto gather the other drivers. They were lucid and did not smell of alcohol. He told them he expected them to speak out if there was something wrong with their trucks.

"Accidents will happen, but this could have been avoided. Treat your truck like it's your own. This is how you make money. If it's broken, you make nothing. If the mechanic is not doing his job, tell Leto. As of now, he is your boss."

#

The offloading of the product into the warehouse had gone smoothly. Resendiz had used some of the security force to get the trucks unloaded and on their way.

It was 2300 when Leto had Ochoa stop in front of the house on the northern outskirts of Santiago de Cuba.

"This is where we live," Leto said. "My parents, my sister and me. My sister and Chepe were saving for a house of their own—the pay from driving was a blessing."

*The blessing is he went fast. The rest is just fate,* Ochoa thought.

Inside the gray cider block and tin roof house, he was surprised to find a light, sand colored tile floor with decorative tiles along the walls. There was a thick wooden mantle over the fireplace, with brightly colored pieces of oddly shaped glass.

"My father works at a tile and glass factory," Leto said. "Everything you see was discarded as imperfect... just as we are before God, no? I will wake my parents, then my sister."

He couldn't make out what was said but saw the sadness in their eyes as the father helped his weeping wife to a chair by the fireplace. The man did not look Ochoa's way. He stoked the fire, then returned to comfort his wife.

A minute later, Leto came out with a young girl who was clearly pregnant and in shock. Tears laced her cheeks and when she saw Ochoa a low moan escaped her throat as she slumped to the floor. Leto sank with her.

Ochoa gently lifted her chin. "He did not suffer. We took him to Funeraria de Calvario, and I took care of the costs. You will pick out a headstone—,"

The girl broke, wailing in Leto's arms.

Sitting with this side of death was not what the major was accustomed to. His feelings swirled and something he couldn't identify tugged at his heart. A knot grew in his stomach, bile rising in his throat, and for the first time in a long time, he felt inadequate.

He stabbed an envelope with five thousand dollars in Leto's face. "You know what to do," he said, then turned and left.

As he drove back to the safe house, he put Chepe's death into perspective.

He wasn't an enemy of the state or a rebel wanting to disrupt the Chinese mining operation.

He was a countryman, eking out a living, trying to make a better life for his new family.

*What would my mentor say if he found me concerned with the death of a low-level worker?*

*It's a weakness I cannot afford if I'm to kill Wolf.*

**26**

─────────

D<sup>AY 5</sup>

Lambarri Apartment Havana, Cuba

Isabel used what little training she had gotten as a junior intelligence officer to drive a surveillance detection route in the morning darkness—which indicated she was clear.

She stopped at a park and her sister jumped into the car. After a minute of keeping her head low, she righted herself and laughed.

"Remember when we played spies and used chalk to mark our meeting locations?" Lisa said.

"Yes... and mom would leave us secret messages in our dead drops." Isabel said.

"And father would check our work and say, 'one day this will be important...'" Lisa's voice trailed off.

"It's important now, more than ever," Isabel said.

The drive to George's took thirty-five minutes. She parked two streets over, and they separated, taking different routes to the walled-in parking area. At the front door two sets of electronic deadbolts clunked open.

George welcomed the sisters leading them upstairs. The house was quiet, the outside world left behind. George ambled into the dining room and pulled out chairs for them.

Isabel realized she'd been cataloging everything: George's mannerisms, the house, her sister's reaction to it all… when George's voice broke through. "Can I offer you coffee?"

"Yes, please. Are we alone?"

"There are others in the house, but this meeting is private."

"What does that mean?" Isabel said.

"I will show you later if you wish. You should know your demand has caused a commotion."

"My sister has told you how I feel?"

"Yes."

"And?"

"And I agree with you. The Americans want what they want—their focus is on the Chinese. There are some who genuinely care for Cuba and its people—your former handler was not one. I am," George said sipping his coffee.

"Keep emailing your uncle in Venezuela for appearances, but I will be your point of contact from now on. I suggest you also pass all your communications on to your sister. She has multiple ways to get to me, as my employee and as a friend of my family. How does that sound?"

Isabel glanced at her sister, who winked. "Good. Did they send you my report on General Delgado's visitors?"

"No. But before you give it to me, I need to ask if you are okay if I bring two more people into the conversation. We can hide your appearance from them, but I believe it's important for them to hear it firsthand."

"Who are they?"

"Americans hunting the Sinaloa Cartel leader, El Chapo."

Isabel tensed, her fight-or-flight adrenaline dump in progress. "Americans?" She turned to her sister. Lisa put a hand on Isabel's arm.

"It's okay sister… please it's okay. They are good people, here to uncover an illegal drug production and transportation scheme operating with help from within the government."

Fear raging through her, she forced herself to relax. "Get me a scarf."

Lisa left the dining room, returning with a beautiful forest green scarf. Isabel wrapped it around her head and neck, so she had only a slit for her eyes.

She took a deep breath and exhaled. "Okay, I'm ready."

With a nod from George, Lisa headed downstairs. Isabel heard a faint noise, then some voices she couldn't make out. Her sister reappeared, followed by a woman who looked South American. Isabel couldn't place where exactly... maybe Columbia or Venezuela.

The man behind her had eyes like Aguila's security guard from the director's office—but different. Not dead, more inquisitive. He was cataloging the threats in the room, deciding if she was friend or foe. But with a lightness the predator did not possess.

*Enigma,* she thought.

"Thank you for meeting with us," the woman said. "I know it can be stressful meeting new people in our line of work. We are here for one purpose and one purpose only. We believe Joaquín Archivaldo Guzmán Loera, also known as El Chapo, has partnered with someone high in the Cuban government. They are growing opium poppies and processing them into heroin to be sold in America. Our goal is to uncover evidence to give to your government and have them take El Chapo into custody."

"For the rest of his life," the man said. "We have seen firsthand what drug cultivation does to the land, and how the people are treated who work it. It starts off seeming to be hard but well-paid work, but it comes at a cost. Once you are an employee, there is no leaving. And if you or anyone in your family talks, you all die. It is a scourge you do not want here in Cuba."

"I understand," Isabel said. "America itself is an example of the disease drugs bring. So, let me start. I witnessed a meeting between the new director for G2, General Delgado, a retired colonel and his two associates. I was not in the room but saw them enter the director's suite."

"Colonel Aguila, right?" the woman said. "He's El Chapo's intelligence lieutenant—we believe he is the broker for the partnership."

"Yes," Isabel said. "The other man with Aguila was short, but clearly in charge. A third man—I call him the predator—he's a bodyguard built like you," she said pointing at Wolf. "He must have been security, as he was told to wait outside."

"You," Wolf said, "just witnessed a meeting between General Delgado and the leader of the world's largest drug cartel, Joaquín Archivaldo Guzmán Loera. The man known as El Chapo."

"This is not good for Cuba. I must go," Isabel said.

## 27

G2 Headquarters Havana Cuba

"Where is the breakfast I ordered? The director and his guests are waiting," Lambarri said.

"My apologies major. We are completing your request now," the captain said, voice cracking.

"I'm coming down. Have it ready."

Isabel dropped the handset in the cradle and left her office, rushing to the elevator. When she entered the kitchen, the captain in charge was admonishing a private who had spilled some coffee on a tray. "Stop! Give me a fresh napkin. I'll take it from here. You are dismissed."

She hurriedly pushed the cart to the director's private elevator. Once the door closed, she reflexively scanned the car and had to remind herself, no one was watching.

Isabel sighed and reached inside her waistband, pulling out the micro dust packets and carefully opened them. She applied the material liberally to the napkins on each of the trays

*The packets feel empty, I guess that's it.*

Isabel put the packets back in her waistband and pulled out a device that looked like a cigar container. Placing it under the cart, the magnets snicked into place. She took a deep breath as the elevator dinged its arrival.

When the director told her to enter, she rolled the trolley to a table and laid out the breakfast. As she filled the cups with fresh coffee, she could feel the eyes of the men watching her.

In particular the predator, who seemed to be noting her every move. Lambarri kept her eyes low. "Will there be anything else, sir?"

"No. Thank you major." Aquila said.

Lambarri was rolling the cart over to the corner when the predator tapped her on the shoulder. She flinched and spun to find him smiling with his hand out. "This fell."

*It's one of the packets!*

Lambarri went to her safe place and pasted on the smile she'd practiced a thousand times. "I'm sorry, colonel, I must have missed it when cleaning up" she said, watching the predator's face.

Delgado laughed. "Ochoa, my friend, you've been promoted."

*So that's his name,* she thought.

But Aguila and Ochoa were not laughing. The predator turned his dead eyes on Director Delgado.

"No amigo," Delgado said. "There is nothing to worry about. Lambarri comes from a family who helped win the revolution and start this directorate. Thank you major, that will be all."

It took all the willpower she could muster to leave the director's suite without running.

She shivered as she pushed the cart into her galley.

Lightheaded, she went to the lady's room, where she relieved herself and flushed the packets.

Her hands still trembling, she washed and got back to her desk.

An hour later after the meeting had ended, the director called and asked her to remove the cart. When she started, the director came to her side and, with a firm grip, grabbed her bicep.

He turned her toward him. "Isabel, do us both a favor and forget the name I mentioned today. And the older man, you've likely heard who he is. You must forget his name, too. Do you understand?"

Isabel paled, her heart skipping a beat. "Yes, sir. You will tell me when I need to know who you are meeting with. Otherwise, I will consider it sensitive."

"Good, we understand each other. I look forward to deepening our working relationship."

Major Lambarri left the director's suite certain she'd just collected information that would stop the scourge.

Back in her galley, she removed the recording device and texted her sister, arranging to meet for dinner.

The minutes and hours ticked by like molasses. When the director finally left at 1630, she took two deep breaths and stretched her neck to relieve the tension.

Setting her backpack next to the monitor to shield anyone from seeing what she was doing, she entered the human resources system and searched for an employee by the name of Ochoa; there were five. Two were retired, leaving a major, and two sergeants.

She accessed the major's record and the predator's file popped on the screen. The record was filled with schools and awards.

Isabel focused and found four items of interest: his clearance, his time as a Black Wasp, the notation of a special assignment, and the lack of anything after the posting two years ago.

She logged off and went through the audit trail cleaning process.

When it was time to go, she forced herself to take her time, saying hi to a few friends before ambling out to the waiting car.

At home, she put on her favorite dress and slipped the recording device into her underwear.

"Are we lucky enough to get what we needed in one attempt?" she whispered to herself and headed to the restaurant.

**28**

———————

Agency Safe House Havana, Cuba

George was alerted to the visitor, the video showed Lisa entering and making her way to the safe room. When he got downstairs, Ilena was pouring coffee.

Lisa sat waiting, her fingers drumming the table. When he appeared, she pushed the recording device across the table with a smile. "Isabel thinks we have something actionable. She was able to deploy the dust and record some conversation."

"Ilena, please get our guests. They're going to want to hear this."

As she walked out, George took the device to a laptop and connected it to a dongle. He moved the file into a directory where the decryption program took over. Ilena returned with Wolf and Elle in tow.

"We're waiting on the decryption program to finish. Our asset deployed the dust and may have some audio of a meeting," George said.

Lisa jumped in. "The asset said the meeting included the director, General Delgado, Aguila, and an active-duty major named Ochoa."

"We have a pretty good workup on Aguila. What do we know about this Major Ochoa?" Elle asked.

"Not much. The asset said high clearance, former special forces, and a note stating special assignment two years ago," Lisa said.

"I bet the special assignment aligns with Aguila's quote 'retirement,'" Wolf said.

"What do you have to back up that idea?" George asked.

"It's been swirling around my subconscious.," Wolf said. "What if the idea to grow here came from here, and Aguila's retirement was part of the plan? What if Aguila was sent to El Chapo with the goal of getting his security and intelligence apparatus right before inking the partnership. And what if it was a plan that then-Director Zaragoza executed two years ago?"

Lisa and Ilena appeared to be considering the idea.

"Personally, I don't think of Zaragoza as that creative," George said. "Which would mean other unknown person or persons are behind this partnership."

"What does it matter how the partnership came to be. We just need to stop it." Lisa said.

"That's true but knowing who the architect behind this is helps us avoid handing over the evidence to someone who would just say thanks and bury it—along with all of us," Elle said.

"Elle's right. We need to know, but it doesn't stop us from gathering the evidence in preparation for delivery to a source high enough to force action," Wolf said.

The laptop dinged, and the screen flashed Decryption Complete. George selected the decrypted audio file and increased the volume. A male voice said, "This fell."

"I'm sorry, colonel, I must have missed it when cleaning up" a female voice said.

"Ochoa, my friend, you've been promoted," a different male voice said.

"No amigo," the second male voice said. "There is nothing to worry about. Lambarri comes from a family who helped win the revolution and start this directorate. Thank you major, that will be all."

A door closed and another man talked about a processing lab

getting back online. A third huffed. "The fire could have been much worse."

George stopped the playback. "So, the first male must be Major Ochoa. The female voice is the asset. The next voice after the asset is General Delgado. It makes the last voice taking about the fire, Aguila."

Elle and Wolf agreed. George hit the play button and the conversation continued. It included Aguila's plan to visit the processing labs one more time to ensure all the product had been transported to the warehouse.

He requested the use of a helicopter, and Delgado apologized he did not have one available. Delgado also apologized that the road into Mensura was in disrepair and promised a dozer and grader to remedy the situation as soon as possible. Then he cleared his throat. "I hesitate to mention this, but it could become a concern we better deal with soon, lest it grow."

"What is it?" Aguila said, a disturbed tone leaking through.

"We have reports that the local men have heard about good paying jobs in the park and are driving and even hiking into the area looking for work. It seems they heard about the generous employer who took care of a deceased worker. We are, of course, turning them away—"

Aguila interrupted. "Good. Keep turning them away and let us know if it escalates. We need to go."

There was some shuffling of feet, then Aguila said, "You should visit the site. You are a critical piece of this partnership and should understand the business better. We won't be here for much longer."

Delgado said he'd clear his calendar and visit soon. There was a brief silence, then Delgado used his intercom to call for a Major Lambarri.

Delgado ordered Lambarri to find time in his schedule and she responded. The rest was muted rustling before the recording stopped.

"What's Mensura?" Wolf asked.

"It's a national park north of Santiago de Cuba," Ilena said.

"That's where they must be growing and harvesting the opium," George said.

"I need to go there immediately," Wolf said. "Can you help me?"

**29**

———————

Agency Safe House, Havana Cuba

"Yes," George says. "But we'll have to drive you there. Taking a commuter plane is too dangerous."

"Good, I need to get eyes on it," I say. "Get some pictures of the fields and the processing labs to start. If I can connect the warehouse, all the better."

"There will be layers of security. G2 works with the Black Wasps so they could be involved too," Ilena says.

"I understand. I have some experience at penetrating layered security, both cartel and military. I'm going dusted so our team can track me. That way there's a record of my route and where I stop if I don't get back right away or can't communicate. My comms will be with our ops center, so if I'm compromised, it doesn't lead back to you. And once I'm in Mensura it's a twenty-four-hour hunt. If I don't find anything, I'll exfil and we can regroup. Agreed?"

"Yes," George says. "We'll turn on a safe house we have on the edge of the city, and you can work from there. I need to stay here and keep to our pattern of life. I have business interests in Santiago de Cuba, but only visit once a month. Ilena can join you full time."

"Good, when can we leave?" I ask.

"Fifteen minutes," George says. "Are you ready?"

"He stays ready. Can you give us the room?" Elle asks.

After the others file out, she gives me the look, so I say, "I'll be careful. Recon and marking only. No engagement unless I need to break contact."

"You know I don't normally ask you to promise me anything, but just this once promise me you won't go hunting, Wolf. We don't have any back up here."

"Okay. And it includes El Chapo too. I know you're going to mention him next."

Elle smiles. "You think you know me Lance Bear Wolf?"

I pull her close and whisper, "Yeah, I've been paying attention," I say and kiss my wife.

"See you in a couple of days when I'm feeling better," she says.

I head to an SUV with Ilena.

*Elle's right.* This is not like assaulting a Sinaloa location with General Gonzalez's men: tons of guns and the full force of the Mexican military for backup if the assault goes sideways.

Not to mention drones, helicopter gunships, and aircraft support. No. This mission is much closer to the singleton missions I've worked in the past.

Like the one where I got chased by Russian Spetsnaz and dog handlers across the southern peninsula of Turkmenistan. I was wounded and out of ammunition when my late friend Colonel Gates pulled me out with my stepbrother Bjorn at the controls of the helicopter.

The lesson from the mission was "Don't Get Compromised."

That is the name of the game on this one too.

We take the A1 south along the spine of the island. I can't see the park in the dark, but I'm surprised by its size. Parque National Cienaga de Zapata. It seems to stretch on forever.

"It goes from here to the ocean," Ilena says. "There are seven national parks in all. About twenty-five percent of the land is parks. There are seven biospheres and three wetlands. Where you are headed is some of the highest and most rugged terrain in all of Cuba."

"Great! I love nasty terrain. The worse, the better. Only the very dedicated patrol those sections, and then only if they have to."

"You Americans call it the suck, right?"

"Yes, we do. Embrace the suck is the motto."

"It's the way of armies, no?"

"True." *Where in the heck did she learn that?*

The next six hours of driving are relatively quiet, except when Ilena points out something significant. We stop in Guaimaro for gas, and the thought this drive might be uneventful crosses my mind.

I fill the SUV while Ilena walks to the restaurant next door to order some takeout. I'm placing the nozzle back in the pump holder when the dirtiest cop car I think I've ever seen rolls to a stop.

I can feel the cop eyeing me, sure he's noticed the new SUV with Havana tags. I keep doing my thing by lifting the hood to check the oil.

*Now that I'm out of sight, let's see what he does.*

I hear the patrol car door open, and I head for my backpack and passport.

The cop, who's about five foot four and as wide as he is tall, comes around the front of the car, hand on his pistol.

I smile and hold out my booklet, waiting for his next move.

He steps forward into my space and yanks it from my hand while attempting to give me the lazy eye version of stink eye.

I'm working to suppress a smile and look down in acquiescence.

"Where are you headed, Mister Zarate?"

I'm about to speak when Ilena appears. "My cousin and I are visiting relatives in Santiago de Cuba."

His hand is still on his pistol while he thumbs through my passport. I keep my hands where he can see them, and Ilena pushes by and sits the food on the front seat.

The cop passes back my booklet. "ID," he says holding out his hand.

She pulls her ID and shoves it to him clearly not pleased with his power play.

I'm amused and simultaneously nervous as she stares down at Jabba the cop.

His eyes narrow. "I want your relatives' names, addresses, and phone numbers."

Ilena rattles them off and I work to memorize them for the future.

I won't always have her or someone else from George's team at my side.

His face becomes a strange combination of screwed up and mean.

He blows out a huff. "You may go, but know I will check these names."

We get in the SUV and she exhales. Handing me my breakfast, she asks, "You have this in America? I've seen it on TV."

I laugh. "Yes. On TV and in real life. Small men with badges. A bad combination."

Ilena pulls away from the pump and parks. The smell of the food is amazing; the pork and eggs with beans fill the hole in my belly and my soul. Delicious.

We're back on the road headed south when she pulls out a map and points. "Here, on the west side of the park, I will drop you off at Biran where the road ends at the trailhead. Then I will head south and spend the night in Miranda in case you need extraction. If we do not connect within twenty-four hours after I drop you off, I will head to the safe house. If you are compromised or late, head to the cement factory at Canapu. It's one of George's business interests in the area. Understood?"

"Okay. I'll see you in Miranda."

"I hope you do."

Two hours later I'm mapped out and ready to go. Ilena pulls over.

"Thank you," I say, exiting the SUV.

It's dusk as I walk into the jungle.

I'm enveloped in the growing darkness which matches my mood.

The black wolf with it's yellow eyes tells me it's time for revenge.

**30**

———————

D AY 4
Parque Mensura, Cuba
The quarter moon is just enough that I can sense the right side of the trail. My plan is to patrol south toward Miranda and Canapu, so I can recon the south faces of the mountains.

If I don't find anything, I'll head north to take another run at it.

The sun has not breached the mountains yet so it's too dark to see tracks right now, but I can tell I've found a trail used by a taller animal like a deer.

The good news is it's headed in the general direction I need to go.

I've got to hand it to animals; we may think they're of limited intelligence, but this trail is making use of the terrain and cover—the exact opposite of the Ranger way, aka, "the shortest route between two points is a straight line." *Embrace the suck brother.*

I'm almost four kilometers south when my nose is graced by odor from a fire. Another one hundred meters and I can make out the men talking and laughing.

I get to the edge of the jungle and the clearing blooms before me.

The multiple fires are scattering enough light so I can make out the processing facility. I back out and retrieve my satellite phone, which I had placed into receive only mode, and note the GPS coordinates.

I follow the trail. It makes a wide berth around the site.

I see the road as the first rays light my way. I won't have the cover of darkness for much longer, but will hopefully be enough to complete the risky part of the mission.

I drop to the jungle floor as two guards walk by only a few feet away. One is trying to talk soccer while his buddy is telling a story about the woman he was with two nights ago. They're a total Frick and Frack duo.

As they pass, I think about my experience with El Chapo and the Sinaloa Cartel. I've seen patterns emerge over the years; more often than not it is a straight-line route between the cultivation plots and the processing labs.

In this case, I'm in an area that looks like your fingers spread out in front of you. Where they join at the "hand," are the south facing valleys. They get the long day's sun. The sun needed to grow opium poppies.

The grow plots must be higher than I am now at this processing lab. I turn left, then left again to intersect another game trail leading into the valley.

The least suck way up the mountain is a trail next to a noisy stream; it helps to hide my approach, but it can also mask others tracking me, so I slow down.

I only need two labs or two fields to get a sense of the operation. I'm into the valley another mile when I come across a muddy path leading to the stream.

I lay down and inch back into the jungle, pulling foliage in front of me. About thirty-five minutes later, two women come to the stream and gather water. They're chattering on about the pig the soldiers brought them to cook.

Their laughter is a break from the serious nature of my objective. But not my vigilance.

As they head up the hill, I follow, staying fifty meters back. Their talking is all I need to maintain contact as they disappear into the darkness of a ravine.

I hear them talk to a guard and I freeze. He is well hidden, and it takes a minute to see his movement. Shifting from one foot to the other, he is the only moving thing in my field of vision.

I scan past him to the use the extra rods and higher levels of Rhodopsin in my eyes, which give me better than average scotopic vision.

Aka night vision. It takes a minute, but I finally pick out his partner, who is motionless.

*The partner is who I need to pay attention to, not shifty.*

I'm moving left when I smell an awful odor. My next step almost takes me into the slit trench. I stumble back, and as slow as I can, sit down below the vegetation line.

Shifty calls out in rapid fire Cuban, asking who's there.

"Probably nothing. Just another pig," his partner says.

They talk for a minute, and I use their noisy conversation to move farther north. It takes time to circumnavigate the field to the southern side.

I sense I'm clear of the guards. Now that I'm in sync with the jungle, I move faster, heading south.

I stop in my tracks and search. I can't see it, but I can smell it. Scanning from the ground up, there it is.

The breeze lets a flash of light in, and its eyes reflect a golden hue. The cat's odor is strong. It hisses at me then slinks back in the jungle. *Someone's exotic pet got loose.*

I remind myself there are no puma or jaguar in Cuba and carefully move off.

My watch tells me I've only got two and a half hours until the sun is overhead.

I need to go faster, or I'll be prey instead of predator.

**31**

---

Parque Mensura, Cuba

I find a low spot along the ridge line and move down, keeping to the trees on the north side. The jungle is thinner here, and I can see my next target and its boundaries below me.

A fire glows in the distance on the southwest corner of the field, and I head toward it, happy to have found a second field confirming my suspicion on the layout of the plots. I follow the ridge with my senses on alert.

Most of the targets my team and I have prosecuted during the drug war have been point targets—except for labs and their relationship to grow plots. The same goes for transportation, regardless of it being land-based or aircraft.

During my one-man war with the Sinaloa Cartel, I found a pattern leading me to multiple clandestine runways and aircraft.

If I remember correctly, I destroyed five of seven aircraft back then. My plan is to do the same to what must be the trucks they use to get the product off the mountain to the warehouse mentioned on the audio file.

But I'm getting ahead of myself and not paying attention to my movement like I should.

Focusing back on being present and working on the problem in front of me, I crab toward the southern edge of the field.

I can't see the fire I saw from the ridge, but I expect to smell it or hear someone in time to give it a wide berth.

Minutes later, I hear a crying female mixed with laughing and jeering men.

It sends a cold shiver down my spine, and clouds of darkness and anger crowd out my rational mind.

I ease to the jungle floor and crawl forward, looking for booby-traps and trip wires as I close in on their position.

I move the vegetation to get a view of a camp on the edge of the field. A young woman is hog-tied on the ground, her clothes ripped off around her.

There are two soldiers with their backs to me, and one to my left. A soldier wearing a black beret comes out of the woods, closing his zipper like he's just relieved himself.

*Sorry babe can't let this go. No one abuses women or children on my watch.*

I promised Elle I wouldn't go hunting, but this is different.

If this is what the Black Wasps are about, I've got a problem. The question is what I can do about it with the suppressed Makarov pistol Ilena gave me.

*Divide and conquer is the way.*

I crawl backwards to a safe distance and take a knee. The sunlight is working it's way down the mountains fast.

I move slowly, expecting some sort of early warning, but find nothing to the north along the edge of the field.

I circle back south, taking a slightly wider route and intersect a well-worn trail which likely leads to the lab. As I head back toward the camp, I find some help.

It's a flashbang the Black Wasps have put across the trail to warn them of someone approaching.

I leave the flashbang and its tripwire; it will alert me if there are men rushing to the soldiers defense. *I hope I don't need the alert—quiet is the best outcome.*

When I get back to their camp, two of the soldiers are racked out, one is playing with the fire, and the other is groping the woman, who whimpers.

I'm not sure how quickly security can get here from the lab.

*It is what it is.*

I spin on the suppressor onto my pistol, then run into the clearing and put a round in the head of the guy molesting the woman.

The solider tending the fire realizes his teammate is dead just before I shoot him through the temple.

I spin back to the soldiers who were sleeping and drop one as he rises.

The other brings his rifle to bear, and I dive behind the soldier who was tending the fire and roll his body up to mine.

The rifle barks on full auto and I can feel the rounds impacting the soldier I'm hiding behind. Suddenly, there is silence.

I look over and see the soldier going through his immediate action drill to clear the weapon.

Unfortunately for him, he forgets he's still in a fight.

I shoot him in the throat and chest. He looks confused, then falls over.

I jump to my feet and gather the woman's clothes, such as they are. I pull a blanket from one of the dead soldiers and cover her.

The chaos has disoriented her, so I find a canteen and splash water in her face. She comes around and stiffens when she sees me.

"You can go now. These men will never hurt anyone again," I say in Spanish.

She stares at me. I try a smile, hoping my face doesn't look too creepy in the firelight. She struggles to her feet, and I help her stand, making sure she is covered by the blanket.

I hand her clothes to her, and she scans the destruction. She kicks the man who molested her, and spits.

"You need to go," I say. I grab an AK, some magazines, and a couple grenades. When I look back, she's gone.

I function check the AK and pick up what appears to be a squad radio. I switch it off and throw it and the pistol in my pack.

I take a second to review my options, tighten the chest strap and waist belt on my pack and run the trail to the lab.

*No one's crazy enough to do that, right?*

As my mentor Colonel Gates used to said, "It's only crazy if it doesn't work."

**32**

———————

Parque Mensura, Cuba

Creedence Clearwater Revival's "Run Through the Jungle" plays in my head as I sprint.

Behind me I hear shouts, and someone rips off a full auto burst from an AK, its sound too distinctive to miss.

The terrain naturally moves me west, so I cut back south again, wading through a stream.

I'm halfway to the top of the next ridge when I hear a sound I hate; dogs howling.

I love dogs, but when they're hunting me, not so much.

The sun has displaced most of the shadows and I'm crouching as I top the ridge, staying low so I'm not sky lighted as I cross over.

There's another stream two hundred and fifty yards to my southeast; I head for it like a madman.

No need to be stealthy now—the dogs have my scent.

I crash into the stream and start following it down, splashing through the pools.

I'm careful where I step, the lush green moss and plants make tracking easy if you know what to look for.

I hop over a rock and fall into rushing water, which pushes me over a waterfall.

Lucky for me, it's only a body length drop, and the dark pool cushions the impact.

I'm about to scramble out when I hear the dogs and shouting men above me.

It looks like they've figured out I'm using the stream to throw off the hounds and are hunting the edges to find my exit.

If I stand now, I'll be seen, so I scrabble between some rocks under an old broken tree.

Just my head is above the swirling stream, which is quickly cooling me off to the point where I am shivering.

I keep the AK underwater to dampen the noise I'd make if I held it at the ready.

*The dogs will be on me in a second.*

I duck under the water and hold my breath.

The dogs are above me barking and howling.

I pull myself around the rocks and find a space large enough for my head and shoulders where I wedge myself into it, cresting the water for a much-needed gulp of stale air.

The handlers yell and pull their dogs back.

My relief is shattered when the air is filled with copper clad AK rounds that smack the water and crack against the boulders.

There are two ricochets in quick succession and more yelling.

The shooting stops and I hear a radio call.

I can't make it out, but it doesn't matter; all I can hear is the stream.

I wait to be sure there are no stragglers, and move up the incline into the jungle.

I ball myself up to conserve what little core temperature I have.

I'm shaking uncontrollably but know it will pass.

After a few minutes, I stand and push the arrogant "you can't catch me" thought from my mind just in time to feel the air pressure change.

I dive under a nearby tree and scan the air.

Through the canopy, it flashes overhead for a split second.

*Crap! A flying tank. Really?*

The suck factor on this mission just went from a solid seven to fifteen on a ten scale.

I've been chased by MI-24 HIND attack helicopters before but had firepower to fight back.

Now I have nothing.

What I wouldn't give for a man-portable air defense missile or even an RPG about now.

Good news is it can't kill what it can't see.

The bad news is it carries troops and could be putting more Black Wasps between me and the cement factory.

*Time to do what they don't expect.*

After the helicopter sound trails off, I slog back up to the ridge.

I'm headed to the lab, which I believe sits west of the last field I identified.

The Black Wasps think they're pushing me downstream into an ambush they are setting.

That's what most well-trained commanders would do.

It takes me close to another hour to cross back over the ridge and start down the other side.

It's another forty after that before I smell the chemicals; a good sign I'm close and downwind.

I take out the Makarov pistol, fold the stock on the AK, and stuff it best I can in my backpack.

I slip a fresh clip in the pistol and jack a round into the chamber.

There are two things I need: a way out of here and the best place for a grenade to keep them occupied.

I skirt the site to the north, then sneak in, looking for transportation.

It looks like an enduro style 125-cc motorcycle and the key is in the ignition. It's small, but will do.

I work my way around to the south searching for a place to deposit the grenade, when I come upon what I call a superfund site in a nod to the EPA.

Like drug labs all over the world, it's where they dump their mostly empty barrels of chemicals.

It's a great place to find incendiary fluids and for getting close if you can stay silent with all the plastic and metal containers.

I weave my way through, shifting my eyes from where I'm stepping to the shed, I'm closing in on.

Some voices are ambling my way, and I hide behind a barrel.

A couple of jugs are thrown on the pile and the voices leave.

I read the jug: Acetic anhydride is some nasty stuff, so I quietly discard it and find a water bottle.

I'm going to make a time delay of sorts, so I don't blow up with the lab.

---

## 33

Parque Mensura, Cuba

The shed housing the chemicals has a metal roof with plastic barrels at each end to catch rainwater. The sides are open.

I creep to the nearest barrel and use my Swiss Army knife awl to make a hole in the bottom.

After I fill the bottle, I stuff the grenade between two barrels with labels saying Corrosive and Toxic.

The spoon is facing skyward; I poke a small hole in the bottom of the water bottle, place it on top of the grenade, and make sure the liquid is dripping out.

I pull the pin with a death grip on the spoon to make sure I haven't made a terminal list mistake.

The weight of the bottle is heavy enough to hold the spoon, and I back away as expeditiously as I can, moving with a purpose, but not so fast I alert the guards.

I arrive on the edge of the jungle about twelve feet from the motorcycle and wait.

I really have no idea how long it will take, and I'm surprised when, a beat later, the explosion thumps the oxygen out of the air.

I'm not looking as I race to the bike, turn the key, and give it a kick.

It starts and I punch it into gear and spin the rear wheel, racing away.

It's not much of a road—it needs serious maintenance.

I push as fast as I can on the switchbacks, focused on staying out of the jungle, when, as sure as my last name is Wolf, I hear the beast.

Its five blades have a diameter of fifty-six feet, and it slams the air to stay aloft.

I can see it in the distance, its nose is down, and it's headed toward the lab.

I slow to make it look like I'm just on the road, not running away.

Death personified flies right toward at me.

*Get ready to bail.*

Suddenly, the helicopter banks and climbs the hill.

With it at my back, I continue my sideways sprint off the mountain.

Surprisingly, it's at least fifteen minutes before the beast decides I'm worth checking out.

I've been generally heading southwest, so when I see a track that goes south, I take it and say a quick prayer for overhead cover.

I hear the beast fly by, looking where I had been headed.

I've only got a few more minutes before they decide I didn't run off the mountain and return.

The cover is getting thicker, but so are the branches and vines that threaten to block my path.

I twist the throttle to the stop; it's an appropriate sentiment, as that's exactly what the engine does. I roll to stop.

There is no reserve setting on the petcock, so I dump the bike and sprint.

It's about six miles to the cement plant, and I run as fast as I can while staying under cover.

Behind and above me, I can hear the beast searching.

Thirty plus minutes later, I slide to a stop.

The side of the mountain looks as if explosives have done much of the work.

It's too steep and too high for a controlled descent, so I trot along the edge until I see a spot where I can slide on my butt, feet out for protection.

I use my hands for stability and as rudders.

At the bottom, I sprint across an open area and hide between some cement trucks.

The one in front is running, so I grab a cell phone transmitter from my pack and let the magnet snap into place.

It's immediately transmitting, and I smile as I hear the driver say something and close his door. I scurry over to the next truck.

The driver goes through four gears just to get the heavily loaded truck rolling. Minutes later, I see the beast roar overhead.

*I'm finally clear.*

I run to the back of the dispatch shed and put the battery in my cell phone. I text Ilena that she can come get me at work.

When I see her drive in, I wave, walk her way like it's a natural thing, and get in the SUV.

She immediately crinkles her nose. "What did you get into?"

"All kinds of fun stuff," I said. "Let's go, I'll tell you on the way."

Ilena has the radio on and all the windows wide-open as we head to Santiago de Cuba. I close my eyes for what seems a second, then wake as I twitch.

I'm fighting an itch I can't reach when Ilena slows and pulls over.

Five hundred feet ahead, a helicopter is descending. It lands sideways in the road, and men jump out and swarm around a cement truck.

Police cars are converging.

Sirens wailing and lights flashing, three zoom by us.

Just beyond the helicopter is the intersection of the A1 and the Carriage a la Autopista Nacional

Both provide freeway-like speeds and easy access to Santiago de Cuba.

"I think it will be safer on the side roads. Security over speed,"

Ilena said. "We can go back to Troncones and head east along the Cauto river."

"They're all focused on the cement truck, let's go."

Ilena checks the mirrors, then crosses the divider to take the road back the way we came.

"Did you have something to do with the cement truck?" she asks.

"Yeah. I hope the driver doesn't get too much grief."

The rest of the drive I fill her in on what I found, and how I killed all of the Black Wasps who were hurting the woman. Ilena sneers and curses the soldiers.

I'm conflicted over my win at finding the drug sites and the loss of having to kill those soldiers. Especially when I promised my wife I wouldn't go hunting.

Right or wrong, I always tell her the truth. She'll understand, but I broke a promise.

# 34

On the Road to Santiago De Cuba

We head north and then east at Troncones, following and eventually crossing the Cauto river to the town of Chile.

Ilena tops off the gas and I stay out of sight this time. She suggests our reroute is not a bad thing.

"It will be much safer to enter the city in the early evening."

I agree. Once we are rolling again, I take out my satellite phone and craft a short message with poppy field coordinates for the ops center.

Ilena has been taking peeks at what I'm doing, but I keep the keypad angled so she can't see what I'm typing. "How much longer to the next town?"

"It's another thirty minutes to San Luis and an hour and a half to the safe house."

I check the constellation and see I've got access, so I hit the transmit button.

As soon as my transmission is received, I expect there to be multiple messages. I wait another three minutes; I still have access to the constellation, but the first message is the only message.

It's short and to the point.

Msg Rcvd. Tracking Stardust. Standby

"What's it say?" Ilena asks, breaking me out of my thoughts.

"It looks like the dust is working," I say and immediately wish I hadn't. She now knows the dust works, and that an American satellite or drone is overflying Cuba.

*Why am I being so paranoid?*

*She just helped me exfil from a tight situation where she seemed calm and matter of fact.*

*She's used to operating in the daylight and I'm not.*

We pass through San Luis, sticking to the side roads.

The sun is setting when Ilena gets a call.

The half I can hear tells me nothing, as she just grunts her acknowledgements.

The last thing Ilena says is, "Understood." She drops her cell into the center console. "Change of plans. George believes the safe house is being watched, so we are headed to an alternate."

"Where's that?"

"It's on the west side of town in the industrial area near the port."

"Let me guess—it's another cement operation."

"Good guess. It does not make the cement, but cement things for warehouses, bridges, and the port. The cement is made next door."

"And it's not covered in dust?"

"It is, just like the dusty and dangerous men who lead Cuba."

An interesting allegory to be sure.

*I have to admit, I would like some cement shoes in El Chapo's size.*

The route to the new location is more convoluted than the one we were on. It is nearing 1400 when my satellite phone buzzes in my lap.

*Why the heck are they calling versus a message?*

"Wolf, it's Kennedy."

I curse to myself. "I thought we agreed messages are safer?"

"Yeah, but I can't put this in a message. Good news is the dust worked. I think we've tracked Ochoa to your sites, and two more."

"Why do you think it's Ochoa and not Aguila?"

"The way he moved through the jungle. Retired colonels don't move like a wolf."

"Funny!"

"It's not meant to be. Ochoa means the wolf in Basque."

*Great, no wonder the asset called him a predator.*

Kennedy continues, "But there's also bad news. The president asked if we have enough evidence to destroy the partnership. Davidson said yes, but reiterated El Chapo is the target. The president doesn't care about El Chapo. He wants to stop Cuba from becoming another Mexico."

"Dang it! How much time do we have?"

"Three days, after that, the president will start to wonder where the evidence is and why we haven't turned it over... Wolf? Are you there?"

"Yeah. It's been a slow start, and I just found where they are growing the poppies. Report follows. Out."

## 35

———————

D<sup>AY 3</sup>
Agency Safe House Havana Cuba

The morning after Wolf left, Elle took the tunnel under the street to the necropolis. George had said it would be quiet; the people of Havana were preparing for church.

She stayed inside the crypt, and, as George had directed, removed a vent grill so her satellite phone could see the sky.

She messaged Morgan, asking for his help. Six long seconds later she got a "message received" notification.

*Morgan's as crazy as a soup sandwich, but he's good for Wolf. And God knows he needs the help.*

Kennedy had messaged her about tracking Ochoa and the president's push to end the mission. But she knew the evidence they had just acquired wasn't enough.

It would stop the partnership, but El Chapo wouldn't suffer any consequence other than some lost investment. Not a big deal for a money printing machine.

*So, how do we tie El Chapo to the product?*

Elle retraced her steps back through the tunnel and joined George and Lisa at the workbench.

"Have you communicated with Wolf yet?" George said.

"No, why?"

"I've gotten reports of gun fire and explosions in Mensura park."

"From Ilena?"

"No. From some other sources."

"Well, if Wolf is compromised, he won't call until he's clear—or more likely at the safe house. While we're waiting, maybe you can help me figure out something."

"What's that?" Lisa asked.

"Let's say he is successful at locating some poppy fields or labs. Short of catching El Chapo during a visit, which is near impossible, what are your thoughts on how we tie him to the opium, morphine, heroin... whatever form it's in?"

"Besides taking a picture of him at one of the sites, it's a pretty short list. We could catch him making a payment to Delgado or another government official. Planting drugs on him is another sure bet. We could also plant them at his safe house or in his aircraft, if it's how he arrived." George said.

"I don't think we should limit ourselves to just the drugs," Lisa said. "What if he was acquiring non-sanctioned weapons or state secrets? Even better, some tech we steal from the Chinese?"

"What's the quickest and safest way to pull it off? I was just informed that we have a couple of days to complete our mission."

"What do you mean?'" George asked.

"Our chain of command is pushing to drop the El Chapo hunt and settle for destroying the partnership."

"Chain of command?" Lisa asked.

"The president."

"Politics," George said inside a growl.

"Stopping the partnership doesn't fix the problem for Cuba. El Chapo will create another arrangement," Lisa said.

"True. He might have already. We're focused on opium. He could be using Cuba as a transshipment site."

"Let's review the facts," George said. "We've just started and must give this time to play out. All we need is one field of poppies or one processing lab, and we'll be able to identify the rest. When we do, we can deconstruct its shipment to Santiago de Cuba and the warehouse."

Elle knew the answer before she asked. "And why is the product going to Santiago de Cuba and not somewhere else?"

"You know why," Lisa said. "El Chapo has everything he needs without the scrutiny of operating in the Havana area. He has a port and airport close by, and I wouldn't put it past him to have created a clandestine airstrip somewhere in the park."

"Agreed. But I suspect he's planning to move the product by sea, not by plane. He can move much more in one load. He thinks in terms of tons these days, not aircraft-size loads," Elle said.

*I can't wait for Morgan to get here,* she thought.

"I think it's best if you two join Ilena and Wolf in Santiago de Cuba. I'll schedule a visit to the plant I have there. Lisa can alert our assets," George said.

"Good. I'm feeling useless sitting here," Elle said.

"I wouldn't worry," George said. "I think this mission is about to get—what do you Americans say, spicy?"

## 36

———————

Mensura Parque, Cuba

Ochoa checked his cell phone and as he suspected, there was no signal in the park. He powered up his Thuraya satellite phone. When it acquired the satellite constellation, he called Aguila.

He answered on the second ring. "Yes."

"Wolf was here. He killed a squad of Black Wasps and damaged a working lab."

Ochoa glanced at his watch as the cursing went on for seven, almost eight seconds.

"Are you sure it was Wolf?"

"Who else would use military tactics during their surveillance and have a micro-transmitter generate a false lead to break contact? The G2 signals specialist who tracked and recovered the device gave it to our Chinese liaison. They said the transmitter was made from Eastern European parts but has an American signature."

*Wolf is here and he has local help,* Aguila thought.

"So, tell me. How did he miss your fake lab and the elaborate trap you set up?"

"Dumb luck. Maybe it was just where he entered the park."

"Listen to me carefully, Major. There is no such thing as dumb luck with Wolf. He did not just happen upon a working lab. He saw through your ruse and made us pay for your arrogance. I'm going to say this one last time, so pay close attention. He is the very best they have, and he's come closer to killing El Chapo than anyone else on the planet, including the Zeta Cartel. Do you hear me?"

"Yes, sir." Ochoa said realizing he would not get another chance.

"Okay. I'll get Delgado to provide more troops. Have them mine the areas around the crops and labs. Can we get your contact to provide technical support?"

"Possibly. It would be a big coup for the Chinese if they found Wolf here in Cuba."

"Yes, but the trick is keeping them insulated from the reason we are hunting him."

"Agreed, I'll start seeding a rogue agent story. He has a grudge to settle with Delgado after he killed some of Wolf's Ranger squad in Grenada during the American invasion."

"Delgado never served in Grenada."

"When the Chinese hack into the database to verify the story, they'll see the classified assignment to whatever the code word for the operation was back then."

"The code name was 'Red Cow.'"

Ochoa balked. "Good. Knowing it makes it easier for my asset to make the change."

"What story are you telling your asset?"

"That it's part of a current operation back story...hold on...there's been another explosion." Ochoa rotated until he oriented to the sound. The boom echoed in the hills, then died away to be replaced by automatic gunfire. He switched to his radio. "Wasp, Lobo. Report!"

"Lobo. Squad in contact, sector three."

Ochoa switched back to his satellite phone. "Squad in contact. I'll message you later." Not waiting for a response, he disconnected the call. The last of the gunfire filtered through the jungle. When he realized it had stopped, he radioed the Black Wasp commander. "Lobo headed to contact."

"Lobo, understood. Squad reports threat neutralized."

Ochoa jumped in his SUV and headed to sector three—the middle field and lab. From his location in sector five, the northern most, it would take an hour—maybe forty-five minutes if he hustled.

#

Ochoa exited his SUV at the closest point to the grid coordinates he'd been given on the drive to sector three. He scanned the roadside and found a track, likely the one used by whoever had terminated the Black Wasps. Eleven minutes along the track, he saw the first signs of carnage.

The dead men had been walking in a file. The last man had been stitched across the chest with rifle fire. The next man up the line had rifle wound, and his arm was severed above the elbow—it lay several steps away. The next three in the line were barely recognizable as human.

The explosion he'd heard had to be the Cuban version of a Russian MON-50 Claymore type mine. Some holes in the parts of the men which were still recognizable were long rather than round. This indicated the mine was an older version, with short steel rods versus the steel balls of the newer mines.

*Not that rods or balls matter to the dead.*

Ochoa walked through the gore. *I bet these guys were just looking for work.*

At the other end called out. "Where's my squad leader?"

*Good,* Ochoa thought as the soldiers appeared from the jungle. *They moved from where they executed the ambush.*

"Report," Ochoa said.

"Sir, we followed orders received this morning to stop any unauthorized personnel from observing the operation. We are one of four squads protecting sites in this sector."

"Did you warn these men or give them any idea they were entering an off-limits area?" Ochoa asked.

"No sir, it was another team's job. Our lieutenant has us set up in protective layers. We've been ordered to terminate anyone reaching our innermost ring, sir."

"Thank you, Sergeant," Ochoa said. The Black Wasps didn't always execute smartly, but they loved their body counts. Useful if controlled properly, and reckless if not. The wives and girlfriends of the five dead men would start asking questions in a day... maybe less.

*How many will die because the cover story was not set before the start of the operation?*

Back at the SUV, he cursed the lack of pre-mission work to set conditions for a successful operation. He'd been taught that in all operations other than extremist hostage rescue situations, there was some level of intelligence preparation of the battlefield.

Most armies, including the American, subscribed to the tenants of Intelligence Preparation of the Battlefield, IPB. The analysis of enemy, terrain, weather, and civil considerations.

*Apparently, there hasn't been any consideration of potential enemies or civilian population interaction. So, now Wolf is in play and the locals think there are jobs in the park.*

Time for some PSYOPs in the area about an unfortunate training accident. A flyer and some radio announcements to keep people away should do the job. A task that Aguila and Delgado should have handled before planting opium.

His boss answered his call on the first ring. "What happened?"

"Five men, likely looking for work were ambushed by a squad of Black Wasps. Good news is no one survived. The bad news is their wives and girlfriends will start asking questions. I'll handle it with the police. I suggest some PSYOPs messaging in the area, and a flyer stating the military has taken over the park indefinitely for training. I also think some radio announcements from the Santiago de Cuba stations about the take-over and training is a good idea."

"It will expose part of the operation. We can't."

"Your lack of attention to the civil considerations of your operation has put it in jeopardy."

"Ochoa, remember your place!"

*He needs to hear this.*

"Sir, let me finish. A minor adjustment will keep everything under control. If, for some reason, it gets out of control, we can give a field or two of already harvested opium to the leadership and the media. It will be a great victory for G2 and Delgado, and a minor inconvenience for El Chapo."

"What you said is true, but this is what happens when working with El Chapo. He does not consider all the variables, nor does he allow time to do the pre-mission work you and I were taught was critical to success. Make the adjustment. We are less than a week away from profits beyond your imagination."

"The money is welcome, but I'm here to hurt America from the inside, using their decadence and addiction like a virus against them."

"If you really want to hurt America, kill Wolf so we can put his dead body on display in Revolution Square. He's the hidden leader of America's drug war, and our biggest threat. Kill him, Ochoa!"

## 37

Cement Products, Santiago De Cuba

It doesn't seem an inspired name for company but as it turns out, glitzy company names are not a thing in Cuba.

Although, George *was* inspired enough to build a three-bedroom apartment over the plant offices. It saved money and acted as a secondary safe house.

Apparently, he did something similar at all of his sixteen cement and cement products plants. This one, on the western side of Santiago de Cuba's upper harbor, is now our designated ops center/safe house.

I wait until 2200 before leaving the facility to call Kennedy.

I walk east over the railroad tracks toward the bay, ensuring I stay in the shadows while I circle around the lights of a Puerto New gas station.

Movement catches my eye and I stop to scan the area; it's a guard patrolling a large building fence line.

*Wonder how much was stolen before they decided to take their security seriously?*

The facility holds my gaze for a beat, then I turn away and stand at the water's edge.

Like most bay backwater areas, this one doesn't get a daily refresh of seawater from the tides like the mouth of the bay.

My nose crinkles at the odor of diesel fuel combined with rotting fish and other debris.

I punch in the speed dial and security codes for Kennedy's line. He, his wife, and their four-year-old have moved back to MacDill temporarily for the mission.

Having my original partner in crime at the operational helm of the organization has given me another excuse to leave my director duties behind and hunt El Chapo.

"Miss me?" I say when he answers.

"Yeah, the paperwork is killing me. No wonder you wanted to operate. You know karma is going to get you when you take Davidson's position."

I laughed. "Scares me. And I'm fearless."

"You must be feeling secure after giving me crap for calling."

"Yeah, sorry about that. The Cubans have some SIGINT here, but it's not threat to our LPD kit. And the Chinese seem to like Havana and not much else."

"We were able to track one of the meeting guests using the dust. According to the Kid, it's a guy named Ochoa. He headed into the park after your run through the jungle. The tech works, but the problem is getting the drone."

"What do you mean?"

"The B-3 drone has been re-tasked. My sources say someone in leadership got the willies transiting the highly sensitive asset over your location."

"That's stupid! It's made expressly for this kind of denied area mission. What about satellite imagery. Get me a satellite launched in the last twenty years and the resolution will be good enough to provide the photographic evidence we need to prove El Chapo's involvement."

"I hear you, Wolf. But to be honest, it appears that we are being denied access to capabilities we routinely source. The word is they are assigned to other priority tasks."

"I don't understand. This is a time-sensitive tasking from the president."

"Agreed… you know I'm trained to look past the labels and false logic of conspiracy theories, so what I say next may sound paranoid." Kennedy says. "I believe the denial of resources is manufactured from within the administration to inhibit our ability to succeed."

"Didn't expect that—but it's possible. I'd bet a certain presidential advisor is pulling the strings. Keep looking into it, but El Chapo is priority one, right?"

"Yes, and to that end, I've been looking at options outside the intel and DOD resource pool. Way out, as a matter of fact."

"Good, I think?"

"I'm going to use NASA's Moderate Resolution Imaging Spectroradiometer, which is onboard the Terra satellite. It feeds their Earth Observing System Data and Information System Worldview application. It's a long shot, but sixty percent of Cuba is agriculture. We can use what it collects and feed the results into Providence."

Providence is our analytic system, built by Kid. It's better, for us at least, than what we would get from Oracle or Palantir. We provide feeds to the El Paso Intelligence Center, the DEA, and the other five eyes partners; the United Kingdom, Canada, Australia, and New Zealand.

"If the NASA bird is a useable workaround, I'll take it. What about our Low Earth Orbit, LEO constellation?"

"We are placing three more satellites in orbit, with Light Detection and Ranging, LIDAR packages to track the dust. You'll have a satellite overhead every thirty minutes."

"Can we switch out the payload for an imagery package?"

"Unfortunately, no. Our window of opportunity is too small." Kennedy says.

"Okay, but the Intelligence Advanced Research Projects Activity, IARPA put our F-15 on hold after the last failure. How are you getting them set in the constellation?"

"You can thank Davidson when you get back. He was able to

scrounge the funding for one more launch. After this, I think we'll be using one of the commercial programs."

"Okay, got it. What about finding El Chapo's safe house?"

"We're scouring the area you designated. We still have access to National Reconnaissance Office, NRO signals and electronic intelligence satellites and the NSA and Cyber Command teams assigned to the mission. It's the new requests that are being denied. I'll keep pushing, but I also need you to start a fire for the NASA satellite. The hotter the better, so it stands out from the agricultural fires."

"But why? Can't you just pull recent flyby data and use the coordinates I sent to locate the fields and labs?"

"There have not been any flybys in the last year. I have to do an off book re-tasking of the satellite to record your activity in Mensura Park."

"Off book re-tasking? K-man, please tell me you're not hacking their ground station.

"No, I am not."

I can read between the lines.

*Kennedy is an intel guru, not a hacker.*

*I don't want to know that it will be Kid on the keyboard.*

"Okay. I have just the thing. The guys at Strategic Command will alert you, but you'll know it's me," I say inside a chuckle.

"Hold on, Wolf. Let's not make the STRATCOM guys jumpy. Just about anything looking like a missile launch from Cuba will hit the president's desk. And that's a bear we shouldn't poke."

"Okay, I'll tone it down. But you'll know where one or more of the labs used to be. The plant next door to our safe house makes cement so they'll have magnesium. It burns at four thousand degrees Fahrenheit... as much as five thousand when water is introduced. And there is plenty of water around the labs. But I need to wait at least a day to let them settle down. The next trip up there is going to suck."

"The word is dangerous, Wolf. Make your own luck, Akduxxiilee." Kennedy said using the Crow word for warrior.

I respond with a 'thanks,' but I'm not feeling like a crow warrior.

Or a spy.

More like a detective working on a homicide where there's lots of information but no facts to grab onto.

As I'm walking back to the safe house, I realize I better become a warrior if I'm to survive another trip into Mensura park.

# 38

D AY 2

Santiago De Cuba

"So, what's the population of Santiago de Cuba?" Elle asked as they passed the welcome sign. "I read it's the second largest city in Cuba after Havana."

"One point five million," Lisa said. "We're on the northwest side of the city. Our safe house is on the southeastern side, almost one hundred and eighty degrees opposite our position. We should get cell coverage soon."

"There are places in America with no coverage. Wolf and I search them out to get away."

"The ability to get away sounds nice."

Elle watched Lisa from the corner of her eye and witnessed the look she'd seen in other women during missions in Mexico and Afghanistan.

The look of a woman wishing for a better life for her family.

Wishing to experience the freedoms available in America.

Lisa drove on while Elle checked her cell, no bars. Her satellite phone was disabled, battery out, and hidden away in a secret compartment beneath the second-row seats.

Elle fidgeted with the cell phone, turning it off and back on to see if it would register into the network. The lack of comms as they entered the city gnawed on her subconscious.

"I'm no tech, but we should have cell service by now, unless it's down."

"It's entirely possible it's offline. We don't produce enough electricity to meet demand."

"Isn't the cell system considered a top priority life safety kind of service?"

"No, not here in Cuba. We are still heavily dependent on landlines. Many people have cell phones, but the priority goes to the government system. The Chinese have loaned the government millions to expand the system, but it's a slow implementation."

"You mentioned a lack of sufficient electricity. What's that about?"

"It's partly due to sanctions, but mostly it's lack of investment. Our power generation is old and at capacity. It's so bad, the government has taken to leasing power-generating ships from a Turkish company. There are six docked in Havana, and four here in the bay."

"I don't want to sound paranoid, but not having service makes me wonder if we've been targeted. We've done it to bad guys before."

"If we are, we'll see them when I run the Surveillance Detection Route in the city. The channelization of the narrow streets makes recognizing a tail easier."

"How long were you in the Army?"

Lisa's tight-lipped smile lets Elle know she was right. "Three years. I was a tactical intelligence specialist until I was injured. They discarded me like a piece of trash. Suddenly, I did not, in their minds at least, have any value. I offered to move to a strategic intelligence position at headquarters, but I was denied."

"What was their problem with you?"

"You haven't noticed? I assumed you were being nice."

"Nope. What did I miss?"

Lisa pulled her pant leg. "My above the ankle amputation and prosthetic. It's good to know it's not easily seen."

*I need to get it together. How'd I miss that?* Elle thought.

You've adapted well. So, why didn't they let you stay?

"It doesn't pay to prove an officer is an idiot. Especially when his father is on the General Staff of the Army. So, my sister and I talked, and we started to search out others who want to rid Cuba of the corruption which has kept us a third world country. The corruption that's led to this partnership with El Chapo."

"If you don't mind my asking, where did you lose your foot?"

"Venezuela, on the border with Columbia. We were gathering intel on one of the paramilitary groups. They'd made some stupid remarks about the president, so the idiot Lieutenant Porres decided we were going to infiltrate their area and call-in airstrikes. We patrolled right into an ambush. As we fought our way out, I stepped on an anti-personnel mine. Our sergeant major carried me out while dragging the idiot lieutenant. Out of eighteen who left on the mission, three of us lived."

"Wow! That's a crazy story. I'm glad you're still here." Elle squeezed Lisa's arm.

"Thanks," Lisa said, a wisp of a smile flashing by. "We're entering the area where I will start the SDR. How do you guys say it? 'Keep your head on a swivel?'"

"Roger that!" Elle said, checking the mirrors.

#

The two-hour SDR completed, Lisa asked, "I'm not seeing anything. Are you?"

"Nothing. If we are being followed, they are either very good or have overhead support. We should stop somewhere like a park to see if they've deployed a drone."

"Good idea. If they have the Chinese involved, I'd expect better SIGINT assets working us, including drones," Lisa said.

"Do you think they'd risk bringing them in?"

"Yes. With the right setup it could be less risky than using additional G2 assets."

Elle whistled.

"The Chinese are a wild card we don't want played," Lisa pulled into a small amusement park. It provided good concealment and line of sight to the sky. The tallest thing in view was the kid's merry-go-round. Elle checked her cell phone, still no service.

Lisa jumped out and Elle followed, stuffing the useless phone in her pocket.

She switched from glancing at the kids to scanning the sky and back again.

Lisa squatted to pet a dog and checked the sky.

Five minutes later Elle nodded, and Lisa tilted her head to the SUV.

Back inside, Lisa said, "I didn't see anything, you?"

"No. I think we're clear." Lisa entered traffic and turned left at the end of the park onto Circunvalacion, then left again to access Avenue de Raul Pujols. She headed west into the city and drove by the zoo and took the first left.

She stopped in front of the seventh house on the left and waited for the garage door to open.

In the garage, Elle jumped out of the SUV and whipped open the second door to get at her satellite phone.

She joined Lisa in the kitchen and assembled her phone, then turned it on.

As soon as it connected, the phone buzzed.

Elle input her security code to unlock the phone, and the pass phrase to unlock the comm's application.

There were five messages waiting.

She opened the most recent one first and read it out loud.

"I have a message from George. He says to stop by the store first. The milk in the refrigerator is sour."

Lisa raced to the front room and peered out.

She cursed and strode into the kitchen, her pistol drawn.

"Sour milk is code for this location is compromised. Follow me."

## 39

Santiago De Cuba Zoo

"Are we headed to another tunnel?" Elle asked.

"No, the back door and into the zoo," Lisa said, slamming a shoulder into the steel door. She halted in the bright sun for a beat, then took off running.

Just then, Elle heard the screeching of tires behind them and the sounds of men crashing in the front door. It was immediately followed by the sound of flash bang grenades and automatic weapons fire.

Lisa didn't slow her pace, running surprisingly fast for an amputee. Elle pushed herself, in her mind, she imagined passing Wolf on the way back to the gym. The shouts faded.

Elle spurted out the words between breaths. "Where...can we... stop. I...need...to call...Wolf."

Lisa took a sharp left, bouncing off the railing into the Big Cats exhibit. She waved at an attendant who moved out from behind her kiosk and rolled it aside. Lisa slid to a stop and disappeared behind the kiosk.

Elle followed; when she slowed, the attendant pointed to a hatch. She went in and the attendant rolled the kiosk back.

On her hands and knees, it was all Elle could do to catch her breath. Lisa pointed a flashlight at the ground in front of her and whispered for her to follow. Lisa slid off a drop and scampered to an area where they could stand.

It took a beat before Elle realized they were in an underground service hallway like those said to support all the workers and shops at Disney World.

"Where are we headed?"

"To a place you can call for help. It won't be long before they swarm in here."

Three minutes later, they were at the top of the fake rock wall overlooking the Big Cats exhibition. The room appeared to be set up for video and audio capture of the cat's activities.

Lisa turned on all the equipment. "The university studies behavior in captivity. Hopefully, turning it on masks your transmission."

Elle's phone had connectivity.

*Must be fiberglass over us.*

Not worried about security, she dialed Wolf. "No time to explain. We need extraction. We're at the zoo. Big Cat exhibit. Bad guys hunting us. We may have to move."

Wolf's voice took on his command tone. "Understood. En route. Keep the phone on so I can track you."

"Roger that," Elle said, then dropped the call.

While Lisa was working to reposition the cameras, Elle messaged Morgan.

If you are here, I'm in trouble and need extraction from the zoo big cat exhibit.

A beat later, the reply said volumes.

10 MINUTES YOUR POS.

"We'll have help in ten minutes or less," Elle said, sagging against a wall. She stuffed her satellite phone into her right cargo pocket, making sure the antenna was extended so it stuck out the front of the flap.

She dug into her pack and traded the Grach pistol for a Makarov with suppressor.

Lisa was working the cameras, but also had her suppressed Makarov out.

"Can you see anything useful?" Elle asked.

"Yes. My people have locked the door leading to this space, so we'll hear them coming."

Elle pushed herself off the floor and sat at the console with Lisa. She scanned the cameras then closed her eyes as she rotated her neck.

"Soldiers," Lisa said, pointing to a camera overlooking the entrance to the exhibit. The soldiers rushed in yelling to the locals to get out, and in the process agitated the cats who paced and roared. Three soldiers stayed at the entrance and watched one of their teammates taunt the lions behind them.

"There's another group here and one here," Elle said, pointing to different cameras.

"The zoo is small enough that they can cover it easily with a single company of soldiers."

Lisa pointed at the camera covering the area outside the door. "They're here," she whispered.

Elle glanced at her watch. It had only been four minutes and thirty-seven seconds since Morgan's response.

She caught Lisa looking and shook her head.

There was yelling and they could see the beating Lisa's friend was taking.

A minute later, they started on another person who handed them the keys.

Lisa left the console and went to a hatch on the wall labeled FOOD.

Elle heard the door open and boots pounding up the stairs. She rushed to the left side of the door and was preparing to defend herself when Lisa grabbed her and said, "In the chute. Go!"

Lisa helped her in, and Elle immediately fell. She arrested her decent by flexing her elbows and knees out, then got traction with her shoes. She held her position and heard Lisa get in and close the door behind her.

Lisa slid to her, stopped, and whispered, "Stay quiet."

Elle could just make out sounds as the soldiers thrashed around the room. Someone in charge commented on the cameras and ordered the men downstairs. "What now?" Elle asked when it was silent.

"We need to get out of here. Wait for me when you reach the room below."

"Okay, descending."

When Elle reached the bottom of the shaft, she could see light around a hatch, so she kicked it open and dropped into another room. She spun and cleared the space, the odor making her eyes water. She kept her ready stance, but glanced down to find she was standing in a bloody mess.

Lisa popped out of the shaft. "We should go."

"Where the heck are we, Lisa?"

"The holding area where the veterinarian works on the Lions." Lisa said, walking to the exit. She peered out and then back to Elle.

"In the lion exhibit?" Elle asked.

"Yes. We should go!"

Lisa exited the room and Elle stayed close, mimicking her moves as she followed the wall around to their left and stopped at a hatch.

The male lions were still at the edge of the exhibit, responding to the soldier egging them on.

Lisa knelt and worked a complex latch system, which open with a thump. She whipped her head to the soldiers, but the Lions roars had hidden the sound. Elle knelt beside her, pistol at the ready.

Lisa wiggled through the hatch and called for Elle just as a lioness came out from behind some bushes and charged.

Elle scrambled into the opening, but stopped with her feet still in the cage, stuck.

She pushed and Lisa pulled, but to no avail.

"No, no, no," Elle said, realizing it was the satellite phone antenna hooked on the frame.

*This is not how I die.* She pulled herself back in and turned, freeing the antenna.

Lisa yanked her out of the cage as the lioness's paw swiped at her foot and tore off her shoe.

Elle snatched herself into the fetal position as the lioness reached through the opening to pull her back in.

When Lisa slammed the hatch shut, the lioness roared—getting the attention of the soldiers who yelled and fired automatic bursts their way.

"Toss your cell phone in the water," Lisa said as her phone hit the water and she started running.

Elle did the same, then ripped off her other shoe and took off after Lisa.

**40**

———

Cement Products Santiago De Cuba

I ran out of the safe house to the maintenance building with Ilena trying to keep up.

As I turn the corner, I see the motorcycle, a Jawa 650 Dakar.

It starts with the first kick.

The shop foreman sees me and starts yelling.

As he runs toward me, I speed off, throwing a roster tail of gray silt.

I race across highway twenty without looking and slide the Jawa through a hard right turn onto De Marti heading east.

Accelerating through the gears until I hit fifth, I blaze through light traffic.

But it's getting thicker, so I downshift to third and weave my way through it at forty-five miles per hour with sprints to sixty-plus for short distances.

*This is taking too much time.*

Ambulances fly out of a hospital exit. Their lights and sirens are a little late for my taste, so I jump the curb.

Pedestrians scream frantically while falling out of the way.

I exit the sidewalk in front of the ambulances and follow the road south, the noise from the ambulances doing a decent job of clearing the road ahead.

By the time the road turns back east, I'm far enough ahead of the ambulances that they aren't clearing the road.

A light turns red, and a taxi jumps into the intersection.

I lock both brakes and slide sideways.

Just before impact with the driver's door, I lift my right leg out of the way.

The Jawa slams into the side of the taxi and my knee goes through the driver's window, knocking the driver out.

I kick to get free.

I spin the tire and maneuver around the disabled taxi, roaring toward the zoo, now less than a half a mile away.

The accident attracts the police; I hear the siren behind me and ignore it and focus on getting to Elle. Twisting the throttle wide open, I'm doing seventy-plus when I see Elle in the distance.

She is running across the street. Behind her, Lisa turns and shoots twice before following.

*Why is she barefoot?* I wonder as I slow to jump the median into oncoming traffic.

The oncoming drivers panic, but luckily, I blow by.

I take a hard left into a residential area, leaving behind crashing cars and honking horns.

I pull in front of Elle and stop. "Get on. Both of you!" I yell as I slide up on the tank.

Behind us the sounds of sirens fill the air; a police car turns on our street.

Suddenly, there is a huge bang and a rending of metal. I turn to see a truck plow through the rear of the police car and spin it around.

I pull my pistol and turn toward the oncoming truck as Lisa jumps off the Jawa.

"It's Morgan," Elle screams.

As the cops exit their police car and start firing at us, Morgan screeches to a halt by us.

"What's the count now, brother? Oh yeah… four times I've had to save you."

*What the heck is he doing here?*

"Take Lisa. I've got Elle."

Lisa jumps in the truck.

I feel my wife lock her hands around my waist and I take off.

Four blocks later, I turn left and enter traffic like we are on a Sunday drive.

"I can explain," Elle says.

"Not now," I say, trying to keep my voice neutral.

We ride on in silence. Sticking to the flow of traffic, we get back to the safe house in just under twenty minutes.

When I stop in back of the office, Ilena comes out, hugs Elle, then looks at the Jawa.

She gives me a roll of bills. "Give it to the foreman to fix the damage," she says.

I nod and drive to the maintenance building, pulling in with the good side showing. The foreman walks around it.

He points to the damage and groans, but I hand him the money roll.

He looks at the damage again, then back to the roll smiling.

I trot back to the safe house, where I find Elle waiting inside the door.

I hold her tightly and whisper, "Are you good?"

"I am now," she says, resting her head on my shoulder.

Elle's voice hitches for a second. "I hope they got away."

"They're fine. Or Morgan would let us know."

"I guess I owe Morgan one too."

"Nah, we had it under control. He was just showboating. You know how he likes a grand entrance."

"I messaged him after I talked to you. I didn't know if he'd made it here yet."

"It's all good. But to be honest, I was angry when I saw him, but happy for the help. This mission is harder than I could have imagined, and having Morgan here will even the odds."

"So, you're not mad at me?"

I smile a tight-lipped smile and furrow my brow to get the effect I'm looking for. "A little."

Elle shakes her head and punches me in the shoulder.

"Ilena," she says. "Can you contact Lisa and have her bring Morgan here."

"Yeah," I say. "It's time to bring the pain."

# 41

SOCOM Headquarters MacDill Air Force Base

Video Teleconference

"General Davidson, I thought we had the evidence needed to destroy the partnership between El Chapo and the Cuban government," the President of the United States said, his voice perfectly clear over the video conference.

"We need this win general," Susan Irwin said. "And we've been very specific on when we need it by."

The video conference with the President of the United States and his, "Let's make drugs legal" advisor was not going well. But Davidson had not led Shadow Tier to its position in the pecking order of US special mission units by being politically naïve.

"Is there a problem getting the evidence out of Cuba?" The Defense Intelligence Agency Director Sam Harris asked.

"Yes, sir. And it's of Chinese and American making," Davidson said.

"What does that mean, General?" President Fairbanks asked.

"Mister President," Davidson said. "The NSA has intercepted signals indicating the Chinese have brought their top-of-the-line SIGINT and drone technology into Cuba. The Agency director can confirm. The second part of the problem is that the Agency does not have the necessary assets to support all the missions under its purview. The single asset capable of extracting the evidence, while simultaneously protecting their team and ours, is currently tasked elsewhere."

Andy Jackson, the Agency director, jumped in. "It's true sir. The asset is tasked to a higher priority mission you authorized in support of national security."

As soon as he'd finished, Davidson could tell the Agency director wished he could take it back. He decided to give the director an out... and maybe get his team more time.

"Sir, we've coordinated with the Agency asset manager, and are told we can have the support of the asset in four days. I know it's past your scheduled date, but it does serve everyone's needs. As it has a higher priority, the asset continues the mission you previously authorized. Meanwhile, my team continues to collect evidence and will look for different means to get it to us."

Irwin displayed her naive grasp of the situation. "General, just have someone swim into the straits and have the Navy pick them up."

The Chairman of the Joint Chiefs suppressed a sigh. "Sounds easy, but the Cubans are world-class when it comes to coastal patrol... and you'd likely be eaten by sharks on the way out. But if you'd like to try Miss Irwin, be my guest."

"Okay, enough," the president said. "General Davidson, I'm giving you three days to get me the information or I'll disband Shadow Tier." The screen went blank.

#

1530 Hours Agency Safe House, Santiago de Cuba

My satellite phone buzzed across the table. I accessed the message. CALL IN THIRTY DAVIDSON.

I make my way southwest toward the nearby food processing plant. A dozen minutes later and I'm across the street from the plant.

This is close enough to the plant office that if someone finds my signal, they'll think I'm in the plant.

I wait another full minute and scan the area with my ears, attempting to catch the smallest sound out of place against the plant's background noise.

There's nothing odd and no movement, so I call Davidson. He answers on the first ring.

"I'll keep it short. You've got three days to get the evidence or the president said he will disband Shadow Tier."

"Screw it. I'll send the data tonight. I value our organization over El Chapo."

"No. Take the time given and bury El Chapo. Three days, Wolf."

"Yes, sir. You're going out with a win if it's the last thing I do."

"I appreciate it, but just make sure you get you and your wife get home safe."

**42**

———————

**M**organ's Safe House Santiago De Cuba

After saving Wolf and Elle, Morgan changed vehicles at a chop shop and drove a lengthy surveillance detection route before stopping at his safe house.

A two-minute drive from the airport, the house his contact had arranged was secluded and concealed from view by woods.

Modern in its concrete exterior, and comfortable in its furnishings, there was an interesting mix of dark wood, chrome, and ivory colored leather furniture.

As the sun set, Lisa was unwinding, or appeared to be, and Morgan understood. The story she'd told of their escape was crazy and he was impressed.

*It takes stones to jump into the proverbial lion's den.*

"Hungry?" he asked, "I make a mean seafood paella."

"We don't have to go out?" Lisa asked, her hands unclenching.

"No, this house is stocked. My friend knows my taste."

"I like your friend already," she said inside a chuckle.

"Yeah. That was enough excitement for one day."

Morgan got out the paella pan, then collected the olive oil and spices. "Can you get the chorizo, seafood, and peas from the refrigerator, please?"

"Sure."

Morgan turned on the stove, added the oil to the pan, and quickly chopped the chorizo, tossing it into the pan to brown.

While he was working the sausage, Lisa prepared the onions and garlic.

Three minutes later, Morgan added the chopped ingredients to the mix and let them soften. Once ready, he added the Bomba rice and saffron until it was coated.

Next, he poured in the chicken broth and brought the mix to a boil before reducing the heat to low and covering the pan.

"Thanks for your help. Wine? I've got a Nebbiolo from Barolo, Piedmont, Italy"

"Thanks. I could use a drink," Lisa said as her cell buzzed.

"What is it?" Morgan asked as he uncorked the wine.

"One of my friends is with Wolf and Elle. They want us at their location tomorrow morning."

"Good. It's time to put a stake in El Chapo's heart."

"What is it with this hatred for him. I mean, I know he's the leader of the Sinaloa Cartel, but it feels like something more. More personal."

"You have good instincts. It is personal for Wolf. As hard as he works to not let it affect him, the fact is, El Chapo is responsible for the death of Wolf's parents and several of his friends. So yeah... it is personal. And if it's personal for Wolf, its personal for me."

"Are you family?"

"Yes, in the way two men are when they share battles and blood. Wolf saved me from a downward spiral after some bad decisions I made. I owe him my life more than once."

"I think I understand. My sister and I have this kind of relationship. We have not fought a war together, but we have both been to war and suffered. We got closer because of it...and by losing our parents."

"Our time here on earth can be seen as one battle after another.

As one loss after another, or as one challenge, one lesson after another. It's all in your perspective—and that's been Wolf's greatest gift to me."

Morgan turned back to the paella, opening the lid to see the rice plump and colorful. He added the seafood. "Another six minutes and it's dinner."

"Smells good. Didn't realize how hungry I was."

Lisa set the table and Morgan brought out the paella. He smiled his famously mischievous smile, raised his glass, and clinked with Lisa. "Here's to bringing down the man who's ruining both our countries. What portion of the paella do you like best?"

"All of it."

"Me too," Morgan said, scooping a large portion onto her plate.

They ate, drank, and talked about childhood, time in the Army, and what they wanted for their futures. All while staying away from cartels, drugs, and especially El Chapo.

#

Morgan was cleaning the kitchen when his cell rang. He answered and stared at the number, not recognizing it. "Yeah?"

"What are you doing here, Danny?"

*Resendiz?* Morgan thought. "Taking possession of an Adams A500 I had rebuilt in Medellin, El Jefe."

"Meet me tonight at twenty-three hundred, hangar seven."

The line went dead. Morgan stuffed the phone in his pocket and ambled into the front room. Lisa sat on a love seat, glass of wine in hand. She smiled as he approached.

"I need your help tonight."

Lisa's eyes closed to slits. "For what?"

"To strengthen my cover story."

"And what's that?"

"I'm contract transportation for the Sinaloa Cartel, and my boss has discovered I'm here."

Morgan's Safe House Santiago De Cuba

"You are... undercover inside the Sinaloa Cartel?" Lisa asked.

"Yeah. That sums it up."

"I don't understand. Why haven't you been working this operation from the start?"

"To protect my cover inside the other parts of the business," Morgan said. "But right now, I need you to be my girlfriend when I go meet El Chapo's lieutenant for transportation."

"Girlfriend? What else is part of your cover story?" Lisa said.

"Nice house in Miami, planes, boats, guns, and girls."

"And drugs."

"Can't forget that, definitely drugs," Morgan said inside a chuckle.

"Okay playboy. But I don't have any clothes."

"True, but you are close enough in size. Let's check the closet in the master bedroom. I think we'll find something there. A dark pants suit, some high heels, and silk top will do."

"You don't want me to look like a street walker?" Lisa asked.

*She's thinking I want her to dress like a hooker, too funny.*

"No, not my style. I'm into good looking and intelligent women. You fit the criteria perfectly."

Lisa blushed and followed Morgan into the bedroom.

#

Hangar seven was code for the only private hangar at Santiago de Cuba International—also known by the locals as the Jose Antonio Maceo Grajales Airport. Off runway 19-1, the north-south runway, hangar seven sat just south of the Cuban Revolutionary Armed Forces base.

The military base housed AN-2 aircraft, MI-8 transport helicopters and two MI-24 helicopter gunships.

Hangar seven reminded Morgan of a forward operating base in Afghanistan—sparse, with minimal equipment and the aircraft always on ten-minute alert.

From previous experience, he knew El Chapo would reduce the alert status to five minutes if the risk profile warranted it.

He'd seen Sinaloa planes spend days with auxiliary power units on and pilots in seats, waiting, just in case.

The Sinaloa transportation lieutenant, Diego Resendiz, was just as paranoid since Wolf had killed his mentor and best friend. On the short drive to the hangar, Morgan explained to Lisa that she would stay in the vehicle while he would go inside.

A guard would be posted at the vehicle as a precaution, but he'd said, "Not to worry. They don't know you."

Three guards walked towards them as Morgan drove in. One of them was on the radio, holding his hand out in front of him for Morgan to stop.

It was just after 2300 when Morgan rolled the window down. "Pedro. All good here?"

"Si, Danny. Leave the truck here. She stays."

"Of course," Morgan said, sliding out of the driver's seat and holding his hands skyward while one of the other men searched him.

"He's clean."

"This way, Danny."

Morgan looked over his shoulder and winked at Lisa. She nodded.

The guards had stopped Morgan 50 meters out from the hangar, which told him Resendiz was in a high state of agitation, likely fearing for his life.

In the back corner of the hangar sat an old metal table and four metal chairs, all positioned facing out. Resendiz watched him amble in and took a long pull from what looked like a double-tall Cuba Libre.

"Got one of those for me, brother?" Morgan asked.

"Maybe. Or maybe a bullet in your stupid head."

"Wait, what did I do wrong? I'm just here to enjoy the nightlife for a day or two and pick up my plane."

Resendiz stood, his hand hanging by the chrome forty-five jammed into his pants. "Take off your shirt."

"Really?" When Resendiz put his hand on his pistol Morgan did as ordered and spun around. "No, I'm not wired."

"We're checking your story. For your sake it better check out. Your timing couldn't be worse. The boss is in one of his moods."

"I can imagine. The heat is on in Mexico," Morgan said, putting his shirt back on. "I suspect you'll be giving the government some useless small wins they can bark about in the press and it will go away, right?"

"Yes, but it will take some time. So, what's with the A500?"

"It's so sexy—and short field performance is like a Pilatus. But mainly, it's sexy."

"You're crazy! You've wanted one since 2006 when you saw the stupid Miami Vice movie."

"Funny, I hadn't thought of it like that. And here we are in Cuba," Morgan lied.

*Good. He's just regular paranoid.*

"Yes, we are. But be careful with your thoughts and words. What we do here will get the best of friends killed. You hear me?"

"Yes. I will take possession of the plane when it arrives and fuel it.

After a quick inspection, I'll leave the same day. Now can I get one of those drinks?"

"What about your woman?"

"She can wait. You and I are family."

Forty-five minutes passed before Morgan headed back to the SUV.

He fist bumped Pedro on the way out and made sure he had memorized the positions of the other guards.

He was surprised to see them in static positions rather than using their normal interlocking roving patrols.

Sporting his signature big grin, he jumped in the SUV and drove away.

"Why the grin?"

"My boss has just become the punch line in a joke El Chapo's going to hate. I stayed for a drink to clone his phone and insert a tracker. Now all we have to do is wait. He will point us to where El Chapo is staying."

## 44

R eset DAY 3

Cement Products, Santiago De Cuba

Due to Morgan's efforts, we now own the cell phone that El Chapo's transportation lieutenant is using, and we have a better than fifty-fifty chance of infecting others.

We are working out my next insertion into the park, when the sunrise follows Morgan and Lisa through the door. It's plain on their faces they enjoyed each other's company last night. My smile is immediately followed by a bony elbow to the ribs.

"Don't be a thirteen-year-old and kid them about it," Elle whispers.

"Yes ma'am."

I stand and man-hug my brother from another mother while Lisa does the same with Elle and Ilena. "Great work, you two," I say.

"Who told you? Kennedy? That communist... I wanted to break the news."

I can't help but laugh. Communist is one of the nicer things we call each other. "And great news it is. Your cover is intact?"

"Yeah. The best cover is the truth."

"I thought you were going to Venezuela to get your Miami Vice toy."

"I've told you before, it's not a toy," Morgan said in a growl "When I got Elle's message it was costly but easy to change the delivery location. I hope you don't mind I'm using cartel money for the payment."

"Heck no," I say. "We should spend more of it!" This brings a much-needed laugh from the team.

"Okay, so while Kennedy and Kid push their code through the cell system here, our team needs to be ready respond to movement of the principals... El Chapo, Aguila, Ochoa, and now Resendiz."

"Who's Ochoa?" Morgan asks.

"Muscle for Aguila," Lisa says. "Former Cuban special forces who works for G2 now."

"Great." Morgan says. "Some other wanna-be thinking he's predator."

"He is dangerous," Lisa says. "With many years working solo to fix G2 problems."

"Yeah, we need to pay attention, but what interests me is finding Resendiz here. Correct me if I'm wrong, Morgan, but I think it means they are shipping the drugs by new means."

"Agreed. I've been thinking about this. If they were using planes or surface ships, he'd coordinate from Mexico. My guess is, they are —or will be—using narco-submarines."

"What's a narco-submarine?" Ilena asks. "Is it different from a regular sub?"

"Yes," Elle answers. "They are different. Most of the time they are semi-submersible, meaning ninety percent is just below the surface. What you might call the conning tower, air intake, and exhaust are all above the water line. Hard to see on radar, riding so low in the water, but their infrared signature gives them away."

"There is a newer version that uses GPS, so only the snorkel is above the water line for air intake," Morgan says. "They're even harder to find."

"Why don't they just buy an old military sub?" Ilena asks.

"Cost to buy and maintain," I say. "The cartels haven't gotten there yet."

"But between the profits they make from heroin and cocaine, they've got to be thinking about taking the next step," Elle says.

"Agreed. But getting back to this mission, Resendiz is an element we need to figure out. Elle, can you work it with your team? Morgan and I are headed into the park. Long story short, Morgan, we lost the overhead asset we were depending on to identify the poppy fields and labs. Plan B is to start a fire a NASA satellite can see. I'm thinking some magnesium will do the trick."

Morgan belly laughs. "Yeah, it'll do alright."

"Lisa, can you team with Elle and be our floater if we get movement out of Resendiz or anyone the asset dusts?"

"Sure. Easier for me to move around town than Miss Venezuela," she says, poking fun at Elle.

*There it is, the joking that indicates a deeper level of trust.*

*We've got a team now.*

"Wait, let's go back for a second. Asset?" Morgan says.

"Sorry... there's a well-placed asset in G2 who supports the director, General Delgado. He's a former peer of Colonel Aguila and is the highest-ranking official with direct access to El Chapo. The asset was able to dust Ochoa with some of Quinn's micro-magic dust and get an audio recording of a meeting. Unfortunately, the overhead asset we lost was our only dust tracking platform."

"So as of now, we have one compromised cell phone and the fact you've seen a couple of poppy fields and wrecked a processing lab. That's it?" Morgan asks.

"Yeah. And we only have two more days to tie El Chapo to all this before President Fairbanks takes the coordinates for the fields and labs to the Cuban President. Fairbanks is focused on destroying the partnership to win points for his party in the mid-term elections. I hate politics, but not as much as I hate El Chapo. I, I mean we, need to tie him to the opium, or this all for nothing."

**45**

S hadow Tier Headquarters, MacDill AFB

Kieran Kennedy sat in his old office at Shadow Tier headquarters. The walls and bookcases now stuffed with Elle's life and intelligence career.

*That was me once. Before the VBIED.*

A vehicle born IED had sent a splinter through Kennedy's right tear duct and into his brain. Many doctors and more than a few of his teammates had considered it a career-ending event; few knew how stubborn he could be.

Elle had taken over his job as director of intelligence, but he'd slowly made his way back, and now led Shadow Tier operations in Europe.

Situated near the primary runway on the southwest corner of MacDill AFB, Shadow Tier had everything it needed to lead, train, and support the unit's three squadrons and support personnel.

Next to the headquarters building, there was the support facility. It was like an Amazon warehouse that included a medical team, a communications element, and lockers for weapons, including American and from around the world.

There were also lockers for mountain gear and free fall equipment, and one with drones and robots for the tech nerds. Three of the biggest spaces were assigned to scuba and watercraft, land mobility, and the parachute riggers area.

Next door to the support facility was a warehouse with sides that could be opened. Wolf especially liked training in the heat and humidity of a Florida summer's day. It housed a state-of-the-art shoot house, with multi-story configurations.

There were overhead instructor platforms with audio-visual aids and cameras throughout. It was busy all the time, as several other special mission units, like Commander Redman's team across the runway, who used it when they were off mission.

John "Kid" Wayne rapped on the doorframe. "Got a minute for an update?"

"Yes. Come on in."

Kid took a chair on the other side of the desk. "Our partnership with NSA and Cyber Command continues. We're ingesting the findings into Providence and running real-time searches against all known activity we've collected against the cartel. No matches yet. The cell phone infection has grown, but as of now, it appears to be limited to Resendiz's security team. He's still at the location from last night, but the in-country team believes he'll travel elsewhere later today."

"Good. Smart thinking on Morgan's part. Resendiz must be in Cuba with El Chapo so their paths will cross. The question is, will it be in the next sixty-five hours?"

"There is one anomaly in our SIGINT and EMINT collection that I can't explain, and neither can DIA nor the Agency."

"What is it?"

"Mind if I use your computer for a second?" Kid asked.

"Have at it."

Kid started a virtual machine to log into Providence, then slipped his secure token into the reader and entered a pin. The Providence UI came up and he selected a map view of Santiago de Cuba. He zoomed in on a warehouse, then backed out the zoom to include a strong-looking fence line and the warehouse access to the harbor.

"What am I looking at?" Kennedy asked.

"Notionally, it's a facility owned by a company called TransCargo. They are primarily engaged in shipping of goods between Cuba and other ports in Central and South America. This facility is also home to their ship repair business—you can see here they have access to the harbor. It all makes sense, right?"

"Yes, but?" Kennedy said, waiting on the punchline.

"Two things are included in the 'but' part of this conversation. One, I ran Providence against three years of data on the harbor, and not once has there been a ship brought in for repair. I also found a link between the movement of money from one of El Chapo's accounts we monitor, to a shell account that paid for the construction of the ship repair facility."

"Interesting, but not helpful at the moment."

"It might be helpful if I was El Chapo and wanted to secretly build a fleet of narco-subs and use them to transport opium to America."

"Okay, I'll give you that. But if they do, we'll see them. What is the second part of the but to the story?"

"Every building inside the fence except for the guard shacks are dark. Not a single emission in any band. The guard's radios are using military-level encryption. NSA said it mimic's an encryption profile used by China's intelligence and special mission units. In my opinion, there is something going on there way more sensitive than some fiberglass narco-subs."

"Could it be a Chinese version of the old Russian signals intelligence facility at Lourdes?"

"Maybe—if they connect to a remote antenna farm or multiple remote locations. But you'd have to consider the site is on the southern side of the island. And it's not conducive to operations against us in any domain other than cyber. No. I'm positive the facility has something to do with El Chapo."

"Okay. Pass the information on to Wolf."

As he started to close the program, the computer chimed, and he saw the icon. So did Kennedy. "Hot dang," Kid said, "Resendiz is on the move."

**46**

---

Cement Products, Santiago de Cuba

"Looks good to me," Morgan says. "The approach sucks no matter where we drop you off."

"Agreed. My plan to infiltrate the park doesn't use the entry or exit points I used during my previous visit."

"Our cover on the way in will be as prospectors who are thinking about buying the closed Mira Loma Alta mine northeast of the target area," Ilena says.

"George owns a share of the mine, and Lisa has a key to the gate. There are plenty of tools, and an old survey kit we can use for a cover story here at the plant."

"I'll insert hidden on the floor of the back seat in the SUV," I say.

"Lisa drives and Ilena navigates. If anyone sees us, they can flash their Pala Mining badges. It will be two in and two out. If I keep to my timetable, I'll set fire to two or three of the labs with what equates to a magnesium flare visible from outer space."

"What if you can't keep your timetable, they'll be hunting you as soon as you start the first fire. Will one be viable from space?" Morgan asks.

"Kennedy says yes, but I want to start more to increase the chances of it working," I say.

"Makes sense. Good plan getting into the area, but what about getting out this time?" Elle asks.

"I'll move east and intersect the road to the mine if I can or go north if I have to."

"North is very hard and ends at the ocean. You can swim with the sharks," Lisa says.

"Okay, I'll try to not to go north. Anyone want a coffee?"

"Not us, Ilena says. "Lisa and I have to go next door to keep up our work cover story. We'll be back shortly."

"Roger that," I say.

"Yes, Morgan says. "I love the coffee here... it's as good as the stuff we used to get in Columbia."

As we stroll into the kitchen, I reminisce. "That seems a world away..." My satellite phone buzzes, and I retrieve the message:

RESENDIZ MOVING

NEED YOU TO CHECK OUT A COMPANY CALLED TRANSCARGO.

STANDING BY FOR FLARES.

I spin the phone so Morgan can read it and call out to Elle to show it to her.

"That's good news. Resendiz's hangover must have subsided," she says.

"Either of you know who TransCargo is? Another business at the airport, maybe?"

Morgan shakes his head. "I'd have seen it when I flew in."

"I recognize the name but can't place it," Elle says. "Let's check with Ilena and Lisa when they get back from the cement plant next door."

#

1400 Hours

Later when they return, Elle brings them to the supply shed

where Morgan and I are arranging tools for the cover story. The "dust" covering everything is perfect.

We can use it to look like we've been out prospecting for a week. When we're done, I feel like pig pen from Charlie Brown. We'll have to make sure Ilena stomps around.

"Have either of you ever heard of a company called TransCargo?" I ask.

"Yes. Why?" Lisa asks.

"We think it's tied to how El Chapo plans to move the opium to America. I'd like you and Elle to put some surveillance on the place while we're gone tonight. We can make a more detailed plan when we get back."

"Sure. It will be easy," Lisa says.

"Nothing is easy here," I say.

"It is when the target is across the railroad tracks. It's a little more than a quarter mile from here. We can put eyes on, as you like to say, from the radio tower here on the plant."

Boom. It hits me. *I was looking at Transcargo last night when I went for my walk.*

"And you'll have cover. I like it!" I say.

"We've got it," Elle says. "Execute your 'I hate Smoky Bear' op and we'll have a plan for you when you get back."

"That's so bad I can hardly bear it..." I say.

I'm rewarded with groans from Elle and Morgan. Lisa and Ilena stare at me like I'm brain damaged.

"Sorry, back to the opp. I'm thinking we should alert the Kakoa brothers. Can you handle it, Morgan? I've got them standing by aboard the Jimmy Carter."

Morgan laughs then leans in whispering. "You've got the Jimmy Carter cruising off the Cuban coast?"

I whisper back. "Yeah, we can't get overhead assets but we still have pull with Joint Strike Command."

"Done, brother."

"Come on Ilena. Let's get you dusty so we can hit the road."

#

Just after sixteen hundred, I feel the SUV slow then stop.

"We're at the mine," Lisa says. I hear the passenger door open as Ilena gets out. The SUV pulls forward and Ilena jumps back in.

"Pull in front of the mine entrance, there's enough brush for Wolf to slip away," Ilena says.

The SUV pulls forward and climbs a slope before stopping again. The back door opens and I squint against the sunlight. I crawl out, staying low. Slipping into my backpack, I tighten the shoulder and chest straps.

Inside are four-quart sized metal containers I've double sealed with Cuban duct tape and insulated with towels to keep them from banging out my location. I also have four magnesium rods.

The sun is low and I'm using the shadows to head back to the two labs I've already identified.

It's ninety minutes later and I'm still two ridge lines away when I see my first indication of the extra security the Black Wasps are implementing to protect the product.

This one hides under some disturbed ground; from the size of the disturbance, I'm thinking it's a variant of the US M-14 anti-personnel mine.

Copied by other communist countries, they were even made by the Vietnamese—who are now our allies against China.

Usually deployed in mixed minefield configurations, it has me looking for Cuban claymores—known as MON-50—which are used to give warning or slow advances on likely routes into a protected area.

I do the opposite, and move through the heavy jungle, spending most of the time sideways or on my hands and knees to get to the first lab.

My target within the lab is the shed where they store the finished product before it's moved to the warehouse.

I'm seventy-five feet out and can barely make out the shed between the thick brush and dwindling light.

The area around the lab is littered with armed men.

Most of them are dressed like locals, with a few in black tactical gear.

Somewhere nearby someone is cooking, and it smells good. Onions and garlic laying the base for a savory meal.

One of the men shouts he's hungry and a Black Wasp tells him to shut it.

I'm prepared to wait. Guards going to eat in shifts will reduce the risk of what I'm about to do.

In the meantime, I procure a discarded tuKola plastic bottle and fill it from a puddle I can reach.

The downside is that I've just stirred up a thousand mosquitos who have to learn the hard way I'm not the tastiest guy in the jungle.

While they puke after trying to feast on me, I slip my mosquito netting over my floppy hat and continue to wait.

It's full dark when the first of the guards are told to go eat.

It reduces the bad guys I have to slip by to two, and both are locals; it's easy to tell they've never been in the military.

Bad decision on the Black Wasps part, good for me.

They move off fifteen meters, and I rush to the back of the shed and slide under.

The lights in the shed are on, and it filters through the floor, helping me in my task.

I remove a canister from my pack and dig a small hole with my hand to steady it.

I'm as quiet as I can be when I jam the tuKola bottle between two floor joists over the magnesium. I unscrew the lid and insert the time fuse.

The length I insert will take fifteen minutes to burn into the magnesium and start the fire.

Once it starts, it will quickly melt the plastic bottle above it and the water will make the chemical reaction burn brighter than a super nova.

I'm ready to light the fuse, but the guards are walking my way.

I search the area around me for something to distract them—I only need a couple of seconds.

*There you are my friends.* Some discarded nails.

I'm hidden in a shadow, so this should work.

I backhand the nails into the jungle behind them.

They spin and walk to the edge of the clearing.

I light the fuse and use the shed to block their view as I slide into the jungle.

I don't stop; I don't turn and look.

It either works or it doesn't.

There is no time to admire my ingenuity.

It's chaos thirty, and I need to get this party started.

**47**

———

Mensura Parque Cuba

"Yes, I'm watching it burn," Ochoa said. "But there's something different about this fire. At its center, it's like someone is welding. I can't watch it but for a few seconds."

Aguila cursed. "The Americans have many different untraceable thermite and magnesium charges. It must be Wolf. He's hunting again."

"Agreed. Can I—"

"Yes, kill him," Aguila said. "I will make the call. The Black Wasps are at your command. Call me when he's dead."

Ochoa ended the call and stared into the middle distance, the locations of the labs in his mind's eye. If taking them from north to south, the burning lab was number two.

*You'll head south. I would.*

*More exfil options.*

*How many more labs will you attack?*

"Lupo to Avispa Seven, set the trap at site three," Ochoa radioed.

The transmission was interrupted by an explosion. "In pursuit," the Black Wasp Captain said.

Ochoa trotted for the helicopter. "Avispa Seven, break contact. Let him believe you lost him." The helicopter squatted as he boarded.

"Acknowledged."

"Go, go," Ochoa said. The pilot yanked on the collective and they surged into the night.

They flew closer to the jungle than Ochoa liked, but they got to the burning lab quickly.

"Pull up and turn on your spotlight," he commanded.

*I'll let him know who the hunter is.*

"Fly a search grid for three minutes, then kill the light and fly me to site four."

The pilot complied. When they landed at site four, Ochoa said, "Head back to site three and continue to search to the south and east... but slowly."

The pilot nodded, and Ochoa jumped out to be met by a captain of the Black Wasps.

"Follow me," he said. "I will brief you on our defenses. I have a rifle and night vision for you."

The double flaps and red light meant the Wasps were serious about maintaining their night vision and security.

"We have deployed mines in a ten-meter-wide pattern at fifty meters from the lab," the captain said.

"We also have technical surveillance scattered from twenty to thirty meters out. My manned observation posts are here to the north and at these sites to the east and west. The only approach we have not oversaturated is the road to the south, where we have an excellent field of fire." The captain indicated the various spots on the map.

"Put a sniper team here," Ochoa said, pointing to the map. "Focus them to the south."

"Yes, sir. Anything else?"

"Yes, a radio and headset. And the communications codes for tonight. I don't want to get shot when I go hunting."

"This way," the captain said.

Ochoa cinched his chest rig tight and added fragmentation grenades to the left and right pouches.

He pulled the suppressed AK sling over his head and practiced bringing the rifle to bear then letting it drop to his side to access his pistol.

His fighting knife was secure, as was his drop leg holster.

The helmet the captain gave him needed an adjustment to the strap at the base of his skull.

It also needed a fresh battery pack, which he installed and tested by powering on the goggles.

He put the helmet back on and tightened the chin strap, then lowered the night vision and rotated his head and nodded to check it was secure.

Satisfied, he stuffed a flash bang into each cargo pocket and hopped to ensure he could move silently. Nothing rattled.

Ochoa handed the captain a device the size of a cell phone. On the display was a map with a pulsing red icon. "The red dot is me. It's your job to make sure your men do not shoot me."

The captain smiled. "I would be honored to join you, El Jefe."

Ochoa regarded the man. *He is a killer, but no... not tonight.*

"An American writer who spent considerable time in Cuba said, 'There is no hunting like the hunting of man.'"

The captain beamed. "Hemingway finished by saying, 'And those who have hunted man long enough and liked it, never care for anything else thereafter.'"

"Bravo Captain! But you forgot one important word. Armed. It is an armed man that is the apex prey. It takes a wolf to kill a wolf," Ochoa said.

Ochoa strode to the exit and turned.

"Move the rest of your men into a defensive line east to west five hundred meters south of this site. Be noisy in the process—I want my target to think this lab is his only option."

Ochoa disappeared into the darkness.

## 48

Cement Products, Santiago De Cuba

"Morgan, wake up," Elle said. "While Lisa, Ilena, and Wolf are driving to the mine, let's go check out the radio tower and put together a surveillance plan for TransCargo."

Morgan blinked and groaned. "Sure, I've got a couple of hours."

*Before what?* Elle thought.

She took Morgan to a window at the end of the building and pointed at the silo out the window. "So, that's why Lisa said the radio tower provided cover."

"I can't tell if it's built into or on top of the silo," Morgan said. "Not that it matters. We can install multiple cameras, and no one will notice."

"Are the wireless versions you brought safe to use given the SIGINT threat?"

"Yeah, and we can operate them remotely. The signal strength is lower than the system you have at home in Tampa. I also have taps so we can hide the video inside the office network."

"Good. Let's get to work then; check in with Kennedy."

An hour later, they had installed three—two daylight and one infrared. Morgan also installed a tap on the office network where it ran against the wall closest to the tower, then he had Elle install a tap on the network cable that terminated in the apartment.

He inserted a memory stick into a Pala Industries laptop Lisa had provided. It took over the system, wiped the existing operating system, scanned the hardware for malware, then rebuilt the laptop with a secure OS and the camera management application.

The wide-angle view and clarity of the camera app surprised Elle. "Holy Moley. That's impressive considering the sun is setting."

"We've got movement," Morgan said, pointing to the window for camera two. "Watch this," he said as he zoomed in on the trucks and brought the license plates into view.

"Notice anything about those trucks?" he asked, a grin spreading across his face.

"Zoom out... They've come from a construction site or up in the mountains."

"Exactly. If I had to guess, it's product delivery. Inside that building they are probably loading up a narco sub so it can sail under cover of darkness."

"Are you sure there isn't anything you want to tell me that Wolf didn't share with the team?" Elle asked. "I know you two—you always have a plan for when Murphy makes an appearance."

"You mean like be ready to save his worthless hide again?"

"Yes, but minus the worthless part."

"No plan," Morgan said. "But he wants me airborne in an hour and I could use your help."

"To do what?"

"To be my date for a midnight joy ride...and my bombardier."

"Wolf is starting the fires, right?" Elle said. "We're not going to try and firebomb the labs, are we?"

"No, but I have a bag of frag grenades that will help divert attention and resources at the right time."

"Well in that case, let's get to your plane. Wait...do I need to dress up like one of your Miami babes?"

"Nah, you're a natural beauty, Miss Venezuela," he winked.

Elle laughed. "Does that line really work?"

"Yes, when it's paired with a nice suit and that confiscated Bentley I get to drive."

He drove the long way around the east side of Santiago de Cuba to the airport, which was shut down for the night.

He stopped by hangar seven, where Resendiz had his plane towed, and greeted the security lead. He handed Pedro a bottle of rum.

"Where is El Jefe?"

"With the big boss. You need to talk?"

"No. I'm taking Miss Venezuela for a little ride. I'll talk to him tomorrow," he said.

Pedro stepped back and radioed his team that Morgan would be taking his plane for a check ride.

"It seems that Pedro is accustomed to you taking ladies for a ride," Elle said.

"True. It's all part of a deep and well-conceived cover story I work hard to live up to."

Elle laughed as they exited the truck. "Well then, let's make it a reality and go see what chaos Wolf has brought to El Chapo's pet project."

**49**

___

Mensura Parque Cuba

*They have to suspect I won't stay around a burning lab.*

The fire I started will throw off their search and flood the area with soldiers. Their reaction will make it easier to get to the next target, so I head north.

But whoever is commanding the helicopter is smarter than I gave them credit for. That is, until he slowed his search pattern.

My plan to skip lab three and burn number four is still in play, but tonight, with the extra security, I can't take an easy route.

No animal or people tracks. Deep in the suck, I'm flowing through the jungle like a shark swimming in the confines of a coral reef.

I'm using every ounce of my night vision, hearing, and sensitive nose to protect myself as I move to the target.

The pulsing rotor blades register a beat before the sound of the helicopter.

I take a knee under a tree as the helicopter searchlight flows over my position then leaves to fly a grid pattern to the north and west.

*Good. They're so attached to their confirmation bias that they will waste resources to see if I'm headed down the mountain like last time.*

*Time to do the unexpected.*

I continue on my heading, keeping east of lab three, when the smell of someone urinating wafts past and I hear rustling.

I freeze and wait for the noise to cease. Breathing slowly, I listen intently; I'm rewarded with a radio squelch break and whispering.

The soldier pulls back his sleeve and covers his watch with his hand to check the time.

I sink to the jungle floor and wait, knowing the listening post check-in times will be useful at the next target.

When I have what I need I pull back to circle the listening post to the east.

*Strange to find Black Wasps so far out from the lab.*

I take a note to make my approach from farther east.

My satellite phone buzzes in my cargo pocket. The display is set to night vision mode, so I pull a NVG monocular from my shirt pocket and read the message.

Airborne thirty mikes your pos

*It's about to get spicy in Mensura Park.*

I push on. When I'm roughly east of lab four, I stop again to verify my position via the satellite phone.

Satisfied I'm where I expect to be, I head south southwest to infiltrate the lab.

I'm coming in from where they would least expect an attack—the dirt track heading off the mountain.

*Have they left any security on the west side?*

*There must be some.*

I'm moving slower now, each step a measured action.

The skills I honed on the reservation and in the army are based in mind, body, and spirit integration.

I acknowledge my spirit guide, sing my death song, and access the bravery of a thousand Crow warriors.

A memory of being chased by a platoon of Spetsnaz flashes in my mind's eye and I take it as my spirit guide telling me to not let my ego get the best of me. A reminder.

*Don't start a fight unless there is no other choice.*

Three minutes later, Morgan flies over, his lights out as planned.

Seconds after that, Black Wasps on my left and right check in, no more than twenty feet apart. I move west, parallel to their positions and hear a third soldier check in.

I back away from the line of soldiers and pause to consider the situation.

Not seventy-five meters from the lab on its south side there is a line of soldiers in a blocking position.

*How does the saying go? For every action, there is an equal and opposite reaction.*

I pull the satellite phone from my pocket and text.

75M SOUTH MY POS

PICKET LINE WEST TO EAST

LIGHT THEM UP

A beat later I get the response that has to be from Elle.

TOO CLOSE

I RESPOND WITH,

DO IT, MOVING AWAY.

ROGER

I don't like lying or stretching the truth with Elle or anyone else on my team, but there is no way she will drop grenades from a plane unless it's a near-death situation.

Morgan has night vision googles, which he has to be wearing—and infrared devices onboard.

They are everyday tools for someone delivering drugs across the southern border of the United States.

*I have to give the appearance of moving away.*

My experience had taught me that in the chaos, there will be an opportunity to slip into the lab unseen.

I'm moving when Morgan comes in, so low I glance up to see the shadow pass not more than forty feet above the trees.

Grenades explode in the trees and a beat later the Black Wasps fire back, tracers every fourth round are lighting up the sky.

Soldiers are shouting as they break cover and I see my opportunity.

A scared soldier rushes my way, and I drop him with a strike to the windpipe. He falls, gasping for air, and I follow him down and put him to sleep with a right to the jaw.

I use the soldier's med kit to fashion a gag, then strip him of his gear and clothes.

Morgan makes another pass in the opposite direction, dropping more grenades. It draws a more ground fire.

*Time to leave, Morgan. Thanks!*

Once I have the soldier stripped to his underwear, I tie his hands and feet behind him, then take off my clothes and put on his uniform and gear. There is only one extra magazine; it will have to do.

I put the satellite phone in my right cargo pocket with the flash bang I found.

The night vision monocular goes in my left, and his pistol in the small of my back.

The soldier's boots don't fit, but it isn't important, I'll go barefoot, no one will be looking at my feet.

I make sure my knife is secure and hoist the backpack and jog toward the site, the chaos continuing around me.

A squad of soldiers rush past then disappear one after another in an rippling series of explosions that slams me to the ground.

I follow their path hoping that it's cleared the minefield. I'm beyond them and still in one piece.

All around me there are wounded soldiers, leaders trying to gain control, men yelling on the radio, and the helicopter overhead.

It is perfect.

**50**

———————

Mensura Parque Cuba

I work my way to the lab via what might be considered the front door.

*Leaving your post to help your brothers is noble, but bad for them and good for me.*

The deception doesn't sit well with me, playing on the heartstrings of soldiers that care more for their teammates than themselves.

I've felt that myself—but this is war, and they stand in the way.

There is no one at the lab or its storage shacks.

I scan over my AK as if looking for the threat, then drop the pretense and sneak behind the processing lab.

It's not built on a raised platform.

The best I can do is hide in the darkness at the back and set up my firebomb on a makeshift stand of sorts.

I take a bottle of magnesium with a time pencil out of my pack and lay it at the base of the processing building wall.

Using three magnesium rods, I make a tripod that I can put my water bottle on to replicate the setup at the first site.

Somewhere deep in my subconscious a warning light flashes, and I roll right as the back of the lab is racked with gunfire.

I scramble on all fours, then drop to my belly and crawl for the safety of the jungle.

The helicopter appears overhead and sweeps the area with its search light.

I watch as a man races to the back of the building and throws the bottle with the magnesium into the jungle.

He turns, and I instantly understand who is commanding the helicopter and who put the picket line in my path: *Ochoa.*

If I'm to even the odds, the search light needs to go.

I fire, taking out the helicopter's light and stitching the cockpit with rounds, then jump to my feet and run.

The helicopter wobbles before it flies off.

Gunfire erupts again and I throw myself to the ground.

I hear Ochoa's AK go dry, so I leap to my feet and run to his left, then drop again.

He replaces the AK magazine with a fresh one, and I crawl to a tree.

Gunfire riddles the tree and strikes my rifle, the ricochet slices through my left hand.

Grunting against the pain, I wrap it with my bandana.

*He's got night-vision.*

I peek around the tree, and I'm rewarded with another long burst of automatic gunfire.

"Wolf, give up. Make it easy on yourself. I promise you a quick death."

*Got to love his arrogance.*

I reach into the small of my back for the pistol and groan—it's gone.

Discarding the broken AK, I check that my knife is where I expect it.

The movement to check for the knife makes me realize I am laying on a magnesium rod.

I slide the rod through the bandage on my left hand so I can hold on to it and draw my knife.

Ochoa is headed to me and I keep low as another burst shreds the ground at the base of the tree.

He's in a combat crouch firing short bursts.

I pull the flash bang from my cargo pocket and cook it off.

When he is less than twenty feet away, I hit him in the chest with it.

He curses and back peddles as the flash bang detonates.

Knife in hand, I run at him as fast as I can through the scrub.

Ochoa is shaking his head and grabbing for his AK when I plow into him, burying the knife into his rib cage.

He howls, drops the AK, and pounds me with a hammer fist to the left side of my head.

He grabs my collar and attempts to use my momentum to throw me on my back, but I keep my balance and use his move to throw him to his side.

When we hit the ground, I twist my knife; he grunts and curses.

I control his right arm with my shin, but I hadn't considered his strength; my ribs crack from a vicious knee strike that gives him room to break free.

In a heartbeat, he is leaping onto me.

His elbow catches my chin and I gray out for a beat.

When I come to, he is choking me. I grab the knife and twist some more.

As I struggle for air, his grip lessens, his body taking on the feel of dead weight.

Wet and warm, I recognize the iron odor of blood.

Ochoa's head slumps onto my shoulder.

I inhale a sharp, pained breath, and push him off.

My left hand is screaming at me, twisted up with the magnesium rod stuck in his chest.

I pull the knife from his chest and cut the bandage free, then get to my feet.

After I wobble for a second, I squat to retrieve the AK. It's operational.

*Why didn't he just shoot me?*

No time for thinking, I rush back to my backpack and find the last bottle with magnesium intact and crush the time pencil.

I lay the bottle next to the rods and take off east toward exfil.

As I crest the first of three ridge lines I have to cross, I gingerly turn to look.

The first lab is more glow than raging fire, but the second looks like someone is welding at the site.

A part of me wants to know the results right now, but my tired and broken body says the call to Kennedy can wait.

There are miles of suck to go, and my focus is singular—put El Chapo behind bars, once and for all.

# 51

DAY 2

    G2 Headquarters, Havana Cuba

    Director Delgado was on his third drink of the morning. He had progressed from coffee with a little chaser to straight rum. Isabel could hear him yelling through the doors.

She had made drinks, summoned Aguila, and canceled meetings. There was a crash, breaking glass, then cursing.

"Major, get in here," Delgado yelled.

Wide-eyed, she cracked the doors open and peered in.

Delgado stood and moved around his desk. "My apologies, Major. It is not you I am angry at. Can you please clean up the mess I've made?"

"Of course," Isabel said.

When finished, she asked. "Is there anything else I can do to put your day back on track?"

In less time than it takes for a heartbeat, she knew she had Delgado where she wanted him. His look morphed from business to insatiable.

"Have the kitchen prepare a late breakfast for three."

"Yes, sir. I assume it will be you and Colonel Aguila. Who, might I ask, is the third?"

"Treat yourself to a good meal, but standby in case we need you."

Isabel let a scarlet heat caress her cheeks. She had worked on her ability to blush on command, and it was proving particularly valuable. After closing the doors, she sat at her desk, taking a beat to revel in her conquest.

*A small one for sure, but priceless.*

She called the kitchen and ordered enough breakfast for five. The leftover eggs, bacon, and pastries she would give to the unseen staff of women who supported bosses with egos of similar size and temperament to Delgado. The simple act of sharing would make friends and turn enemies into neutral observers.

It was 0815  when Colonel Aguila strode past. He was through the doors to Delgado's office before Isabel could finish rising from her chair. His clenched jaw and white-knuckled fists indicated he was just as angry as her boss.

Chasing after him, she got the expected: "It's okay. Close the doors and let me know when breakfast is ready," her boss said.

Isabel backed out, closing the doors behind her. Agitated that she had not been able to position the breakfast cart before the meeting started, she picked up the phone to call the kitchen. Someone answered the phone just as the elevator chimed and a soldier pushed the trolley into the galley. She dropped the phone and rushed to inspect it.

*Take a breath. Don't give them anything to suspect.*

Isabel counted off her requests out loud, noting the items on the cart. She acknowledged it was all there and dismissed the soldier. After taking her plate and the extra food off and setting it to the side, she dusted the remaining napkins and secured the recorder.

She pushed the cart to the doors and knocked. "Your breakfast is ready," she said through the door.

"Yes. Bring it in."

When she opened the doors, Delgado and Aguila looked as if they flunked a test and were wondering what to do next.

They reminded her of a bootleg movie she had seen about a jewelry heist where the gang of criminals suspect one of them is an informant.

*Something about dogs.*

She kept her head down and focused on preparing the cart and serving coffee.

When she got back to her desk, the word *intense* came to mind. The feeling in Delgado's office was like a smoking campfire about to burst into flames. She dove into her breakfast.

Finished, she returned to her work.

*You're not a super spy. Do the work, stick to your cover.*

It was just before noon when Aguila left. He seemed stressed, but less so than when he had entered the office. Standing in the doorway, she asked if it was okay to take the food away.

Delgado grunted a 'yes,' and headed to the bathroom. She took the cart to the galley and had the recorder in her hand when Delgado surprised her from behind. He leaned into her.

She replaced the recorder on the underside of the cart and spun to face him, only to be surprised again when he kissed her. She responded with a groan. He stepped back, a smile on his face.

"Another time Isabel, when we can be alone," Delgado said, then returned to his office, closing the door behind him.

Turning back to the cart, she hid the recorder inside her uniform pants, hoping her wobbly legs would be taken as desire rather than panic.

She did some deep breathing to center herself and went to her desk to alert the other women that the cart and extra food were available for pick up.

*It must have been important. I need to get this to Lisa.*

## 52

Cement Products, Santiago De Cuba

I appreciate the fresh set of clothes, a bandage, and wipe down with a wet towel. But the ride back to the plant is painful. Three hours later, I groan as I crawl out of the SUV.

Elle's face is scrunched up in worry. "You look like crap. What'd you break?" she asks.

I gingerly lift my shirt, the bruising along my side, black and purple. "Couple of ribs and a ricochet hit my hand. It feels crunchy."

Morgan walks out from behind Elle. "Take a deep breath," he says. As he probes my ribs, I inhale between my teeth.

"Yeah, broken, let me see your hand," he says. "Besides the hole the round left, your pinky finger metacarpal is broken, and it feels like you dislocated your ring finger. Get cleaned up and I'll wrap your rib cage and hand so they're not flexing so much. Do you want something for the pain?"

"Not until we after we debrief."

Later after my hot shower, the team and I are sitting in the kitchen. I have my shirt off and Morgan is wrapping my chest.

"Lisa and Ilena why don't you start," I say.

Lisa nods. "After we dropped you off, we spent three hours at the mine, working our cover. We then drove out to La Deseada and stayed the night. The next morning, we left at six and drove back to the mine and stayed there until we received the pickup location. There were no police or military. No one gave us a second look."

I grunt as Morgan pulls the tape tight. It takes fifteen minutes to brief them on what I did. How the first lab attack went to plan and how Ochoa then tricked me into an ambush.

"Moving north fooled no one, so I decided to skip the next lab to the south and head for the fourth site. Expecting heavy security, I wanted to circle around it and come in from the west. I was right but did not plan for a picket line and minefield just south, and—."

Ilena interrupts: "What's a picket line?"

"A defensive line of soldiers designed to catch an enemy trying to move through an area," Elle says.

"When I realized I was being pushed into the picket, I had Morgan and Elle make a couple of bombing runs. The chaos it created was impressive—I was in business as the saying goes. I captured a soldier—no, I didn't kill him—but I took his clothes and gear. I made it to the lab undetected... or so I thought. Then it went sideways."

"I'll say! My first time in an airplane that Morgan is flying and I'm playing bombardier. Then the sky fills with tracers and he's laughing like a maniac. The glow across his face from the cockpit instruments, combined with a voice demanding we pull up was like a Nightmare on Flight Street," Elle says, eyes wide in mock horror.

I can't help myself. I'm laughing and crying out in pain. Morgan is looking at Elle and me like, 'what'd I do?'

I wipe the tears from my eyes. "All good, brother. The wound to my hand is from a ricochet that disabled my AK. Lucky for me, Ochoa was an arrogant son of a gun. He could have just shot me, but he lost control and decided to kill me with his bare hands... hence the bruising on my neck. When he jumped on me, I unknowingly impaled him with one of the magnesium rods I had stuck in the bandage on my left hand. I was lucky... after that, it was a long painful walk to the exfil site."

*That was the closest to death I've ever been.*

Elle squeezes my arm and I give her my best "I'm okay" look.

"Well," Morgan says. "That was the most fun I've had flying in a long while. Elle and I went to the airport where she met some of my cartel friends. According to his security lead, Resendiz was with the big boss. And yes, I can't wait to hear how the cell phone infection has spread. Anyway, it was an easy flight to the park, and once we had the picket line location, Elle used an IR scope to confirm their relationship to Wolf. That's when I sent them welcome packages in the form of frag grenades. The winds were a all over the place, but we got it done."

"Once is enough for me," Elle says. "Flying at stall speed in the mountains, at night, no more than a hundred feet above the trees and often lower... it was terrifying. Now I understand what the guys mean when they say Morgan's crazy."

"Welcome to my world," I say, continuing to inhale through clenched teeth. "What's the word from Kennedy?"

"The fires worked," Elle says. "Kennedy said there is a dramatic difference between the sugar cane burns and yours. Kid told me the infection is spreading, but the three new phones that he acquired only stayed on the net for a couple of hours. He suspects they are rotating through burner phones every twenty-four hours."

"That means one of those phones likely was in the hands of El Chapo."

"Lisa's cell rings. "Yes..." she says. "Okay, we'll be here." She turns to us. "George is coming. He has a recording from a meeting between Delgado and Aguila. It seems both men had a stressful morning."

"Excellent. A bad day for them is a good day for us," I say.

**53**

---

El Chapo Safe House South of Santiago De Cuba Airport

Aguila had gotten the damage report via Delgado. The general was so worried about profits that he almost forgot to mention that Ochoa was dead. Aguila's blood pressure soared into dangerous territory.

*Two processing labs burned to the ground.*

*Sixteen Black Wasps dead and wounded.*

*Ochoa dead.*

*Can it get any worse?*

Aguila stormed to the airport and caught the first flight south. He stared out his first-class window, the lush green and its abrupt transition to dark blue had a calming effect.

His mind wandered to the perfect house he had designed for the ten acres of beachfront land he owned in Costa Rica. He sighed.

*Yes. It could be worse.*

*We've got eighty percent of the harvest sitting at TransCargo, waiting on Resendiz to finish refitting the submarine.*

Product sitting idle is always a higher risk than in transit, and there was fallout from the attack to consider.

Rebuilding the processing labs, of course, but *where did the plane come from and who was flying it?*

*How did they know where the soldiers were deployed?*

*Did Wolf kill Ochoa?*

And as had been pointed out at the meeting he had just departed, the Black Wasp's leaders would have to be paid to stick to the classified "training accident" story concocted by Delgado.

"Sir, are you okay? Would you like a drink?" The flight attendant asked.

"Coffee please."

She'd caught him murmuring to himself.

*Focus Ignacio, pay attention to your surroundings,* he thought.

Two hours after taking off from Havana, he was onboard an MI-8, headed to the site where Ochoa was killed.

They were entering the park when the crew chief sat across from Aguila. He reported that the wounded Black Wasps were in awe of the ghost that moved through them, taking lives as he pleased.

He grunted, and the crew chief went back to his station.

*Just what we need, the Black Wasps conferring Wolf with supernatural powers.*

From the air, the wisp of smoke and charred remains of the lab were easy to spot. He waited until the MI-8 landed and the dust settled before exiting.

He was met by a Black Wasp Captain who would take him to the burned lab.

"The lab is of no concern. Take me to Ochoa," Aguila said.

"Yes sir. This way," the captain said and turned to a small shack. Aguila pulled back the fabric door and saw the body bag on the lone table.

He unzipped the bag and stepped back, the odor attacking his senses and causing him to pinch his nose. He blinked then recovered sufficiently to ask. "Do you know how he died?"

"Yes sir." The captain pulled a dull silver rod from the other side of the table.

"This pierced his heart and was sticking out his back when we found him. There was also a short dagger stuck his chest, but the medic said that was recoverable." He handed the rod to Aguila.

"Any idea what this is?"

"Our pioneer officer said it's magnesium. He confirmed it via the residue at the center of the fires."

*Where do you get magnesium rods in Cuba?* "Take me to the lab," he said. "And have his body put on the helicopter."

The captain led Aguila to the remains of the processing lab. He walked into the charred rubble, then looked to the north.

"How far to the other site that was attacked?"

"Nine miles. He probably covered thirteen to get here."

"How do you know that?"

"During planning for the processing sites, we were tasked to clear any camps and villages within three miles of each site. It took us four days."

"That will be all Captain," Aguila said looking east, then south, where he imagined where the line of listening posts had been.

The jungle looked different, disturbed. After staring for a minute, the damage became clear. Broken branches, fresh wounds to the trees, and an occasional out-of-place scrap of white.

*Combat dressings.*

The urge to find where Ochoa died clawed at his psyche. He huffed at his emotional leash to the young man.

He'd always wanted a son, and the brash Ochoa had reminded him of his younger self.

His fatherly feeling was drowned under the realization of what he faced.

*To survive, I need to take Wolf out of his element and bring him into mine.* "And I have just the bait to do it," he said to no one.

**54**

---

Shadow Tier Headquarters MacDill AFB

The scuttlebutt around the NASA program concerning strange fires in Cuba was limited to a team of three inside a sub-project concerned with the global warming effects of fires and deforestation.

Their excitement was dashed when a deeper review of the data found two mountain fires of limited duration and scope.

Kennedy thanked his contact and invoked national security concerns.

The icing on the cake was his hinting at the appreciation of the Director of National Intelligence.

He ended the call and winked at Kid. "Good thing they didn't perform a spectrum analysis. Magnesium fires in a remote location of Cuba would spark community-wide intel interest."

"Your network has saved our bacon more than once."

"Yeah, it proves it's worth once again," Kennedy said. "Now that we have the alignment of the labs, we can use the NASA program information to identify all of them. Have you completed the upload to Providence?"

"Yes. And I've retrieved another twenty-four hours of cell phone logs. There is an interesting pattern emerging from the infected phones."

"That's quick. I expected it to take a few more days."

"No sir," Kid said. "The burners are new, but they are being used in two primary locations—south of the Santiago de Cuba airport and in the city itself. They're a little scattered, but I'll have actionable data in the next twelve to twenty-four hours."

"Excellent… oh shoot. I need to brief Davidson and he wants it in person. Why don't you join me."

"Yes sir. Always interested in what goes on at SOCOM head-quarters."

"Ha! Just don't expect it to make sense," Kennedy said inside a chuckle.

#

Fifteen minutes later, Kennedy knocked at the general's door.

"Enter." Davison said from his desk. "Gentlemen… We've got a situation—Shadow Tier is on the precipice of being disbanded if we don't get the president what he wants. Where do we stand?"

"We will have the locations of the processing labs and opium plots by the end of the day," Kennedy said. "We are twelve hours from having El Chapo's safe house location, which I believe is between Santiago de Cuba airport and the ocean. Likely closer to the ocean, so it can be used for exfil in extremis circumstances."

"Tight but doable. Has the Agency been helpful?"

"Yes. We wouldn't be where we are without the Cuba cell. Their asset inside G2 has helped identify the Cuban side players and others are providing direct support to Wolf and Parker."

"Are the LEO satellites operational?" Davidson asked.

"Yes, sir." Kid said. "And it occurs to me that we can use them to create a high-fidelity map of El Chapo's project quicker than the old school method we were considering. It will highlight the fields and processing labs, the disposition of the Black Wasps, and anything else they have hidden in Mensura Park."

"I look forward to the results," Davidson said, ending the meeting.

"Yes, sir," Kennedy said. He waited until they were several offices away at the stairs. "I'm not worried about giving the president something useful by the deadline, but I'm stumped on how to get El Chapo into the park so we can capture images of him with the product."

"I'd bet my last dollar Wolf has some ideas," Kid said.

"Oh no doubt about that. If it's outrageous and dangerous, he's already thought of it," Kennedy sighed.

"I've never told anyone this, not even my wife, but this is the point in our missions where I lose sleep. When it gets tight, Wolf tends to improvise and operate outside our ability to support him... so, we might as well hear it from the horse's mouth. Let's check in with him when we get back."

**55**

———————

Cement Products, Santiago De Cuba

I'm groaning through my drug and nap induced fog as the buzzing continues. I toss my legs over the bed and push myself erect, taking several slow and shallow breaths before picking up the satellite phone to read the text.

Call at next available, K.

I toss on a t-shirt then slide my hand along the wall and shuffle to the sound of voices.

As usual, Elle, Lisa and Ilena are around the kitchen table. This time, George is with them.

They are having coffee and partaking in some good-looking pastries.

I'm pleased to not get the motherly treatment when I gingerly sit and accept the coffee George offers.

"Where's Morgan?" I ask.

"Installing surveillance on the far side of TransCargo," Elle says.

"Are you okay, Wolf?" George asks.

I paste on a tight-lipped smile. "Yeah, I just need a little rest. Ops wants to talk."

I call Kennedy's number and lay the satellite phone on the table with the speaker on.

"Jimbo's pit barbecue. Can I take your order?"

"Why you so mean to me, brother?" I ask, mouth watering.

"You might have been compromised, beaten up, and had your phone taken."

"Partially right. Elle is here, and we are with our partners. Why the call?"

"To let you know the fires worked and that Kid has made some adjustments to the LEO satellite data processing. We're using them to create a high-fidelity LIDAR-generated map of El Chapo's farm and processing labs," Kennedy says.

"Good idea. What else?"

"I was wondering how you are going to get El Chapo into the park," Kennedy says.

"I'm not. Been thinking—yes, everyone tells me that's dangerous, I say acknowledging the nod from my wife.

"The park was my initial plan. Do so much damage, he shows up, blah blah blah. But here's where the thinking comes in. Call it a stroke of luck or whatever, I'll take it. I'm talking to you a quarter mile from TransCargo and Morgan agrees with the Kid that it's a narco sub facility."

"Wait! Your safe house is that close?"

"Yeah. Morgan and Elle installed cameras on our side while I was on the way to the park, and Morgan is installing more cameras as we speak. Did he send a request?"

"Yes. We didn't know he was with you until we got it."

"That's good, actually."

"The Kakoa's are sailing into position. They will be on station at twenty hundred tonight," Kid says.

"Good. My plan is to get El Chapo to TransCargo. Much simpler than up in the mountains. If Morgan and the Kakoa brothers can start a fire that damages the product, it will get El Chapo and Aguila to the site. Speak of the devil, here he is now."

Morgan appears in the doorway to the kitchen. "Why's everyone staring at me? Is Wolf showing off more of his spirit warrior 'I heard you coming a mile away mojo?"

Elle laughs. "Yes, and you're just the guy we need to talk to. Kennedy and Kid are on the horn."

"Kid, the cameras are operational and hiding in the Pala company network in an encrypted IPSEC tunnel. Two IR and four night-vision capable. I'll send you access." Morgan says.

"Okay nerds, if you're done?" I say. "What's your plan for tonight, Morgan?"

"The Kakoa brothers will use some new high endurance scooters to move up the bay. My plan is to link up with them off the pier at Punta Perro. Once inside, we'll tag any narco subs we find. They're also bringing isotope tags that we can place in the product if we get a chance."

"That's cool," I say. "But I want you to start a fire. Not the burn-the-place-down kind, but something to get their attention. We want to piss off El Chapo so he's driven to visit the site. Do you have any cameras left?"

"Yes, at the plane. You want us to place them inside the facility?"

"Yes."

Kid says, "It won't do any good. The facility is a pretty good approximation of a SCIF. You'd have to place a repeater on the outside wall... and I'm still not sure it would work."

"Putting up a repeater is too risky," I say. "If they do scans, they'll find it anyway. The devices have onboard micro-SD cards, right?"

"Yes," Morgan says.

"Make sure their wireless signal is off. If needed, we can have you or the Kakoa's retrieve the SD cards."

"Morgan, can you plug them into outlets? They're small enough that it's unlikely they'll be noticed in a facility like that. It's possible I can find them," Kid says.

"I like it," Morgan says. "Tag the subs. Place the cameras. Start a fire. Sounds like my kind of mission."

"You're not going, right?" Elle says looking at me.

"I'd be a liability. I'm happy to sit this one out and wait for the results. Lisa, can you support Morgan while he retrieves the cameras from his plane? And Morgan, before you go, make sure Kid has access to your surveillance package," I say and smile.

"You know what—all this pain and suffering we are about to put on El Chapo has me feeling better already."

**56**

———————

El Chapo Safe House

*What was that driver's name?* Aguila thought, looking out over the ocean.

His shoulders drooped and he took a deep breath as the sounds of the waves rolling to the shore brought a moment's respite.

Ochoa had mentioned a smart young man who had shown some leadership after the truck crashed off the mountain at the start of harvest deliveries.

*When was that... let's see.*

It took a moment to reconstruct the episode: Vega, Leto Vega.

Leto had demonstrated a desire for a better life, and willingness to follow orders. He would be the perfect foil for what Aguila had planned. He picked up his cell and called Resendiz.

"Resendiz, it's Aguila. Is there a shipment scheduled for tonight?"

"Yes, twenty-three hundred. Three trucks this time. One partial load after this, and the submarine is full."

*Unbelievable. The street price must be close to a billion dollars US.* "I still think it's unwise to put all your eggs in one basket, as the gringos say."

"I don't disagree, but it's what El Jefe wants."

"I'm going to need a couple of kilos to set a trap, my friend."

"No problem. With the last load, I have ten percent overage factored in for screw ups and damage."

"Wolf bait?" Resendiz asked.

"Yes. He's putting my life on the line in the park. I want to draw him out here in the city. In my element."

"A predator has no element, Aguila. It just hunts. Countless Sicarios, soldiers, and even El Chapo's best, Antrax. Many men have tried… and died." Resendiz said.

"Good, I relish the challenge, and pray he comes to the trap as arrogantly as his legend portrays him," Aguila said and disconnected the call.

*Wolf's invincibility has found its way into El Chapo's leadership. This needs to stop now.*

Aguila turned his attention to the magnesium rod. The blood on it was black and flaking off with every touch. Beneath it, the magnesium was gray, cold, and unaffected.

It didn't care; it had a job to do. But now that job was to pinpoint where Wolf had gotten the rod and who was supporting him. Unable to do a google search like when back in Sinaloa, Aquila called his contact in the G2 foreign materials exploitation unit.

Lieutenant Colonel Javier Torres would probably hold that rank for the rest of his career, and Aguila knew that was fine by him. His scientist friend wanted nothing to do with people, budgets, or interdivisional politics. Javier picked up on the third ring.

"Lieutenant Colonel Torres."

"Javier, its Aguila."

"I'm on my way to a department meeting. What can I help you with?"

"Magnesium rods. What are they used for?"

"Magnesium metal is used in aluminum alloys, iron, and steel production. Here in Cuba, it is mostly used in phosphate form as a component of fast setting cement. Do you want me to continue?"

"No, that's good."

Torres ended the call. *I need the G2 database.*

He changed out of his casual shirt and shorts to a starched shirt, cargo pants and hiking boots befitting his rank of colonel, retired. The drive from the compound at the beach to the G2 facility at the northern edge of the airport was quick.

Inside the modern, monotone, single-level facility, Aguila was given an office and an account name and password for the computer. He said a silent prayer of sorts that the computer and its connection to the central database would work.

Minutes later, he was in the database, accessing the business intelligence section. Every business in Cuba was granted a permit to operate only after they were thoroughly investigated and found to support the communist party interests.

He typed 'cement,' and fifteen seconds later the system returned two thousand four hundred entries with the key word cement. Aguila huffed.

*Too broad. This was easier when I had subordinates.*

He returned to the search page and entered 'cement, Santiago de Cuba."

#

Five hundred and forty-two miles to the north, an alert popped up on Major Isabel Lambarri's screen. The alert appeared to be an undecipherable computer system message about a failed search parameter.

George had given Isabel a device she sat next to the network cable. The malware it had installed was hidden inside the system bios , and it had one job: early warning.

Delgado was at the capital in a meeting with the president and military leaders. An early lunch and a little shopping was something she had done before.

Isabel performed several rounds of quiet but deep breathing cycles to center herself before logging off and telling the chief of staff's assistant her plan to return in an hour.

Isabel called her sister during the four-minute walk from G2 headquarters to the outdoor shopping mall. Lisa did not pick it up, so she left a message that she was dying to see her.

The breeze chilled the sweat along her back, and she shivered. She wrapped her arms around herself and prayed.

"Lisa, George and the others are in danger, I have to let them know," she whispered to herself.

**57**

———————

Bahia de Santiago De Cuba

Morgan slipped into the bay next to the pier known as Punta Perro and as he kicked, he saw a dark form moving toward him.

A jolt of fear flowed through his body for a beat as Tom Kakoa pulled him under and bear hugged him.

Morgan could see him laughing, even in the full-face mask. His brother, Jerry Kakoa, was just behind him, holding Morgan's rebreather system.

*Tom is going to be the first to leave my plane without a parachute.*

He pulled on the mask and cleared the water. "Not cool!" he said over the diver-to-diver intercom.

"Blame it on Wolf. He told us you're not a big fan of sharks," Tom said.

"Time's a wasting. Let's go," Jerry said.

The Kakoa brothers grabbed a line and swam into the darkness, with Morgan close behind. Fifteen meters away, a trio of dive scooters waited.

The brothers clipped themselves to a scooter and pointed to one for him.

Tom pointed to a digital navigation board with a lime green icon and made a tapping motion; Morgan gave him an okay symbol.

The brothers both tapped the icon and headed towards the target. Morgan attached the safety line from his rebreather system to the scooter and followed.

Twenty some minutes later, they were in the channel to the TransCargo facility. Ten meters from entering the facility, they tied off the scooters to a piling.

Jerry pulled a minisub looking device from a bag attached to his hip.

Using a handheld device to direct it, he sent the drone on its way. When the device surfaced, on the other side of the doors, Jerry manipulated the camera.

Morgan's eyes went wide. "Holy crap. That's... ah..."

"What have you gotten us into Morgan?" Jerry demanded.

"That's an advanced German electric diesel attack submarine," Tom said.

"Okay, same mission, less work. Let's get it done and split."

Jerry extended the drone's periscope camera to sweep the facility.

"On the side closest to us, there is a collection of racks, containers, and pallets. I think they're loaded with replacement parts for the submarine. We can exit the water there and reassess," he said.

"Priority one, tag the sub so we can track it," Morgan said.

"We'll take care of it—you being skittish in the dark and all," Tom said.

"Thanks. I'll make sure you get an extra ration of sardines for your trouble. I'll deploy the cameras."

The brothers swam away. Morgan finned to his left and surfaced under the pier side overhang then moved along the overhang to the first ladder.

He slipped out of the rebreather system and used the safety harness to tie it to the ladder.

His knife, dry bag, and the suppressed SIG P320, Tom had given him were all that he would take top side.

Two rungs up, Morgan got a better view of the sub and dock area.

There were two armed men at the north end of the building; one was talking on the radio as both looked toward a door.

He took advantage of their focus on the radio chatter and climbed the ladder, his scuba skin and rash guard shedding water like a duck.

On the concrete floor, his water shoes provided all the traction and stealth he needed to reach the container.

From beside it, he watched the men walk through the door.

He took out a camera, set it to wide-angle, and slowly rotated to take in everything inside the covered dock—including the submarine.

Task complete, and with no one around, he scampered to the crane backed against the west wall.

He wasted no time climbing the ladder to the operator's perch and installed a different camera in an outlet outside and below the operator's line of sight.

Back at the crane ladder, he heard voices. He pushed himself into a shadow and waited.

Three men exited the submarine, and its diesel engines came to life.

They walked toward the door the security guards had left through, laughing about a boss who had evidently been chosen to accompany the submarine on its maiden voyage.

A voyage scheduled to depart in two hours.

When they were gone, Morgan slid down the ladder sides. He dropped the last four feet and ran for the open pallets.

Some were stacked with heroin base and others with what looked to be finished product.

Morgan slid to the pallet on his right. Underneath the plastic he found solvents used in the processing of opium. *Perfect.*

He went back to the pallet with product, used his knife to slit open the wrapping at the bottom, and removed two half kilo bags.

He pulled a four-inch-long thermite device from his dry bag replacing it with the product.

The device looked like a black toilet paper tube with a pull pin actuator.

A voice from the doorway caught his attention; he chanced a quick peek toward the voice then dropped.

*Aguila. Is he sailing with the sub?*

Eight minutes later, when Aguila finally disappeared into the submarine, Morgan scrounged a cigarette butt from the floor and dropped it near the pallet.

He then pulled the pin, sat the device in the solvents, and sprinted to the ladder.

Back in the water, he donned his rebreather and finned as hard as he could to the meetup point.

The Kakoa brothers were waiting. "They were charging their batteries," Tom said. "The battery charging will take a while, so I'm thinking they're planning to sail later today."

"Agreed. We detected lots of voices, like the crew is onboard," Jerry said.

"Let's go," Morgan said. "I need to tell Wolf what we found."

They stopped where they had met and huddled.

"Do you want us to track the sub?" Tom asked.

"Yes," Morgan said. "Those pucks you applied to the hull will insert malware into the nav and comms systems, so the sub will self-report. Prep a squad of SEALs for us. I expect Wolf will want to hit this site tomorrow when the fire does it's job."

**58**

TransCargo, Santiago De Cuba

Aguila startled at the warbling sound of the fire system. It was followed by an announcement that he could not understand. He rushed into the submarine control room, his eyes flitting from person to person until he found the captain.

"Get us out of here," he demanded.

The captain faced Aguila and scowled. "We will sail when we're ready."

To a man, every sailor in the control room had turned to face the colonel.

"There's a fire. We can't lose this product or the submarine."

The captain accessed the intercom. "Engineering, status?"

"Ready in all aspects."

Aguila sniffed the air. "That's an order."

"I take orders from Resendiz, not you. Arturo, escort this man to my quarters and make sure he stays there."

The man grabbed Aguila's arm, his other hand on a pistol. They were stepping through the watertight door when Aguila overheard "Captain, message from El Jefe. Sail immediately."

"XO, take us out."

Ten minutes later, the captain entered his quarters. "I do not apologize for my earlier actions. There is only one captain of the boat, and we were never in any danger. El Chapo was onsite—he gave the order to sail."

"And?" Aguila asked.

"And now that we have sailed, I'm to take orders from you."

"Good. I admit I know nothing about submarine operations. The only orders you will get from me going forward will concern the completion of the mission. You are responsible for the safety of the boat and your crew. Agreed?"

They shook hands just as the boat heeled over. Both men grabbed the table to steady themselves.

"What's happening?" Aguila asked.

"My navigator is showing off. We are maneuvering around the wreck of the USS Merrimac—an American ship sunk in the mouth of the harbor during the Spanish-American war. In minutes, we will be in the Straits of Yucatan, on course for our first stop at oil rig number three off the Louisiana coast."

"If I understand this part of the plan correctly," Aguila said. "We have three oil rigs retrofitted to our purposes. Two off the coast of Houston and one off the coast of New Orleans. The rigs are configured as warehouses for the opium, each with its own crew to provide security and dispense product to distributors. On subsequent trips, you will be stocking the warehouses."

"Yes. When we return to Cuba, we will pick up the rest of the product—if there is any left after the fire—and sail to Mexico for another load."

*Interesting,* Aguila thought. *El Chapo's paranoia keeps him from sharing his plans with his leadership.*

#

El Chapo was in his office reviewing the production numbers when the alarm sounded. He followed Resendiz into the dock area and found the source of the alarm; a pallet was burning brightly.

An explosion echoed through the enclosed space and several pallets around the original were engulfed in flames or had flaming piles of plastic atop them.

Resendiz grabbed security guards and extinguishers, rushing them off to the fires.

"Have the submarine leave immediately!" El Chapo said entering the operations center.

"They are in no danger," a supervisor said.

El Chapo's gold Beretta was out in a flash, the gunshot dropping the supervisor and making the men and women duck under their consoles.

He pointed his gun at the one woman still standing. "Tell the submarine to leave."

She glanced at her dead supervisor. "Si, El Jefe at once." She typed out the message and hit send. "It is done."

"Good. You are now their leader. Feed this man to the sharks," he said pointing to the dead man.

He strode out of the operations center to the dock and growled, seeing the submarine where it was minutes ago.

Angered, he was about to go back to the operations center when sailors appeared and removed the lines holding the sub to the pier.

The hatches thudded closed, and the submarine sank into the dark water.

The fire was still raging. Resendiz was on the radio, telling the security team to collapse on the dock and bring extinguishers with them. Guzman cursed and rushed over to the fire sign on the wall.

*I can't lose this product, or I'll have no cash to pay the Cubans.* He punched the red button.

Resendiz looked to the ceiling wide eyed, a grimace forming on his face as the foam sputtered then dropped from the ceiling in huge waves.

**59**

———

DAY 1

Trituradora de Soya Plant, Santiago De Cuba

*Red lens flashlights, old school but effective,* I thought as I stood just after midnight with my back to the wall of the pump house.

The soybean plant is quiet. A lone guard is stationed at the main gate.

Morgan slips down from the tree he has been waiting in and pulls me close. "El Chapo has a real sub," he whispers.

"Holy crap. Is it an old Russian diesel boat?"

"No. Tom was jabbering on about it being a German 209-model electric-diesel. No worries though... it's tagged."

"That's a serious escalation. Let's get back to the safe house. We need to call Kennedy," I say.

An hour later, after making sure we are not followed, I assemble the team in the front room.

Lisa and Ilena are at their company apartment; I will ensure they are brought up to speed when they arrive during normal working hours.

Morgan stands drying his hair after a quick shower. Elle and George are on the couch.

"Run us through your operation, brother," I say.

"The Kakoa brothers are jerks," he smiled. "They know I don't like what I can't see, and they grabbed me from below."

I laughed. "Morgan thinks all dark water is infested with sharks."

"You don't know! Anyway, they brought some new, long-endurance scooters instead of a minisub. They worked great with the Drager full face mask rebreather. Easy comms, great vision. At the entrance, Jerry deployed a drone that captured El Chapo's new electric-diesel attack submarine and got us a view of the dock area."

"I have some knowledge of this type of submarine," George said. "German-made electric-diesel. Single hull designed for the Baltic and shallow water operations. Carries eight torpedoes. The Cuban Navy has been trying to buy one on the secondary market for years, but sanctions and lack of cash have kept that from happening."

"Cash is one thing El Chapo is not short of," Elle says.

"If they're carrying torpedoes, they are a serious threat," I say.

"The Kakoa's tagged the sub while I placed a camera. I was going to deploy more cameras, but Aguila showed up and entered the sub. I found a pallet of solvents and it got a thermite treatment. We left in a hurry, but I suspect the Kakoa's got an up-close view of the submarine as it sailed by."

"We'll tell Kennedy when I call," I say. "Did you see any response to the fire?" I ask my wife.

"Yes. Guards ran into the warehouse. Some were carrying fire extinguishers. Seconds later, a generator started, and the windows shuddered. Probably the fire suppression system."

"Anyone else show up during or after the fire?" I ask

"Nope," Elle says. "Strange, isn't it? We all thought that destroying product would draw out El Chapo, but it doesn't appear that it has."

"Unless he was already there," Morgan says.

"It's possible, but let's update Kennedy."

I call his number and put it on speaker for everyone.

"Joe's mortuary. You stab 'em, we slab 'em," he answers.

"Did you hit your head and go back to the sixties?" I ask.

"Talk to a retiree on base… they'll tell you it was a fun time."

"That's great. George is with us. And in other news, El Chapo has gotten his hands on what might be a German made electric-diesel attack submarine. Check with your friends at DIA and see if there have been any sales in the last year."

Over the speaker we hear some shuffling, then, "Kid, my office." A door closes and Kennedy says, "Kid's here. Wolf needs you to check your sources for submarine sales in the last year. Start with South American countries."

"Yes, sir." Kid says.

"What else?" Kennedy asks.

"The Jimmy Carter should have a track. I want you and Alpha squadron to prosecute any targets that come from the submarine. It has to stop somewhere along the coast to unload product. Anything new come from the cell phone infection?"

"Roger that. And yes, on the cell phone side. We have a target area, but it's not as focused as I'd like. Although with the limited time we have, it's worth checking out. I'll send it after this call."

"Good. We think we may have drawn El Chapo to the TransCargo site, but we aren't sure."

"Excuse me for interrupting," Kid says. "The Venezuelan Navy is down to three submarines. They bought four German model-209 boats. I'll confirm with my contact at the Office of Naval Intelligence."

"Okay. My first priority, is to use the information we have to get us another 48 hours with the president. The diesel attack submarine should do the trick. Let's get on it. Wolf out." I say and disconnect the call.

"George, I know you've got to make an appearance at work, so we'll wait for Lisa and Ilena before we start surveillance of the target area Kennedy is sending. In the meantime, let's review the video Morgan took and the external camera recordings to see if we can identify El Chapo."

"If he's already inside I need to retrieve the SD card," Morgan says.

"Agreed," Elle says. "But they're on edge over there. Let's let them cool off and get back to normal before you go in. If he's on camera, we're golden. If not, we keep working."

"We've got one shot to take out El Chapo for good," I say. "We can't let it slip. Not this time. Not now."

## 60

Shadow Tier Headquarters MacDill AFB

Kennedy had called an all-hands meeting. He strode into the packed SCIF conference room and stopped just inside the door. Kid closed the door, and the Top Secret/SCI light flashed then stayed lit.

"Kid and I just learned that El Chapo has purchased a modern, German electric-diesel attack submarine and that it has almost certainly sailed for somewhere along our coast."

A hand rose. "Sir, we can eliminate an at sea transfer."

"My apologies that I have not had time to meet all the new faces. Who are you?"

"Victor Martinez, sir. Former US Navy, special warfare. At sea transfers require submarine crew and receiving crew expertise. The submarine captain will not let an unknown captain and his boat alongside. We can limit our search to fixed docks."

"How does that help?" Kid asks. "We've seen that docks can be hastily erected anywhere."

"Check," Victor said. "But if our identification is correct, the submarine El Chapo purchased requires at least forty-five feet of water to stay submerged. The captain is going to want more to keep from being visually detected. We can limit searches of the NGA database to locations with that depth or more."

Ryan Nevis, from the WizKids who worked exclusively with Providence posed a question. "If we know it sailed, did we tag it?"

"Good question, Ryan," Kennedy said. "The answer is yes. But I don't trust that the tag will report in time to be of any use."

"At some point, the captain will need to communicate to the receiving party or parties that they are ready to be unloaded," Victor said. "We'll get a ping when that happens. Then he's ours. I'll coordinate with my anti-submarine warfare contacts at Pensacola. They've caught narco subs, they'll catch this one."

"Excellent. Victor, pick three of your teammates. Search the map database and feed the locations to Ryan... he'll get them into Providence. We've got less than 24 hours to help Wolf tie El Chapo to the opium."

#

After the meeting broke up, Kid joined Ryan in the analytics vault. "Are they keeping up their burner phone hygiene?"

"Yes," Ryan said, ambling over to his computer. "With a few exceptions where someone was late deconstructing a phone. Let me show you on a map."

He brought up a map that bloomed with red dots. "The dots are hits from infected burner phones pinging cell towers. As you can see, most stop at the circle leading to the Santiago de Cuba airport. We have one outlier to the southwest, at a restaurant called Paladar Miguel Angel. The other concentration is the hangar where Morgan found Resendiz and his security team."

"Can you enlarge the map and center it on the intersecting runways?" Kid asked. "That's it. What's out this dirt road? Looks like shacks."

"Yeah, we've been focused to the west and the Piscina de Hotel to Antonio Macea area. Easy access to the airport and the water," Ryan said, adjusting the center of the map.

"Dang it! Why didn't I think of it before," Kid said.

"Since we are still being denied satellite support, let's use our satellites' LIDAR capability to link cell phones pings with vehicles. They're overhead every thirty minutes—we could get lucky with an off angle shot of a license plate or visual of El Chapo."

Ryan slapped his desk and stepped back in excitement. "We've been collecting and storing SIGINT and LIDAR data since the first of our satellites was launched. It's stored in the Agency's classified cloud. I'll get Providence on it right away."

Kid fist bumped with Ryan. "The odds are in our favor that we have at least one vehicle we can pinpoint that takes us to El Chapo's safe house. I'll let Kennedy know."

Headed to Kennedy's office, Kid said to himself, "El Chapo, you can run but you cannot hide. Not from us."

---

## 61

Cement Products, Santiago De Cuba

"Wolf, Lisa and Ilena are here," Elle says, leading them into the kitchen.

Morgan rises from his breakfast to greet Ilena with a fist bump and Lisa with a hug. I limit myself to a tight-lipped smile.

*Definitely something going on between the two of them.*

"Great timing," I say. "Let me bring you up to speed."

"Before you start," Lisa says. "I got word from the asset that someone with access to G2 databases was searching for cement product companies in Santiago de Cuba."

"Expect G2 to swarm all the registered companies," Ileana says.

"If they make the connection between TransCargo and these plants, we're done!," I say. "They can't go big, it would give away too much of their operation. I'm betting it will be a small team under the guise of safety or registration checks."

"We need to increase our counter surveillance," Elle says. "Morgan, can you make sure we've got camera coverage of the gate and front offices."

"Roger that."

"We're out of time and they're closing in," I say. "Good thing

Morgan started a fire inside TransCargo, last night. They did not call for outside help—we, of course, know why. During his sojourn, Morgan saw that El Chapo has upped his game with a modern submarine. We should have listened to Ilena."

My wife smirks.

"Okay, I should have listened to Ilena," I say inside a chuckle.

The rest of the team gives me the duh look so, I continue.

"Resendiz—the Sinaloa transportation lieutenant—is in the facility, and Morgan saw Aguila board the sub just before it sailed. We suspect El Chapo is still on site, but we are not certain. We've reviewed the camera recordings and can't tell either way, as all vehicles enter the large door we see from here, then wait for the door to close before exiting."

"Just before this meeting, I received the cell phone target area Providence highlighted," Elle says. "We need to split into teams—one here, watching TransCargo, and one checking the area southwest of the airport for indications of a protected safe house."

"Lisa and I can take the safe house tasking," Morgan says. "I need to stop by my airplane and fuss over an engine problem to keep my reason for still being here viable. Maybe I can get some more intel from his security team... they're not the sharpest tools in the shed."

"There are only two ways out of TransCargo," I say. "I'll stay here and be ready to tail any vehicle that leaves headed into the city. Ilena can you to cover the—"

"I know you're trying to cover all the angles," Elle says. "But working as a couple in a nondescript car is better than solo on a motorcycle. Plus, Ilena knows the city better than you. I say we ignore vehicles headed to Mensura. We know El Chapo's safe house is not in that direction."

"You're right, you're right," I say. "We need to focus where the data is pointing us—the area around the airport."

Morgan rises from his chair, staring through the kitchen doorway to the laptop and its tiled windows streaming the camera feeds.

"Looks like you're about to get in the game Wolf. An SUV just pulled up to the guard shack and the driver lowered his window."

My coffee spills as I rush to Morgan's laptop. "Do you know this guy?"

"No, but I've seen him. He's one of El Chapo's bodyguards from Los Antrax. Either El Chapo is in the SUV, or that guy is here to pick him up."

"Ilena, start your car," I say. "I'll be down in a minute. We will pre-position on the route back into the city. Morgan and Lisa, you trail behind us. We can tag team them to keep from getting made. Elle, you're on over-watch. Grab the tag number when he enters the building, and ping us when he leaves."

"That SUV is a rolling armory, Wolf. We need to go heavy. Pistols won't do it."

"Yeah. Agreed."

Elle's face scrunches in worry. She grabs me by the arm and hands me a palm sized camera. "We need evidence El Chapo is here... not a gun fight you can't win."

Hugging her as hard as my ribs permit, I pull her close and whisper in her ear, "My number one goal in life is to grow old with you. I'll come back. I promise." I release my wife and smile. "Wipe that smirk off your face, Morgan. By the end of the day, I'll be saving you again."

Morgan laughs. "We'll see, brother."

Elle closes her eyes and shakes her head at our exchange, then watches the laptop and jots down the license plate as the SUV stops in front of the roller door.

Morgan and I perform our weapons checks, then head to the cars. When we pass, Elle holds out the note with the license plate. I briefly squeeze her hand as I take it.

I ask my spirit guide to give me another day with my wife and my vision of her turns a roiling black as the yellow eyes of the dark wolf pierce my soul.

A whisper lingers. *Kill him Wolf, for your parents.*

**62**

———

Santiago De Cuba

Tucked into the trees surrounding the Bacardi Rum factory museum, a block north of TransCargo, Ilena and I have a view to any of the east-west streets the SUV might take.

We can also see to the south along Avenida Jesus Menendez. "They could go north, but it would be part of an extended surveillance detection route," I say.

"Into the city is the better SDR, with kilometers of dense city traffic and intersecting roads to check for a tail," Ilena says.

"Agreed. This will give us a good idea of what level they think the threat is."

"I would think no more than moderate—even if they believe you are here. With police and G2 everywhere, they must know that we are restricted in our movement."

"A rational person might," I say. "But El Chapo takes paranoia to a new level. In his line of business, everyone is a threat. Even his lieutenants and their crews. It's the mid-level guys and gals that get cocky and make mistakes. When the SUV moves, it will do so with a counter-assault team just like our presidents do. El Chapo plans for the worst and can pay for support to get him out of trouble no matter where he is in the world."

My satellite phone buzzes. It's a text message.

Two SUVs headed to city.

"They're on the way," I say, checking the rifle between my legs.

I look up and see them turn south on Menendez, then continue onto Sao Del Indio. "Okay let's go. Nice and easy."

A minute later, Morgan texts:

On your six one block.

"Morgan and Lisa are one block behind us," I say.

Ilena keeps her eyes on the SUVs.

"How far does this road go?" I ask.

"It changes names, but you can get to Altavista, which is just north of the airport. Wait… ahh, they're turning left onto Avenue 24 de Febero."

I text Morgan to leapfrog us as the SUVs accelerate. Morgan and Lisa fly by and hurtle down the avenue. Ilena downshifts and floors the go pedal to get as much as she can out of the compact car.

My phone rings and I put it on speaker.

"We lost them," Morgan says. "Lisa thinks she saw them turn right around Virgen. We're taking the second right to see if we can box them."

"Take del Morro south to Chicharrónes," Iliena adds. "They'll SDR in Mariana De La Torre or Vista Hermosa, then rejoin."

"Roger that." I disconnect.

"Why not leave the line open?" Ilena asks.

"Respect for Cuban intelligence and the new Chinese equipment they are installing. Let's head to the intersection she mentioned and standby."

#

My phone rings. It's Lisa. "Head south to First Avenue and position so you can see the exit for the Hotel Versalles," she says.

Lisa and Morgan drive by us. Ilena stays back as the SUVs continue by the hotel and stop at a supermarket.

Morgan calls. "This makes no sense. They pulled into a supermarket and the drivers are out, headed into the store."

"Darn it! They weren't running an SDR, they made a vehicle switch. Can you tag the vehicles?" I ask.

"Lisa can. I'm giving her the combo units that ping location and infect cell phones." Morgan says.

"Good. We'll let the tech do the work, and maintain your cover. Get back to ops so we can figure out if we're blown."

## 63

Cement Products, Santiago De Cuba

"Be honest with me. Was it a lack of training or resources?" I ask after the team joins me in the apartment.

"In relationship to what?" Lisa asked

"Sorry, I meant that for Morgan...we lost El Chapo when they made a car switch."

"The answer is resources, and it's my fault," Lisa said.

"I expected one behavior, and they did something different. If I hadn't told you to wait, we might have caught the switch."

"You made a call, I agreed, and we were wrong. It sucks, but no one died. So, we re-set."

Lisa gave a tight-lipped smile that I take as a thank you.

"Let's continue this in the kitchen," I say. "I need some coffee." We all gather around the table.

"I hate to spoil the party," Elle says. "We are not sure El Chapo or anyone else of consequence was in those vehicles. They could have been red herring runs for all we know."

"True." Morgan glances at his watch.

"But we'll have cell data in another thirty-five minutes, and that will indicate if there was more than the driver in those SUVs."

"'Likely' but not definite—we've all carried multiple cell phones," Elle says.

"Debbie downer is right. We need that camera, Morgan," I say.

Elle punches me in the shoulder, and I wince in mock pain.

"You're right. It's our only chance at video evidence that ties El Chapo to the opium and the submarine," Morgan says.

"It's a start," I say. "If the video is good, we're done. If not, we can use the submarine to draw him back to the site."

"So, there are several threads we are pulling," Elle says. "The video, the tagged vehicles, the infected cell phones, and the support team hunt for his safe house. The question is, will any of them lead to the evidence we need, the clock is ticking. To use an American football analogy, my Broncos are fourth and one on the nine-yard line. There's time on the game clock for one more play. They can kick for three and tie the game or go for it and the win. Which is it?"

"We don't know what that means," Lisa says.

"What I mean is, we have nothing to lose, short of getting rolled up by G2," Elle says. "While you were gone, the cameras caught a truck entering the property. I have a good image of the driver—a young guy. I think we should—"

"Target him to get one of us inside," Lisa says glancing at Ilena.

"It's an option but Elle and I can't go. If El Chapo is inside, we'd be recognized immediately. And Morgan would have no reason to be there. His even knowing of the site would get him killed."

"I hate getting killed," Morgan says.

The team laughs at the absurd comment.

"Let the locals handle this," Ilena says.

"With no time on the clock, we need something to hook him immediately if we are to make this work."

"I have just the thing. A kilo of heroin I took from the docks before I set the fire. While you're blackmailing the target, I'll retrieve the camera," Morgan says

"You're going in daylight?" Elle asks.

"Yeah," Morgan says. "I'll be taking a fishing pole, fins, and a spear gun with me to the break in the mangroves where I came ashore. It's a remote area, and I've got the dive scooter and the rebreather cached there. Both will be good for one more trip. If someone catches me coming out of the water, I'll have the spear gun as my cover. Never know—I could come back with dinner."

"Okay, Elle and I will work with Kennedy to get El Chapo to TransCargo... or keep him there. First though, I need to beg for more time, we're so close."

## 64

Cement Products, Santiago De Cuba

Morgan ambled downstairs to check his gear. Lisa and Ilena talked through their initial contact plan then went next door to the cement plant and their cover stories.

Elle called Kennedy. "K-man, you're on speaker with Wolf. Any update on the submarine?"

"No. Waiting on them to surface or pop a comms buoy," he says.

"We've been thinking about how to use the sub to drive El Chapo to the TransCargo site," I say. "I want Kid to prep some malware for delivery. If the malware stops the boat or makes it run on the surface without endangering lives, that's best. If we can convince El Chapo his multi-million-dollar boat and its billion-dollar load is in jeopardy, he'll want to manage the crisis himself."

"Will do," Kennedy says. "We'll have to deliver the malware with embedded commands, so if the connection drops it will at the very least introduce a navigation system fault. I'll have him trip a fire alarm too. One of our former Navy Special Warfare guys said that freaks out submarine crews."

"I can only imagine... and never want to find out," Elle says. "Has

Providence mined any more cell data? After our tracking the bad guys went bust, we're looking for any help we can get."

"Nothing yet. The pings stop at the airport and the infections, if any haven't—"

Someone knocked on Kennedy's door, then it was the Kid's voice, "Boss. We've got a lead."

"Close the door. Elle and Wolf are on speaker."

"Oh, sorry. Uh... yeah. From the tags earlier today. One of the three cell phones at the supermarket was at a house on the southern end of the north-south runway. It was there for twenty-three minutes before it went offline."

"Any useful images from our sats?" I ask.

"Yes. But the roof of the house is metal, so nothing inside. We do have a low-angle view under a carport—the partial plate we see is a match for one of the SUV's from earlier. There is also a track, partially hidden by the trees, that is a direct route to the runway."

"Send us the coordinates... and check for fishing boats and fast movers up to ten miles out," I say. "El Chapo has probably deployed the boat crew he used to get Eliana Cortes off the beach when the Tijuana Cartel attacked."

"What's your plan?" Kieran asks.

"Recon. Find out if El Chapo is there. If he is, create a plan to hit the place tonight if needed. Morgan is retrieving the camera he placed inside TransCargo. The recording could make any further action moot."

"And if you see El Chapo?" Elle asks.

"I'll improvise."

"That's what I'm afraid of," Elle says as she faces me. "I'm going with you. At the very least, I can provide another exfil option. If Morgan gets back in time, he can be the QRF."

Our satellite phones buzz. "Got the coordinates," Elle says. "Did you send them to Morgan?"

"Yes. Do your thing and we'll keep him updated," Kennedy says.

"As your neighborhood friendly SIGINT expert, I suggest you take one phone and keep it off unless you find Murphy in your op,"

Kid says. "One of those shacks could house the Cuban or Chinese equivalent of a tactical signals intelligence team."

"Agreed. El Chapo is paranoid enough to pay for SIGINT and electronic warfare capabilities like we take on missions," Elle says.

"Good catch, Kid. We'll dust ourselves so you can track us with the LIDAR sats. Out here," I say.

"Make your own luck," K-man says.

Elle disconnected the call and took the battery out of her phone.

Before we head out, I need to call Davidson," I say punching the speed dial button and selecting speaker.

"Are you secure, Wolf," Davidson asks when answering.

"Yes, sir and I have good news," I say. "We've located the warehouse where El Chapo stores his drugs and hides his submarine. The team also located his safe house here in Santiago de Cuba. I'm headed there shortly but wanted to get you the latest in hopes that it would get us another 48 hours."

"Wolf, while that is positive news, the president was very clear that he wanted whatever information you have today. Not tomorrow. I know how you think and operate. And I've been good with it because you back it up with results. The president and his administration does not work that way. I'll go to bat for you, but I expect an immediate no. The fate of Shadow Tier depends on what you do next."

"Yes sir, I understand. Out."

I turned to Elle. "I say we continue to operate as if we have more time, what else can we do?"

"We could package up what we have and leave but you're not going to do that are you Lance Bear Wolf," Elle says.

I flash a smile. "How many times have I said, 'we're so close'?"

"I've lost count but not faith in you, husband," she says. "We never quit, and I agree we *are* close. My reason for continuing is you go, I go. And there's that freak submarine he bought. We must see this through and trust that the people who believe in us and what we do will prevail over politics."

*How did I get so lucky that you chose me?* I think.

Elle starts grabbing kit and I hand her an AK. She checks it is loaded and on safe before she bumps into my body and stares into my eyes.

"Where's your head, Akduxxiile?" She asks, using the Crow word for warrior.

"If I'm lucky, I'll just be outgunned twenty to one. My plan is recon, but if I get a high percentage shot, you know I'll send El Chapo to hell."

"Yeah, I get it. I want him too. But no one is more important to me than you," Elle says. "I can't do this without you."

She kisses me then pushes me away, to focus on her kit.

"One of these threads is going to break our way," I say. "My spirit guide says this is the one."

*Why does it have to be the dark wolf, the harbinger of death?*

## 65

———

Trituradora de Soya Plant, Santiago De Cuba

Morgan rode the motorcycle to the soybean plant like he didn't have a care in the world. He had dressed in local clothes, paying attention to the way they were worn in this part of Cuba.

His Mexican passport and cover story—visiting his uncle—were provided by George and a well-paid plant worker.

The fishing pole, spear gun, and motorcycle gave him an island gypsy look.

He slowed as he neared the front gate, a pack of workers were leaving the plant. A boisterous group, he heard them talking about a cantina and beer.

A hundred meters down the road, he took the dirt track that led to the water.

At the tree line, he drove between two trees and leaned the motorcycle against one. He untied his gear and walked the last 100 meters to the little beach.

Morgan had to shield his eyes from the setting sun as he looked across the placid water.

*A little shack, a girl, and some beers... I could be happy here.*

He found an adequate branch and broke off the long end, jamming it into the sand to prop up the fishing pole

After he cast the lure and laid the pole against the stick, he stripped down to his swimming trunks, happy for the bug spray Lisa had liberally applied.

With his mask and snorkel around his neck, fins and spear gun in hand, he waded into the water until he was chest deep.

He slipped into the fins first then pulled the mask over his arm. He finned north to the mangroves, where he had cached the scooter and rebreather.

Taking a deep breath, he dove ten feet to the bottom, and slipped on the Drager purging the water from the mask.

After he lashed the other mask and the snorkel to the mangrove, Morgan righted the dive scooter and powered on the navigation computer.

With a deep, slow breath to center himself, he slid his left hand into the safety lanyard and cinched it tight. On the way out the first time, he had set waypoints in the navigation system.

He hit the icon to follow them in reverse.

It blinked three times and the scooter accelerated, taking him parallel to the shipping channel.

According to his watch, it had been twenty-seven minutes since he had left the beach area.

*Maybe the tide is outgoing. I should have checked.*

Six minutes later, the navigation computer icon blinked, and the scooter slowed to a stop.

He pulsed the motor and saw where the rocks at the mouth of the TransCargo facility changed to a cement wall.

The setting sun was reflecting on the massive doors that sported their company logo. He pulsed the motor again.

In seconds, he was under the doors and could make out the ladder.

Morgan drifted and tied the scooter and rebreather to the bottom of the ladder, fifteen feet below the surface.

He took one last deep breath and slowly made his way up, pausing with just his head out of the water.

He cleared his ears and listened.

A radio squawked, but he could not make out what was said. Slinging his spear gun around to his back, he climbed to just below the dock and brought his feet up another rung.

*A quick look to decide which route to take.*

When his eyes were above dock level, he stopped and breathed through his mouth to stay as silent as possible.

There was a guard sitting on a nearby pallet, having a cigarette.

He was at the guard's back but could see there was a lot of cigarette left to smoke.

He stepped down a rung and locked his left arm around the ladder to wait.

*Cut it short dude, if that doesn't kill you, I might.*

He could hang onto the ladder for a day if he had to, but every minute on the ladder meant another minute that Murphy could show up and cause all kinds of havoc.

He might make a noise that would alert the guard.

Time seemed to slow in situations like this for Morgan. Not nearly as patient as Wolf, he was more prone to make something happen and adjust to the changing circumstances.

Just when he was getting irritated, he heard the guard's radio crackle. A voice told the guard to relieve the front gate.

It laughed, then mentioned bad food. The guard acknowledged and walked away; as he did, he created a sound Morgan couldn't identify.

The area was clear, so he scampered over to the parts racks. He feet made the same noise he heard from the guard.

*Why is the floor is sticky?*

The racks were scorched and smelled of smoke. There was crystallized foam in some places. The center pallet he'd set afire was all but gone, and the ones to the right and left were half empty.

The guard entered what had to be the office space. Morgan

moved along the racks to where he could get a better look at the vehicles parked inside.

Along the way he tried different methods of movement to limit
the noise from the sticky floor; on the balls of his feet worked best.

*I must look like a prancing idiot.*

There were three SUVs. One appeared lower than the others,
which likely meant it was armored.

Morgan used mnemonic linking to memorize the license plates.

The crane was in the same position as when he had attached the
camera. He stayed low against the wall until he got to the derrick,
then used a wheel to hop up and ascended the ladder to the cab.

*Everything is sticky... must be fire-retardant foam.*

Locking his legs into the ladder to free his hands, he reached
around the front to peel off the camera. Even it felt sticky.

He placed it in his dry pouch and squeezed the air out before
closing the double zip locks.

Morgan cringed at the noise as he climbed down the ladder.

He jumped off the derrick and sprinted to the racks, just slipping
behind them as two guards entered the dock area, weapons at the
ready.

They moved to the crane, obviously searching. One was
advancing on the derrick, focused on the wheeled base that moved
the unit.

Morgan used their focus to dash to the pallets and then to the
ladder.

He grabbed the side rail and flung himself over the edge, using
his other hand and feet to quiet his landing on the cement wall.

In the water, he moved to the right side of the ladder and against
the wall.

*They won't be able to look straight down. Time to go.*

He pulled himself down and donned the rebreather mask, which
he cleared.

He untied it rebreather and slipped into it, then freed the dive
scooter and powered on the navigation computer.

As the scooter accelerated down the channel he thought, *Please be on the recording, so we can leave before Wolf gets himself and Elle killed.*

**66**

———————

Lambarri Apartment, Havana, Cuba

After work, Isabel checked her personal email. Lisa had sent an image, which she copied to a thumb drive.

She shut down her computer and made dinner, then watched the news until eight pm—which was her custom.

Back to her desk, she opened her work laptop and attached the network cable. In theory her super-user role should have been more closely monitored.

She hadn't found it to be the case, but kept to an easy-to-track routine.

That way, outlier times of network and odd systems access could be easily explained by the director's schedule and his support requests.

Once inside the network, Isabel accessed the facial recognition system and its growing database.

A staggering leap in capability had recently taken place, thanks to the Chinese.

Isabel copied the photo that Lisa had created by replacing the head of a former military friend with that of the truck driver.

She then entered it into the recognition application and highlighted the man's face.

In less than a minute, the application came back with Leto Vega's government ID, driver's license, and other personal information. Isabel scribbled his information on a pad of paper.

She circled his name and wrote—is my sister safe with him—to throw off anyone questioning her about the ID check.

It needed to look like nothing more than one sister looking out for another. She texted Lisa his age, and address, and that he did not have any radical indicators and added the warning that Lisa should forget him if he lied about anything.

#

Lisa smiled at the ruse and handed Ilena the phone. Together they headed for Vega's address on the north side of Santiago de Cuba. They found a nondescript, gray cinder block-and-tin roof house.

Before Ilena exited the car, she wedged her hand through a slit in the bottom of the seat back and withdrew two G2 credentials. Ilena tossed Lisa hers and they ambled to the front door. Standing shoulder to shoulder, Lisa knocked, then whispered, "Like they say in America, I'm good cop; you are bad cop."

Ilena smiled, the wrinkles at the corners of her eyes telegraphing her excitement at the opportunity. The young man they had identified as Leto answered the door, and they immediately flashed their credentials.

*Good, he's worried,* Lisa thought.

Ilena pushed by Leto but stopped when she saw an older man and woman in front of a new TV.

"Where can we talk? We have some questions," she said to Leto in a whisper.

His face paled, his Adam's apple bobbing up and down. "In in the kitchen. Can… can I get you some coffee?"

"No, we are not here to check on your coffee making," Ilena said curtly.

"I would like a cup, thank you, Leto," Lisa said and smiled.

When they entered the kitchen, Ilena huffed and moved to the window as if checking their security. "Who else is here besides your parents?"

"Just my sister, who is mourning."

"My condolences. May I ask who passed?" Lisa asked.

"Her husband."

Ilena got in Leto's face. "The trucking business is dangerous, but pays very well, no?"

"The payment was for his death." Leto stiffened.

*That touched a nerve. Time to set the hook.*

"Can I get that coffee?" Lisa asked. Leto poured himself a cup, handed Lisa one, then took a seat at the table. "Please, sit," He said.

They sat on either side of Leto. "Let me get to the point of our visit," Lisa said. "We are investigating a drug operation in Parque Mensura that appears to be tied to TransCargo. We have video of you delivering opium to TransCargo and want you to get us inside."

Ilena thumped her hand on Leto's shoulder. "The alternative is that you and your family go to prison. Your parents will die there. The medical care is not good."

"You... you have the wrong person. I just delivered engine parts to TransCargo."

Ilena laughed. "You are a terrible liar."

Lisa dropped a bag of heroin on the table. "We have the rest that fell off your truck. Half kilo bricks. We have video. We know you were working for a man we know as Ochoa. Six two, two hundred pounds, dark hair, lifeless eyes..."

"Ever hear the name Resendiz?" Ilena said. "He leads the transportation side of the operation."

Leto stared at his coffee. She squeezed his arm. His shoulders slumped as he sighed.

"Listen to me," Lisa said. "The only way to save your family is to work with us. Right now, you are not a named suspect, and we can keep it that way. And as a show of our appreciation, we will let you keep the trucks, so you can start a legitimate business."

Leto stared into the middle distance.

*He's decided,* Lisa thought.

"These are dangerous men," he said. "They do not hesitate to kill. You must promise my family protection."

"We agree. It's best if your parents and sister take a vacation. We will make arrangements," Lisa said.

"When is your next delivery to TransCargo?" Ilena asked.

"Tonight. It's the last shipment of the first harvest."

"Good. I'll drive. It will be my final test to see if you are going to hire me." Ilena said.

"No, no, no," Leto said. "They will check your background and we'll both be killed."

"Not to worry. We have taken care of that. She can drive anything in Cuba."

"I don't know," Leto said. "It's too fast."

"Leto, look at me. We do this tonight, or the deal is off," Lisa said.

He closed his eyes and sighed. "We'll get the load and you can drive once we are out of the park."

*If Isabel can't get the records changed in time, we'll never see Ilena again,* Lisa thought.

**67**

S hadow Tier Headquarters

Kieran Kennedy stared at the result of the question he'd asked Providence earlier in the morning. It had answered him much quicker than he anticipated. The response glared at him on the screen.

*How many times have we been this close, only to lose him.*

His door flew open. Kid and Victor rushed through the door. "We got em boss!" Kid said.

Kennedy turned off his screen. "Okay, okay. Spill it!"

"Yes, sir. Position and track. It leads to a derelict oil rig off the Louisiana coast south of New Orleans," Victor said.

"Derelict oil rig. Why that location?"

"One, it's over the horizon," Kid said. "Two, it's not patrolled, Three—."

Jennifer Lynn appeared in the doorway and interrupted. "Three, it's where El Chapo plans to store drugs for distribution. I found out the same shell corporation bought two other derelict rigs off the coast of Houston. The sub can sail back and forth on its own schedule, a billion dollars of drugs per load. They need somewhere to stash it."

"Innovative on Resendiz's part," Kennedy said. "Also pushes more of the risk to the distributors, who must travel offshore. Any indications of additional buildings being erected on the platform? They're not going to all that trouble to have product sit out on the deck."

"I haven't found anything yet, but I will," she said mischievously. "I'd bet they've cleared out the oil equipment and control systems, so they don't need to build right away."

"Back on the submarine for a minute. Victor, any chance they will surface before reaching the oil platform?"

"Not unless we force them to," Victor said.

"That begs the question. Do we force them to surface before or after they've offloaded the product?" Kid asked.

"What do you suggest?" Jennifer asked.

"After," Kid said. "That way we can take it down, no pun intended, without the buyers knowing. We can take over the platform and sell the product ourselves. By tagging it and the buyers, we could go deeper into the distribution network than ever before."

"Jennifer, what do you think?" Kennedy asked.

"I'm with Kid. We can't pass up the opportunity," she said.

"Victor? Thoughts?"

"I agree with Kid, too. Let the cartel do all the hard work of unloading tons of drugs, then send Charlie squadron to take over the rig. They have experience acting as cartel members."

"That they do," Kennedy said. "But it will be Alpha squadron. Charlie's up to its eyeballs in Afghan opium. Kid, have Leblanc spin up Alpha. I'll contact Wolf and have him sign off on our plan. And before I forget, I just want to say I appreciate your leadership on this mission. And let your teammates know we value their hard work. But make sure they know this isn't over yet... not until Elle, Wolf, and Morgan are out of Cuba."

There was a chorus of *roger that*, and they left the office. Kennedy closed and locked his door, then called Wolf via his encrypted phone.

"Good news or bad news," Wolf asked.

"Good news, brother. We own El Chapo's submarine. It's headed to a not-so-derelict oil rig off the Louisiana coast south of New Orleans," Kennedy said.

"Submarine. Oil rig. Tons of drugs. Sounds like an Agency operation."

"Hey, they're probably listening. All joking aside, it's pretty darn innovative, and scary."

"Agreed. We have plenty of terrorist organizations that would pay as much as those drugs are worth to slip their goons into the United States undetected," Wolf said.

"We're thinking we'll take some of our moves from the Marseilles operation. Let the sub unload its cargo, then have Alpha take over the rig and go undercover as cartel. We can sell the drugs ourselves after we tag them. We should have seven to ten days of sales before we are burned. It will give us a lot of the Sinaloa network we have never had before."

"I love it. What about the sub?" Wolf asked.

"While it's unloading, we'll place a trojan in the life support software. It will shut down the air systems and disable the snorkel. The captain will have no choice but to surface. We'll have the Coast Guard and a Navy destroyer on hand to help them out and take them into custody."

"That's perfect," Wolf said.

"That will give the Cuban president TransCargo and the drug linkage," Kennedy said.

"Hey," Wolf said. "Got to go, Morgan's back with the camera from inside TransCargo."

"Roger that." Kennedy said, then entered his password to opened his screen. Centered in the window, the results mocked him.

EL CHAPO: INCARCERATION OR DEATH - 18% PROBABILITY.

WOLF, PARKER, MORGAN: INCARCERATION OR DEATH - 70% PROBABILITY.

## 68

L eto Vega House, Santiago De Cuba

Repeat it back to me, Ilena said, putting a hand on Leto's arm. Instead of it relaxing him, he startled.

Leto stared at his shoes. "You're my girlfriend, a former truck driver in the Army. I'm training you as my backup driver."

"What's my name and birthdate, and where was I born?"

"Ilena Serrano, July 23, 1999, Las Flores."

*It will have to do,* she thought.

When the new asset started his truck, Ilena was in the passenger seat. The vehicle was a commercial version of the transport Ilena had driven when on active duty.

Three hours later, after a fill up at a gas station and forty minutes of first gear grinding up the dirt road, they reached the opium lab.

Leto and Ilena jumped from the cab and circled around to the back. Workers already had the tailgate down, and two had hopped into the bed to stack the product.

They were watching the loading when an overweight guy in dirty jeans and t-shirt ambled up and pointed his AK at Ilena.

He scowled and flipped the safety to full auto. "Leto, who's the Chica? Did you bring her here for me?"

"Put your rifle down, Alvaro. She's my girlfriend, I'm testing her to become one of our drivers. The next harvest will require more trucks. Ochoa ordered me to prepare."

"Forget him. He's dead."

Leto stepped between Ilena and Alvaro. His brows knitted together. "No, it can't be. Don't joke, it's not funny," he said.

Alvaro grunted. "We've been attacked three times now. Ochoa and a lot of Black Wasps are dead. No one can stop him."

"Who is he?"

"He calls himself Wolf. The word is he's hunting El Chapo. Ochoa just got in his way."

"Is this why this load is so small?" Leto asked, looking inside the bed of the truck.

"No, it's just the last of the product. But I did overhear Colonel Aguila talking about setting a trap to kill Wolf and his team."

Leto grabbed Alvaro's arm with trembling hands. "Here in Cuba… Are they watching? I'm not a fighter. Send two… no send four of your men with me."

"Stop!" Alvaro said, peeling Leto's hands off his arm. "They won't attack you, just be extra vigilant when you drive your surveillance detection route."

"Chica, you were in the Army. You understand what I'm talking about?"

"Yes, I have experience leading clandestine resupply convoys in South America and Africa. Two of your shooters will suffice."

"I like your Chica—." Alvaro said.

"It's Ilena. Ilena Serrano," she interrupted. "Leto let's go."

The big man belly laughed. "Be careful my friend, she's going to take over the whole operation one day."

The workers closed and latched the tailgate, then secured the flap covering the back of the hoops and canvas cover.

Leto started the truck and waited until he felt the guards jump in the back.

He took off but, kept the truck in second gear to save the brakes on the way down. Ilena scooted next to Leto and let her lips brush his ear before she whispered.

"You are good at making people think you are scared."

"I am scared. It only gets more dangerous when we arrive at TransCargo. If El Chapo is inside, the guards will be more than on edge. Before this day is over, we could end up fish food."

"One problem at a time. We proved the cover story works… and it will again," she whispered, then moved back across the bench seat.

**69**

———————

Front Gate, TransCargo Facility

"I'll pull up to the gate just like every other delivery you have done. It will be fine," Ilena said.

The sun was setting, a brown orange glow brought on by the sugarcane harvest. As Ilena stopped, flood lights switched on.

She squinted as she rolled down the window and handed their Vega Trucking badges to the guard.

The guard eyed them, then Leto, then stared at her. When he radioed for backup, he tried to hide the movement of his rifle safety to a firing position. At the distinctive clicking sound, she slowly raised her hands.

"She she... is with me," Leto stammered.

"Both of you out. Keep your hands where I can see them," the guard said.

Two more guards ran up, weapons at the ready. "What are you doing Leto. You can't bring someone we haven't cleared in here. You know that," a man with captain's bars on his hat said.

"Sir, I am following Ochoa's orders to train new drivers. Ilena was a truck driver in the Army. She has experience in South America and Africa."

"Ochoa is dead."

"Yes, sir. We were just told when we picked up the load."

The sound of canvas being thrown out of the way turned everyone's head.

The two security men from the lab site fell out of the truck, laughing and clearly drunk.

A bottle of clear liquid broke on the pavement just before an AK clattered to the ground.

"Get them inside. Now," the captain ordered. Then he spun to Leto and Ilena. "You two, back in the truck. I'm going with you."

He jumped in the front next to Leto and drew his pistol. "This is a bad time to be stupid."

Leto's face was drawn and pale. "But sir. I'm following orders."

"And you just violated our operational security by bringing her here. When we are inside, I will hold her until we can check her history."

"But she is my girlfriend. Ochoa vetted her."

Ilena focused straight ahead.

*Leto is fast on his feet, and Ochoa isn't around to deny it.*

She stopped the truck in front of the roller door and waited. When the door didn't open, the captain radioed the operations center and the door clanked and creaked open.

She drove in and waited again. The door closed behind them, and another door opened to their front.

"Park over here," the captain said, pointing to forklift with a metal tray on its arms.

Parked, Ilena took in as much of the facility as she could. The captain came around to her side of the truck, opened the door, and stepped back.

He motioned to the guards that stood on either side of Leto. "Take her to interrogation. You're coming with me."

She let the guards manhandle her. Along the way, she shook and let her eyes go wide as if in fear.

They pushed her into a room and shackled her to a large eye bolt but left her standing.

There was a drain under her feet and a water hose was coiled up in the corner. The walls and ceiling were gray, making it hard to tell one from the other.

*Are those blood stains?*

"Hands behind your head," one guard said as the other gave her a rough pat down. He spun her around, took her driver's license and Army ID from her back pocket, and forced her into a chair.

When the guards left, she looked around as if trying to figure out what was going on.

She put her head in her hands and sobbed, knowing it was how they expected her to react.

There were two cameras, a microphone, and a not-so-subtle loudspeaker, all easily spotted. She hoped they enjoyed watching.

*If they bust the door open, it will mean Leto broke.*

*If the captain comes back, we're good, but in for some yelling and screaming.*

#

The captain led Leto to the office, which was dominated by a large wooden desk and several overstuffed leather chairs. There were no windows, and nothing on the walls. Not even a phone on the desk.

A short stocky man stomped into the room.

He strode around the desk and repositioned the high back leather-covered chair so he could look straight at them.

"What is this about, captain?" El Chapo asked.

"Sir, Colonel Aguila is not here, so I had to come to you. This man, Leto Vega, is our transportation leader. His job is to ensure the safe transport of your product from the park to here. But he has just violated operational security by bringing a stranger to the facility."

"Speak!"

"Sir, ah I'm following Senor Ochoa's orders to hire new drivers. And... and... have them trained before the next harvest. I vetted the woman as best I could and brought her here to test her driving and have Colonel Aguila's people finish the process," Leto said.

The man played with his gold-plated Beretta pistol. "I apologize El Jefe. I was not told about the process."

"Your fate rests in the hands of the woman. If she is as you said, I will show mercy. If not, your deaths will be slow. Chain him to his truck so he can hear her screams."

# 70

---

TransCargo Facility

A man dressed in a tailored gray suit opened the door to the interrogation room.

He had polished cowboy boots, but unlike the picture of cartel leaders she had in her mind's eye, he hadn't adorned them with silver or gold.

He looked like a banker or businessman you might find in Havana and the pistol at his side was not drawn. She didn't see any guards behind him. He closed the door and locked the deadbolts from the inside.

She wracked her memory and then it came to her. *Ah, it's Resendiz. El Chapo's transportation lieutenant.*

He ambled to the table and grimaced when he flexed his shoulder. "Ilena Serrano, you are a problem. Leto was unwise to bring you here. We are researching your history. If it looks suspicious, you will not live to see the sunset."

"Sir, my boyfriend is not wise to the ways of clandestine operations. It is unfortunate that the Mister Ochoa he spoke so highly about did not push that part of his training. However, I have been trained. While my background will show me as a lowly truck driver, I was, in fact, in intelligence, running covert resupply missions to our partners in South America and Africa. I can be an asset to your organization by improving the operational and logistics security of the team Leto has assembled."

"So, you're a truck driver and a spy. Who are you spying for?"

"No one, sir. I just need a job."

Resendiz stepped back and drew his pistol in one fluid motion. "You have one chance to answer the question!"

Ilena tried to throw her hands up, but the chain kept them at chest level. The blood drained from her face as she cringed. The boom from the pistol was deafening. She spun to find a hole in the wall at eye level. She snapped back, "G2. General Delgado!"

He dropped the weapon at a low carry and stared into her eyes. "Delgado... so what's your mission?"

"After the death of Ochoa, the general tasked me to assess the security of your transportation between the labs and TransCargo."

There was banging and yelling from outside the door. Resendiz thumped the door with his free hand. "Stand down," he said turning back to her. "So, you know who I am?"

"Yes, sir."

"Who can I call to validate your claims?"

"Sir, if you have pen and paper, I can provide my handler's contact."

He holstered his pistol and sat a pen and business card on the table. "Write!"

Ilena scribbled a number, and a passcode on the back of the card. He snatched the card and unlocked the deadbolts. "For your sake I hope this is true."

He opened the door and motioned for a guard to enter the room. "Bring Vega in here and get them some water."

"Si, El Jefe," the guard said.

Resendiz pocketed the card and headed to the operations center. Inside, he told an analyst to take a break and sat down at his station. He dialed the number and was about to hang up when a female voice came on the line. "Authenticate Delta Kilo Bravo Two Niner Six."

He activated the voice scrambler and read back the passcode Ilena had provided.

"Authenticated. Do you need assistance?"

"Mission accomplished. Awaiting new orders."

"Will relay to director. Standby for tasking. Out."

The line went dead. *So, she's real. Now I must flip her.*

#

The gunshot startled Leto. Muffled as it was, it was distinct.

He yanked on his chains and cursed. "Ilena! Ilena!"

When he didn't receive a reply, he slumped back against the truck.

Resendiz exited the room and held a short conversation with a guard. Leto waited for Ilena's lifeless body to be drug out.

*I should have never taken the job. All the death...*

The guard acknowledged Resendiz's order and strode over, unchained Leto and deposited him in the room.

"You are lucky, the guard said. "Your girlfriend is not who she appears to be, but in a good way. Your prospect of leaving here alive tonight has grown."

## 71

Cement Products, Santiago De Cuba

We've watched the video from the camera Morgan has retrieved at least fifty times. We replay it every way we can think of then break it down frame by frame. I identify El Chapo's voice, it's clear, but he doesn't enter the camera's field of view.

It's beyond calling it luck. He has a preternatural gift that keeps him from my grasp.

*Resendiz is easy to ID, is that, combined with the submarine enough? I wonder.*

"Morgan," I say. "Package up the relevant portion of the video and send it to Kennedy for analysis. Let's see if Providence can find El Chapo in a reflection or something we haven't seen. We need a break."

#

I'm pacing as Ilena pulls the truck up to the guardhouse

"Two guards just left the building. They're running toward the truck," Elle says, pointing at the corner of the screen.

Lisa's face clouded with emotion. "That can't be good."

Elle, Lisa, Morgan, and I are in our hasty ops center. We have four cameras collecting data from the west side of the facility and two in the north.

The east and south faces of TransCargo are surrounded by the bay, Bahia de Santiago de Cuba.

"I told her to pull forward so the guardhouse wouldn't block the view," Lisa hisses.

I put a hand on Lisa's shoulder. "It's okay. We assumed they would freak out when she drove up to the gate. Time to find how good Leto is at keeping to the story."

We observe Ilena and Leto scoot along the bench seat to the driver's side and disappear along with the guards. Suddenly Leto and Ilena jump back in the truck.

A guard with silver captain's bars on his patrol cap climbs in the passenger seat and bangs the outside of the door. The truck drives to the large door and stops to wait for the overhead roller to open. It seems to take forever, but the truck finally rolls in, and the door slams shut, gravity doing the work.

They're in, and we are blind—for now. Time to close some other loopholes. "Morgan, I need you to go to the airport with Lisa and figure out what plane or planes El Chapo has on standby."

"Roger that. I haven't heard yet, but I'm certain the Kakoa brothers are using all of Jimmy Carter's considerable tech to locate and track any fast movers El Chapo might use for a seaborne escape," Morgan says.

I crack my neck and sigh at the pleasure.

"One day your head is going to fall off, brother," Morgan says.

"True. We've got two escape options covered. Any thoughts on other ways he might bug out?"

"Paging Doctor Wolf... Doctor Wolf?" Lisa says. "Elle, is he asking what other ways El Chapo can escape?"

My wife is about to burst at the seams; all she can do is nod before breaking out into laughter.

"Come on, guys. I promise to keep the words small so you can comprehend what I'm asking."

"If I was him and had General Delgado in my back pocket," Lisa said. "I'd have an MI-2 for myself, an MI-8 full of Black Wasps, and an MI-24 on standby in case I needed to make a statement."

"Not much we can do about that if it comes to it—although it will be hard to cover up the aftermath.

"Do you think El Chapo has Delgado in his back pocket? Or is the spy master playing him?"

"According to the asset, Delgado has a reputation of being, how do you say... Teflon coated. I have been thinking about this a lot in the last twenty-four hours... I believe Aguila might be involved in the play with Delgado."

"If the arrangement continues unobstructed," Lisa answers, "Delgado and the colonel reap a good portion of the benefits. If not, they take as much as they can from the Sinaloa Cartel, then make El Chapo the scapegoat."

"It feels right," Elle says. "Why would El Chapo run from the heat in Mexico only to land in a communist police state? He had to have some assurances. Aguila, his man with all the connections, probably ran a pilot program to validate his personal security and the opportunity. The dollar signs in El Chapo's eyes and his gigantic ego cloud his vision and the next thing he knows, he's been conned by a couple of grifters who went for the big score."

Morgan slides next to me, draping an arm over my shoulder. "Wolf, I understand you're obsessed—sorry, 'focused'— on getting him behind bars. We all are, but this mission has run its course. We will still put a hurt on his reputation and the cartel, so why don't we take it? Send the package to the Cuban president and it all falls apart, right on El Chapo's head."

*I want to pound the wall like a frustrated kid.* "Thanks Morgan. I understand. It's a good course of action, but I can't let it go. I need to think."

I head into the bedroom, closing the door behind me. I drop to my knees and sit back on my ankles. Three rounds of four count breathing will still my mind and let me discern the path.

The world outside slips away and I am with my spirit guide,

looking out across the plains from the Big Horn mountains. I ask for guidance and receive laughter. I concentrate harder; the voice grows dim, so I relax again. My white wolf sniffs the air and steps closer. His mouth isn't moving, but his voice is in my head. *You know the way. The path of many is love.*

The scene dissolves and I'm at peace... until my satellite phone buzzes. As soon as I answer, Kennedy is in my ear, his excitement infectious. "We've fixed El Chapo at a specific beach house south of the east-west runway. I'll send you the coordinates. We've also identified a company sized security element that includes his gunmen and Cuban soldiers with armor."

"This is the break we need!" I say.

## 72

D AY 0
I'm not sure how much time has past when I hear Kennedy. "Wolf… Hey Wolf! Are you there?" He calls out over the phone.

To be honest, I'm not. My mind has raced ahead, testing options, calculating risk.

In the past, Shadow Tier has supported Mexican Special Forces under the leadership of my friend, General Gonzalez.

We've used company-plus sized forces to overwhelm El Chapo's security and still haven't captured him.

*I can't attack at the beach and be sure he won't slip away.*

*No. I need to put him somewhere more contained.*

"Yeah, I'm here. Great news, brother. The question is, where is he now? He could be at the beach, up in the park or… right across the street in TransCargo."

"True. Now that we know where he beds down, the best bet is to do what you do."

"What's that? Mark the site for a cellulose wrapped, thousand-pound, laser guided bombs?"

"No, that only happens in movies. You sneak in, Native American style, and emplace trackers and one of our infected burner phones. Then one of El Chapo's knuckleheads takes the burner inside and boom, electronically speaking, we own all their cell communications," Kennedy says and chuckles, seemingly happy with himself.

"If we had more time, that would be a great course of action. But time is the one thing I'm short on. I expect to get an end mission call from Davidson any minute now. What I need is a compelling event that brings El Chapo, Delgado and Aguila to the same location at the same time. Preferably at TransCargo, where we face limited security and have containment."

"Hold on Wolf, Kid is making faces at me and waving his hands. I think he's stroking out."

I hear Kid mumbling, then Kennedy switches his phone to speaker. "Sir, Wolf... ah... what if we give the infected burner to the G2 asset. If she can place it close to the director's phone when she gets to work in the morning, I can own his phone in thirty minutes or less."

"How is that possible, Kid? Isn't the G2 network isolated?"

"No, not according to a friend at NSA—"

I interrupt Kid. My mind is racing forward again. "That means we could text from the general's phone and have El Chapo and Aguila meet him at TransCargo. I'll call you back. I've got to put the team in motion. Out."

Back in the ops center, they are all looking at me.

"Everything okay?" Elle asks.

"Yeah. Better than okay. Morgan, how many infected burner phones do we have left?"

"Three."

"Good. Here's what we're going to do. The first one goes to you, Lisa. I need you to get it to the asset so she can place it next to General Delgado's phone. I know it's last minute, but if we can infect his phone, Kid says he can own it in thirty minutes. Will she try?"

"Yes," Lisa said.

"Once we own it, Kid will text El Chapo and Aguila to meet at TransCargo at noon today."

"Aguila is on the sub," Elle says.

All I care about is El Chapo," I say. "But if Aguila gets the message he'll make every attempt to show, especially if he's Delgado co-conspirator."

Morgan gives us his patented lady magnet smile, but I have direct experience and pay attention to his eyes. They tell me his devious mind is in high gear.

"I'll have the Kakoa brothers bring the SEAL squad to the party," he says. "That way, we'll be able to keep them in the kill zone."

"Yeah, that works. Have Tom and the SEALs plan to pick me up where they met you."

"I'm going with you, brother," Morgan says.

"No, I need you at the airport to find and disable the aircraft he has on standby. Check?"

"Sure," Morgan says, a surly undertone to his response.

"While you're at the airport," I say, "I'll take one of the burner phones and some trackers to where El Chapo is staying."

"Come on, Wolf. Let's make him dead and go home."

"I wish it was that easy Morgan, there's company of soldiers pulling security. I'm going to emplace the tech, hoping we can infect their cell phones before the meeting."

"I'm going with you," my wife says.

"Sorry, I appreciate the thought, but this is what I do best, and I do it best alone."

She points a knife hand at me, but I interrupt her. "You'll be with Morgan, less than two miles away if I need help."

Elle grits her teeth and glowers but nods her agreement.

"It's coming up on 0100, which gives me, Morgan and my wife plenty of time to accomplish what we need to do and return here to prep for the meeting. Lisa get some sleep, and meet the asset before work, then come back here. It's going to be a busy day."

# 73

Cement Products, Santiago De Cuba

Morgan and Elle head for the airport; the knot in the pit of my stomach tells me I should check in with General Davidson. I want to know if the new information got us more time.

I could also receive a direct order to head back to Tampa. My satellite phone is in my hand, but I pause.

*It's easier to ask forgiveness than get permission.*

Over the course of Shadow Tier's short history, this has been my *modus operandi* once given a mission.

As the Shadow Tier Deputy Director for Operations, I've been assigning the missions and owning the responsibility for their successes and failures.

Our high ratio of success has led General Davidson to provide me with the operational latitude to execute our missions as I deem appropriate.

So, asking forgiveness may be the right path forward, but it has consequences— my early retirement if I am lucky, but as dire as the disbanding of Shadow Tier if I am not.

\#

I straddle the rice-rocket style motorcycle and pop open the gas cap to check the gas level. It's enough, so I pause and visualize my route.

I'll drive around the east end of the airport, where I'll hug the trees until I'm north of the target.

From then on, it's all improv. I'll probe and test until I find my way inside the inner cordon.

*Semper Gumby. Always flexible.*

The sky is mostly clear, with an occasional cloud obscuring the quarter moon. As I circumnavigate the city, it opens to a rural setting.

I can make out the airport beacon rotating in the distance. Very few people are out on the roads tonight.

*Or at least on this side of town. Have I made a mistake?*

Evidently, Murphy thinks so, as two Army pickups with armed soldiers fly by in the opposite direction.

No big deal, right?

Until I glance in the mirror and see red lights.

I switch the lights off, down shift and peg the throttle to accelerate, shifting up through fourth into fifth gear. My eyes and brain are barely keeping up with the yellow line.

The off ramp that comes up on my right is flat and I'm hard on the front brake. The rear wheel is off the ground, and I sense the motorcycle's frame protesting my rookie version of MotoGP.

I need to alter the rice rocket's geometry, so I slide back in the seat and feel the rear wheel make contact so, I accelerate again but stay in third gear, scanning ahead for any turn off this road I can take.

The next right is a dirt road and my senses alert me that the suspension is compressing just before the backend bucks. The next thing I feel, the motorcycle has become a full-on shimmy machine.

Off throttle, I throw out both legs and slow way down. *I can't do this. I'm leaving a trail a blind squirrel could find.*

I lower my head and steer into the trees. A dozen feet in, branches are smacking me.

*That's going to leave a mark.*

The motorcycle splashes into some thick muck and I struggle to hold on. I switch the key off and tear my helmet from my head. The rice rocket is ticking as the engine and exhaust cool.

Luckily, the muck is only ankle deep where I am, so I trudge to the dirt track in time to watch what must be the trucks roar by.

*Great. I didn't need to stick the bike in the muck.*

I look back at the motorcycle, then to the road. I find what I need and work with a palm frond to erase my track to where I turned into the mud. As I complete the task, my mind is calculating the odds of the soldiers alerting Shorty's security.

*Do they have a clue what's going on at the beach house?*

*Do they consider some lone biker a threat?*

It doesn't matter; I have a mission to complete. I take a beat to reorient myself, then follow the dirt track to where it stops.

Before me is the eight-foot-high chain-link fence with razor wire on top that surrounds the airport. To my left and right are signs I don't take the time to read.

There's a ten-foot clear space between me and the fence, so I head toward the target in a distance-eating lope.

I'm within 300 meters of the target when my satellite phone buzzes. I have Davidson on a special notification, so it has to be either Morgan or Elle.

I step into the trees and take a knee before getting it from my backpack. I hide the phone in my shirt to block the red background of the screen.

It's Elle; they are task complete earlier than I expected. I text back to stand by for ninety minutes, if possible, as I may need them for exfil.

I receive the acknowledgement at the same time I hear voices nearby. I shut down the phone and place it back in the flap. I'm mid-thought that the voices are an outer band of patrol when I catch female voices laughing.

I creep around to the south of them until I have visual confirmation that it's a party, not a patrol.

Moving on, I stay inside the palms and scrub oaks until I'm 150 meters out. On my belly, I crawl to the edge of the wood line and get my first glimpse of what I'm up against.

It's bad.

It's cold war era soviet technology, a BTR-60 eight-wheel armored personnel carrier with a heavy machine gun.

Not something you take lightly.

And where you find one, you will find two—and likely three.

Each with their own squad of infantry, or, if I'm unlucky, more of the Black Wasps.

Now is when the hard work starts.

**74**

———————

Closing on El Chapo's Safe House
I reverse my crawl back into the trees and sit to sing my death song.

I'm determined not to turn this mission into a one-sided firefight, but if it ends up that way, I will die with honor.

For the first time I can remember, my biological father stands with my mother and stepfather on either side of my spirit guide. The moment I drop out of my meditation to think about its significance, they are gone. What is left is a feeling I'd describe as family.

Nourished by the three minutes of stillness, I suppress a smile and take my bearings.

My absolute boundaries are the ocean to the south and the airport fence to the north. I've moved to within 75 meters of the north boundary and facing west.

Moving in concert with what the trees and scrub give me, I pass through one natural drainage then to another, where I find a pond and pipe heading toward the ocean.

I follow it until I find a lane cut through the scrub. In its center is a recently dug and filled up trench. It's wide enough for two more pipes but doesn't intersect the pipe I've been following.

I step across and focus on my heading. My pace count says I'm within 30 meters of my target, so I stop, listen, and smell the air. The cool air current is flowing from the airport to the ocean.

As thin as a fleeting thought, it's the odor of a cigarette—a good indication that it's one of El Chapo's hired guns or a regular army soldier.

*A Black Wasp would not make that mistake.*

The smoke comes from upwind, which is both good and bad.

Good, that whoever it might be can't smell me, bad that my scent is being carried to the target. The best route would be to come in from a downwind location, but that's the ocean in this case. Not an option.

I'm closing in when I sense movement to my left.

I lower myself into the scrub and listen to what must be a squad of soldiers. They are on a parallel route to mine and appear not to be worried about noise discipline.

As they crash through scrub, one of them orders the others to head to the water source.

*How do they know where I've been?*

*Did I miss a remote sensor, trip an alarm? It would seem so.*

*Now I have to be extra vigilant.*

I change my route to the west, thinking it's time to go to the other side of the target. I glance at my watch again and find that 'my slow is smooth, smooth is fast' recon is burning time.

I pick up my pace and soon find another recently dug trench in my path. Instead of leaping over it, this time I follow it from inside the trees. I'm closing in on the target when lights come on and the roar of diesel engines sound.

I sprint away from the lights as the armored personnel carriers crash through the trees, most of them small, and easily knocked over by the multi-ton behemoth.

The lights are dancing just behind me, so I take a hard left to move out of their path. After another 50 meters, I turn north again and find them headed in my direction.

My mind is racing as I try to break contact.

One of the heavy machine guns opens up and I throw myself to the ground.

*I didn't see any sensors or tripwires… just trenches.*

*How are they on me?*

*Ahh, the trenches are the sensors.*

I'm familiar with a physical security sensor system called leaky coax that is used in arid conditions around Department of Energy and US Air Force nuclear weapons sites. The trenches must house something similar.

The heavy machine gun stops firing for a beat and I'm up. The only way I can stop the gunner from firing is to run for the north side element, so I run right for the second APC.

I make sure I hop over the trench again, then parallel it before diving into the scrub. Both APCs start firing and I crawl like a maniac out of the line of fire.

I draw my pistol and bounce three rounds off the BTR-60 to the north. The soldiers scurry inside and button up. I've moved farther east by the time the hatch reopens and the KPV gunner rips off a long burst at where I was hiding.

The other KPVs open up, and the roar is deafening. To my relief, a loud ricochet pings off one vehicle then another.

The machine guns fall silent, and I visualize the commanders yelling at each other to cease fire.

I grin at the chaos.

The APCs behind me have stopped their advance, so I make use of the confusion to head straight for the beast to my front. As I close in, the gunner secures the hatch amid much yelling and confusion.

I move around to its rear and find a fire with several rucksacks nearby.

*Heck, if I can't get the burner phone to the target, one of these guys will do it for me.*

I execute a quick scan and pick a rucksack I believe belongs to the officer in charge. It's new, clean, and sits alone. I remove the infected burner phone from my backpack and make it look like I was rummaging through the officer's rucksack. The burner is in the pile of stuff I create.

Happy with my creation, I run hard.

When I'm 600 meters to the east, I stop, catch my breath, and text Elle to pick me up along the highway.

I break into an easy seven minute a mile pace and wonder what more I could have done. It's unlikely the infected phone will come in contact with another more useful handset.

I hate to say it, but we could be out of time and luck. But as we say at Shadow Tier, never quit!

I've got one last card to play.

*If I live, Elle is sure to leave me and I'll probably get committed.*

Insane doesn't begin to describe it.

## 75

East of Santiago de Cuba Airport

Elle and Morgan have just picked me up alongside the highway. Of course, her first question is a Parker-patented two-for-one.

"Were those APCs firing their KPVs at you?"

She must have recognized the sound from her tour in Bosnia and our recent missions in Afghanistan.

Morgan, my good buddy, is sporting a Cheshire grin and his eyes are on fire—like they often are when one of us is saving the other.

"You got them shooting at each other, didn't you?"

"It was not my intent, seeing that I only carried a pistol. I tripped some kind of buried alarm and had to improvise."

Elle's scowl indicates she's not impressed, but that doesn't stop her from telling me so. "Lance Bear Wolf! When we get back—if we get back—we're going to see a professional. You need to look at your penchant for creating chaos so you can improvise."

Morgan sees my dilemma. "It could have been the same buried, fiber optic cable that El Chapo has installed around his mountain homes. I've read it's stolen DARPA tech the Army is testing for forward operating base security. It's a pair of cables—."

"Thanks brother. I'll geek later. It was a fortress. I wasn't getting in, so I got them chasing me. Must have not have infrared. Anyway, I left the infected burner phone behind. Maybe we'll be lucky, and the officer will turn it in."

My wife and Morgan look at me like I'm crazy. "How'd you guys get done so fast?" I ask.

"We only found two aircraft on standby. One in hangar seven where I met Resendiz, and another at the commercial fixed-base operator hangars. Unless he's got a deal with the Cuban Airforce, it seems odd," Morgan says, keeping his eyes on the road as we enter the city.

There are lots of other airports—some just a hunk of pavement that he could jump to. "We need the Wizkids to search for those," I say. "They could confirm aircraft on standby using our satellites."

"Good idea." Elle says.

"Agreed," Morgan says. "El Chapo would likely have one or two more alternates. Knowing their locations is a key element of containing him if he squirts."

"Let's put the Wizkids on this," I say. "Any movement at TransCargo?"

Elle's satellite phone buzzes and I remember I have not turned mine back on. She accesses hers and shows me the screen; it's Davidson. I take several deep breaths. She answers, "Yes sir," then hands me the phone.

"Wolf," I say.

"Do you have a specific reason you've gone dark?" he asks.

"Putting you on speaker, sir. It's myself, Elle, and Morgan."

"Good! You all need to hear this."

"Yes, sir. As for going dark, I was just picked up from my attempt to penetrate security at El Chapo's beach house. It is a fortress. No joy," I say, using the expression for mission failure.

"That's too bad, Wolf. I'm in need of more information to stall the White House. President Fairbanks is in a foul mood and his advisor is stirring the pot. You can expect a presidential order to hand over what you have to Cuban authorities no later than twelve hundred today. Irwin is already leaking information of an upcoming explosive revelation regarding a Caribbean nation and Mexican drug cartels. The administration wants to dominate the six o'clock news cycle."

Morgan fixes me with the violent stare that he reserves for high-ranking military idiots and politicians. My wife's mouth is open, and I realize I'm catching flies too.

"Sir. We are setting the conditions for an El Chapo, Aguila, and General Delgado meeting at thirteen hundred today. We have people inside TransCargo, and we will own General Delgado's cell phone by ten hundred. The Kakoa brothers are on alert, and we have a SEAL squad in support. All this to say we will have El Chapo in a contained environment where we can pit the Cubans against the cartel. They'll do the rest. Or be exposed as part of the conspiracy."

"Excellent plan, Wolf. But it's a day late and a dollar short."

"But sir, the plan will work. And it's just a couple of more hours."

"I want you all to listen carefully to what I'm about to say. If you are not out of Cuba or on the way out by noontime local the administration will provide the entire world the details of the Cuban drug conspiracy. G2, the military, and every police officer and informant will be hunting El Chapo and unnamed agents of the United States... that's you guys."

"We can handle that, sir. We just need two more hours. They will still have plenty of time to dominate the news cycle."

"Wolf, I'm sorry if I wasn't clear enough before. We're talking disavowed. You and Elle will be out in the cold by yourselves, while Morgan dives back into his cover story."

In the rearview mirror, Morgan's eyes are filled with concern.

I put my hand on my wife's shoulder.

*I know what I'd do if I was alone.*

"Sir. We are committed to seeing this through. Two hours is all we need. If you can't get it for us, we'll see you when we see you."

"Roger that. Make your own luck," Davidson says and disconnects.

Elle grabs my hand and squeezes. "Nothing's changed. You go, I go."

# 76

Day - 1

Lambarri House, Havana, Cuba

The beeping from the sensor at her front door jarred Major Isabel Lambarri from her sleep.

She peeked at her bedside clock and spun her feet to the floor. Her pistol was within easy reach. She grabbed it and strode to the kitchen. There, she slid the curtain back just enough to see Lisa at the front door, fumbling with her keys.

Isabel unlocked the door to find her sister red-cheeked and scowling. "What are you doing here so early, Lisa?" she asked, and pulled her in.

"I need a drink," her sister said.

"I'll make coffee," she said, and walked back into the kitchen. Lisa followed her and slumped into a chair. Isabel started coffee. She welcomed the smell as it brewed.

She sat across from her sister. A ray of streetlight pierced the curtains and splashed the wall in front of Lisa. *Film noir. How appropriate,* Isabel thought.

"So, I'll ask again. Why are you here?"

"The Americans. They are down to their last, ahh... what's the term?"

"I believe they call it a *Hail Mary*. It's something from American football that denotes a play made in desperation with an exceptionally small chance of working. But in this case, they want me to make the play, right?"

"Yes. It's a technical attack they can exploit if you can put this phone within a foot of General Delgado's cell. Once the infection is complete, they will send a text from Delgado's phone to El Chapo and Colonel Aguila to meet at TransCargo."

"What or who is TransCargo?"

"It's a shipping business that also repairs ships at the top of the bay. That's where they deliver the opium before shipping it out via submarine."

"Wait, what? A submarine? What else has George been keeping from me?"

"I'm sorry. I would have thought—"

"No, it's okay. I don't check in with George until Sunday. Tell me about this submarine. Our Navy should be detecting a submarine—unless they have paid the Navy for their silence, too."

"No, from what I have been told it is a sophisticated electric attack submarine made in Germany. The Peruvian Navy originally bought it, but when their government needed money, El Chapo made them an offer. Our defenses are not as good as the Navy claims."

"There are many aspects of our military that are not as good as advertised," Isabel said. "Is there anything else I should know?"

"Yes. Ilena let herself be taken hostage. She's in the TransCargo facility while they check out her cover. She and I turned a young truck driver and used him to penetrate the facility."

"Ilena is scary crazy. It sounds like something she would do just for the rush it brings."

"Wolf said it's only crazy if it doesn't work," Lisa said, breaking into a grin.

"The Americans all talk like that. But what we do... It's more nuanced. An intricate ballet of moves and countermoves. Don't let the mystique draw you in. We are helping where we can, but we must foremost protect ourselves and our family."

"You mean George and Ilena?"

"Yes, they are all we have now—besides each other," Isabel said as she looked at the kitchen clock. "Almost time for me to wake and go for my run. Why don't you get some sleep. We'll talk when I get back."

"Does that mean you won't try?"

"No, I will. But when I do, it will not be a *Hail Mary*."

---

## 77

Shadow Tier Headquarters MacDill AFB

Kennedy's door was open, but Kid knocked on the frame to get his attention. "Sir, we're live in the ops center."

Until recently, watching operations live was a dream. Kennedy had begged Customs and Border Patrol for the use of two drones and promised a large takedown in return.

The CBP was open to the offer, hoping it would change the president's—and the American public's—negative view of the agency.

Now, with a dual drone rotation overhead, Shadow Tier would have round-the-clock high-definition video of the oil rig and any visitors. And they could switch the video stream to infrared based on the time of day or the weather at the oil platform.

They watched the sunrise on the digitally connected screen made of sixteen displays, showing the oil platform and submarine in orange glow. A bar at the bottom of the screen with three Xs indicated targets outside the current view.

Kid clicked on the bar, and a notes window appeared, stating that there were several patrol boats holding a 300 yard perimeter. In the upper right of the screen there was an icon indicating what the Predator sensor operator suspected was a helicopter.

"Amazing. Those two conveyor belts are a slick way to get the product off the sub quickly and efficiently," Kennedy said.

"Reminds me of the conveyor we used to get bales of hay in the barn back home," Kid said.

"Yeah, but your bales weren't worth thirty thousand a piece," Victor said.

"It's still going to take them three to four hours to unload the sub," Jennifer said.

She pointed at the screen. "Holy Moley! That's Colonel Aguila."

"He doesn't look happy, does he? Could it be an indication that he got my text?" Kid asked.

"We'll know shortly. If he heads for shore, that means 'yes.'" Kennedy watched his analysts.

*Two nods, one shrug. Good to see the lack of group think.*

The icon for the helicopter moved toward the oil rig, eventually coming into the field of view and landing atop of the platform. Colonel Aguila headed up the stairs but stopped partway.

"Grandpa has to catch his breath," Victor said, glee in his voice.

Kennedy huffed. "Don't let that fool you. He can still make you dead before you realize it. He's got hundreds of Sicarios lined up to make a few thousand dollars and get bragging rights for killing a member of Shadow Tier."

*Why am I being so negative? This is the path our missions take.*

"What the boss means is that the time for spy moves is gone and it's full on kinetic from here on out," Kid offered.

"Yeah. Sorry about the dead stuff," Kennedy said.

"We all know that can happen at any time. Wolf, Elle, and Morgan have been here before, and understand the threat. It's our job to provide them with every advantage we can. One way or the other, this will be over in a matter of hours. So, while watching the product transfer is riveting, and we all want to shoot down the helicopter Aguila just left in... let's get back to work."

Back in his office, Kennedy closed the door behind him and went to the sideboard for coffee.

*How long has it been since I slept more than thirty minutes?*

He stared at the Tandberg video conferencing system.

After a long sip from a steaming hot cappuccino, he picked up the Tandberg handset and dialed the three-digit code for Alpha squadron. Interested in the value of video conferencing, he had added communicators to the Alpha support package.

Commander Oleos Leblanc and his Alpha teammates were on fifteen-minute standby. The MH-60 Direct Action Penetrators crews waited in their helicopters for the execute order.

From their staging area at Naval Air Station Reserve Base New Orleans, they could be over the oil platform in twenty-three minutes. Master Sergeant Ron Brown answered the call. "Headquarters, this is Brown. Copy?"

"Brown, it's Kennedy. Go video."

"Yes, sir," Brown said as the video bloomed to life.

"I see you five by."

"Roger that. Same here. Put Leblanc on for me."

"Yes, sir."

Brown left the screen and Kennedy heard him call out for the Alpha commander.

After ninety seconds, Oleus appeared. "Dude," he said. "When's the last time you got some shut eye. You look like crap."

"Oh thanks. Love you too."

"You know me, brother. All about big love for my teammates. What's up?"

"As slowly as they are unloading the sub, it's at least another three hours before they get near the end," Kennedy said.

"How will you know when they're close to being finished?"

"Victor knows almost as much about submarines as Commander Andrews. It will ride higher in the water. He's calculated a whole displacement thing. It's voodoo to me."

"Just saying, I'd rather launch early and loiter to catch them with their hatches open then be late."

"Got you covered. The Navy steamed the USS Hudner out of Tampa Bay last night—it will hold over the horizon as your backup. I know you want to get all pirate and capture the sub, but the platform is your mission."

There was a knock at the door. Kennedy yelled to come in.

Victor entered but stopped just inside the doorway.

"What is it?" Kennedy asked.

"Sir. Message from the USS Jimmy Carter. The Kakoa's launch at 1130 local."

"Got it." Kennedy turned back to the screen. After the door closed, he said, "Did you hear that? We need to coordinate our actions with Wolf's assault at 1330 Cuba time."

"Roger that," Oleus said. He turned away for a moment, then came back with a smile on his face. "Your intel nerds are barking that we are taking all the bandwidth. So much for video."

"Yeah. Listen brother, do me a favor and remember El Chapo's guys got nowhere to go. After you sink the boats on the perimeter, they have no other option but to fight to the death."

"No worries, I got you. It's in our job description. We'll make sure they visit their ancestors. Out here."

Kennedy stared at the floor. *Why do I sense impending doom?*

## 78

Cement Plant, Santiago De Cuba

"What's the good word, brother? I'm looking at Trans-Cargo via our video feeds and you're on speaker. Elle and Morgan are here."

"Hey guys," Kennedy says. "I've got three good things. First, they've flown Aguila off the platform and we believe it's an indication that Kid's takeover of Delgado's cell worked. Second, Alpha is ready to assault the oil platform. They're using dual conveyor belts to move the product from the sub to the platform. Alpha will assault between 1300 and 1330, Cuba time. Leblanc, wants to be the first in his family to capture a submarine. Knowing him, he'll be sporting the Jolly Roger."

"Pirates, really? Don't release him until I signal. If he executes too early, the sub will receive word and that could make him bolt. If the sub slips away, you have a backup, correct?"

"Yes. The USS Hudner, an Arleigh Burke-class destroyer. If we can't make the sub come to the surface, they will."

"You said there are three things. That's only two."

"Ah, right. Number three. Tom Kakoa will meet you with his

squad of SEALs at the same location where they rendezvoused with Morgan—at the north end of the bay."

"Excellent. So, the meeting request went to Aguila with the requirement to ensure El Chapo is at the meeting. What about getting Delgado to show up?"

"Yeah, Kid wiped the outgoing text from his cell phone history and inserted an incoming text from Aguila, urgently requesting the meeting. The asset should be able to confirm he's going."

"Right—if the asset has time and a secure location to communicate through their in-country handler."

"She and her handler are smart," Kennedy says. "They'll figure out a way."

"How do you... ah never mind. I don't want to know."

"A wise choice, my friend," Kennedy says.

"Hey, Lisa's back. Got to go."

"Yeah. Win the fight and come home, brother."

"We will. It's a promise," I say, then disconnect.

As I set the phone down, Elle greets Lisa. They walk toward our hasty little ops center stuck together like two peas in a pod.

Morgan gives Lisa his 'is everything alright' look. He holds his breath until she nods. His shoulders drop and he smiles.

*Morgan really cares for her. That's good. We need to maintain our humanity, 'cause it's about to get dark.*

"The meeting is on Delgado's schedule," Lisa says. "But he's concerned. He tried to reach Aguila, but it didn't connect, so he gave up. The asset said he'll be there."

"Okay, let me run it down and see if you agree... The principals all appear to be headed to the meeting."

"Yeah," Elle says.

"Check. We have coverage for any seaborne or airborne escape."

"To a point," Morgan says. "More so for seaborne. If El Chapo tries to take a plane, it will be chaos with commercial flights coming and going. We need to confine him inside TransCargo."

"Okay, let's discuss. I was planning to use the SEAL squad as a blocking force. What else can we do to keep El Chapo from running?"

Morgan's wicked grin alerts me to the crazy he's about to bring. "We can't make him stay unless he wants to. But you know what? If he sees you, that might change his mind."

"You done pulling my chain? I shouldn't have said we can keep him confined. As always, we'll have to adapt to his moves once we kick off the party. That's why you and Elle will be at the airport. If he runs that way, all the better."

"If he heads to the mountains or an alternate landing zone, we make a pass. If it fails, we E&E, period. End of mission," Elle says, daring me to disagree.

"Agreed," I say with as much conviction as I can muster. "Back to the checklist. After confirmation that the principals are on site, we attack TransCargo from inside. And that leaves us with the fate of Ilena and Leto. My plan is to free them, first. Before I capture El Chapo."

"You mean, kill him, don't you?" Lisa asks.

"Capture first, kill if forced to," I say stating our standard operating procedure.

Elle's satellite phone buzzes, and she opens it. "Not sure if this is Ilena's doing. Someone plugged in their phone to recharge, and it beaconed out. Kid has access and has turned on the hotspot transmit feature. He expects auto-connection from other powered up cell phones inside the secured space."

"It's just what Seneca said, 'Luck is when preparation meets opportunity,'" Morgan says.

"All that security and they didn't filter their electrical power. I'll take it," I say.

"Not to be Debbie Downer, again," Elle says. "But aren't we well past our presidential mandated time limit?"

My wife forgets nothing. I also know that Davidson and Kennedy back channel her information that is intended to reach me when I may not be in a listening mood.

"Forgiveness over permission. Just like the rest of our ops. We're good until shut down, right?"

"And what if we're in the middle of a gunfight?" Elle asks.

"We do what we always do—we win the fight. And in this case, we go home."

"After we free Ilena," Lisa interjects. "We have to free her."

Elle slips an arm around Lisa's shoulders and squeezes. "We leave no one behind."

I grasp Lisa's forearm. "I can assure you; it will not come to that. Presidential order? Don't care... I will free Ilena. It's what we do. It's at the core of who we are. Family first. And you, Ilena and George are family."

"He's not joking when it comes to family," Morgan says. "I've seen it myself. Check the time, Wolf. You need to go fishing."

"Roger that," I say. Savoring her smell, I hug Elle and kiss her neck, then push her to arm's length and stare into her beautiful face. "If this all goes wrong, you bug out with Morgan. I'll go with Tom and the SEALs. See ya back in Tampa."

As I'm leaving, she whispers, "Yeah. In Tampa."

## 79

Helicopter over Gulf of Mexico

"Just like Delgado to demand a meeting when he knows I'm away," Aguila said to himself as he boarded the helicopter.

The crew chief slammed the door and the noise level lessened. He was handed a headset and shown the push to talk button.

Aguila put the headset on.

*This better be important, or El Chapo will kill him outright.*

Tense with the thought, he attempted to focus and mentally jot down his new to-do list.

First, call Delgado and find out what the meeting is about.

Second, call the boss and make sure he gets to TransCargo by 1 p.m.

Third, call Resendiz and report offloading going well.

Fourth, reschedule distributor security audit.

Aguila retrieved his satellite phone from his aviator's bag. It had buzzed seconds after he had left the submarine.

Upon reading the text, a lump formed in his throat and his stomach soured.

News of a leak that Delgado was not sure he could stop was not what he'd expected at this point in the operation.

He tried Delgado's cell three times; it rang and rang without being picked up.

Heat climbed his neck and he focused on his breathing. He stab-dialed Major Lambarri and waited.

"Director's office, Major Lambarri."

"Lambarri, Colonel Aguila. I need to talk to the director. He's not answering his cell."

"I understand, sir. The technicians are looking into it."

"I need to speak with him now. Forward me to his replacement phone.

"Yes, sir. Normally I would, but he's in a meeting with the president. The director instructed me to tell you he will see you at the thirteen hundred meeting."

Aguila cursed, then disconnected.

*Has Delgado been telling stories to his girlfriend?*

*Where could the leak be?*

He dialed his boss.

"Report," El Chapo said.

"We arrived an hour earlier than the estimate. The unloading is going quickly and smoothly. The team will be ready to start business in four hours."

"It sounds like you are on a helicopter, why?"

*I need to play this off as a Delgado problem.*

"Delgado texted me to set up an emergency meeting between the three of us at TransCargo today at 1300. So, I am headed back. He said there is a leak he is not sure he can stop."

"No. That is his job, and I pay him very well. He needs to terminate the leak and I don't care who it is."

"Si, El Jefe, I agree completely. If he can't, I will."

"The weakness of Cuban leadership astounds me. Do we need to be thinking about a replacement for Delgado?"

"In the long run, yes. But not right now... so soon after the death of General Zaragoza."

"Ochoa's deception worked, did it not?"

"Yes, it did, but another death less than a week later would be investigated with presidential oversight."

El Chapo grunted. "I am here at TransCargo. I will stay for the meeting."

"This is good. I should see you around twelve-forty."

"The sooner the better. That way you will have time to interrogate the spy Delgado sent to check on our lab to TransCargo truck routes. She's smart and has already pointed out a couple of things for Resendiz to consider. If you clear her, you will hire her as our double agent."

"Yes—," Aguila started to say before the call disconnected.

*It always ends badly when El Jefe thinks he's a spy master.*

He checked his watch and peered through the cockpit window, then closed his eyes, knowing that he'd wake on touchdown.

The momentary break renewed him. He grabbed his bag and opened the door before the crew chief could get to it, then jumped to the pavement and strode directly to the waiting jet.

As soon as he was by the forward galley, the attendant closed the door and the pilot powered the jet onto the taxiway then the runway for immediate take off.

The Falcon rotated and soared into the sky.

Aguila smiled at the pretty flight attendant as she braced her feet against the bulkhead.

El Chapo's three engine Dassault Falcon 7X had been upgraded to push the jet past Mach 1.0, if needed.

As the plane leveled out, the attendant unbuckled. "May I get you something, sir?"

"Yes. Rum and Coke, please. How long until we land?"

"You will exit the jet in one hour and ten minutes."

"Thank you."

*That gives me time to find out the truth behind Delgado's spy.*

He dialed Resendiz. As it rang, the attendant handed him his drink and a small tray of meats, cheese, and crackers. He pushed the food aside to take a long pull on the drink.

His call was answered on the third ring. "Resendiz, it's Aguila. Can you hear me?"

"Yes. I hear you are flying back. Does Delgado's spy have anything to do with your return?"

"Yes, she is an issue. But there is something bigger going on. Delgado demanded an emergency meeting with me and the boss. What's your security situation?"

"We are good. Full staff, all systems operational—except for Vega breaking protocol and bringing the spy here to TransCargo."

"You've tested the escape plans yourself, right?"

"Yes, of course. "What's going on?" Resendiz asked. "Has the threat increased? If it has, I need to know."

"I'm not sure, but we can't be too careful. Have your watchers on the lookout for signs of military activity."

Resendiz went on a cursing jag and Aguila yelled to break in.

"Diego! I'll be there within the hour. In the meantime, I suggest that you quietly prepare for a gunfight and ready our escape plans."

**80**

---

Trituradora de Soya Plant, Santiago De Cuba

I roll to the departure location using the same motorbike and gypsy fishing setup Morgan put together two days ago.

If I can see TransCargo, then it's appropriate to expect they can see me—at least until I drive through the wooded area on the south end of the soy products plant.

I'm not too worried. My ball cap, cheap sunglasses, and bandana pulled over my face make me almost impossible to identify.

Up in my head, in risk management mode, I almost crash as I slide to a stop.

Luckily, my subconscious processes the rusty cable that has been pulled tight across the path to the water.

The sign dangling from the cable says, "No Motorized Vehicles."

I try not to be the old guy who thinks that every response like this is caused by the stupidity of young kids, but it occurs to me, and I chuckle.

It reminds me of my stepdad, Andy, a Vietnam vet.

Just as quickly, his words from our first bear hunt pull me back to the seriousness of what I'm about to do. We had communicated using the hand signals he taught me.

The Grizzly bear was less than sixty yards away, and the wind favored us.

I'd brought my rifle up, and he gently pushed it down before leaning close. "It's easy to be brave from a distance."

I sense the lost minutes and park the motorbike, locking the handlebars. Grabbing the fishing and snorkeling gear, I walk around the cable to the water.

At the water's edge, I cast the fishing pole.

When it splashes in, I immediately step into the bushes to switch into trunks, leaving my clothes hanging in the bushes like I don't care.

I scoop up the snorkeling gear and step into the cool water.

I slip the mask on and take long, slow, deep breaths to reduce the carbon dioxide and increase the oxygen content in my blood, then duck under.

I'm not sure how long I'll have to stay under until Tom Kakoa picks me up; more oxygen is a good thing.

I swim in the direction Morgan gave me. Ahead is the rebreather system. It's on a line that plunges into the darkness. I'm checking the gauges to see if I can determine how much time is left when I feel a hand grab my ankle from below.

I know it's a hand via simple deduction; it doesn't hurt and it's not shaking me to pieces. I wait as Tom climbs up my body.

His face is disappointed; I wiggle a finger in his face. He pulls up a full-face mask rebreather. I take off my mask, put the rebreather on, and clear its mask.

"You're not as scared of the water like Morgan is," Tom says over the comms system.

I fumble for the PTT and Tom reminds me, "Just talk. Its set for voice activation."

"Unlike him, I've never been attacked by a croc as I crossed a river. Yeah, true story. Where is the SEAL squad?"

"On the way to the doors where they will hold," Tom says. He clips me to his harness. "We'll let the scooter do the hard work."

It's another twenty or so minutes later when Tom turns off the scooter and attaches it to an anchor point where there appear to be four others. A baby-faced kid and an early-thirties guy appear.

"Where do you want the SEALs, brother?" Tom asks.

"Two on the north side, four on the east side, and two with us inside. The perimeter mission is containment. Keep the tangos pinned in the facility if possible."

"Check," the baby-faced kid says.

"Rules of engagement. Destroy any cartel QRF and engage Cuban military just long enough to break contact. Our fight is not with them. If they show up, it's a good thing. Same with cops."

"First time I've heard that," the older guy says.

"We've got until 1300 to get into position. That's when the high value individuals are scheduled to meet. The building is shielded, so don't expect comms. There will be an explosion to signal the assault has started. Any questions?"

The kid glances at the old guy, who nods. "We're good," baby-face says.

"Make your own luck gentlemen," I say, and watch them swim off.

Two other men join us; one hands me a dry bag.

I point a knife hand at the submarine pen, then swim under the door with one thing—one person—on my mind.

# 81

———

TransCargo Facility

The four of us are huddle around the ladder. I take a minute and slip into the body armor and function check the suppressed LSA TX4 the Kakoa brothers have brought me.

One hand at a time, I feel and visualize the chest rig.

The pistol rides high on the right-side cummerbund. It's a SIG P320. Next to it, there's a long cylindrical pouch, then a radio and three double stacked magazine carriers. On the other side, I have a first aid kit and tourniquet, then more pistol mags and some grenade pouches.

I slip on the radio earpiece and whisper, "What do I call you guys?"

Tom points to the taller one. "He's S5, the other is S6."

Roger that. I'll lead out." I swing the rifle around my back and slip the pistol from its holster.

My arm is crooked as I inch up the ladder, pistol in front of my eyes, scanning for threats

Just below the hard deck, I hold.

When I peek over the top, the view is complex, so I scan to get the physical layout of the pallets, equipment and doors.

I squat down and whisper via the team channel for Tom and the SEALs to follow me.

Morgan's intel is good; Leto's truck and a couple of nearby guards are the only deltas from his drawing.

I'm up and moving behind a series of five-foot-high pallets that provide cover and concealment. I glance down at the sticky floor then check my watch.

*Twenty minutes until the meeting.*

I take the suppressor from the pouch and screw it onto the pistol. Tom and the SEALs do the same.

"Tom and I are moving closer to the wall. Somewhere over by the truck, there are two hostages I need to free when this kicks off. S5 and S6, you stay between here and the water so we can catch the tangos in a crossfire," I say.

Their quiet confidence is infectious, and I relax my shoulders as I take a deep breath and let it out slowly.

There are five more pallets of drugs between us and the open area where Leto's truck is parked.

We move to the last one and I get on my belly to peer around the corner. Beyond the truck, I see two doors. At the closer one, there is a guard—if you can call him that. His hands are in his pockets, and he looks bored.

*Fifteen minutes.*

My back to the pallet, I form my plan and smile at Tom. "I'm moving to the truck, so I'll be close to the guard at the door when we kick this off. That's probably where they're holding the hostages."

"Agreed," Tom says. "I'll move to the front of the truck when you execute. That will provide a no fire zone around the back of the truck to the water. Question—what entices your three HVIs to meet in this part of the building versus the office spaces intel said are in the front?"

"That explosion I mentioned is an asset with an RPG. As soon as the tangos enter the building, the asset will send the hate right through the front door. That should do it."

Tom suppresses a laugh. "Subtle, Wolf. Very subtle."

*Twelve minutes.*

I sneak another peek around the pallet.

*I sure hope Kid's got control of the cameras out here.*

Rifle up, I move to the underside of the truck and hug the rear differential. Looking over the rear wheels, I can see all the way along the wall to the office door.

Once Lisa lights up the front of the building, the door to the offices will become the chokepoint and priority target for our crossfire.

I freeze as the two wandering guards amble towards the door guard and stop for small talk.

One of the guys describes a new hot spot for girls who like cartel money.

The guards continue their route. Good for us that they don't check between the pallets.

As they move off, I take a minute to sing my death song to myself. I can't close my eyes, but my spirit guide is with me.

I finish, and a moment later the door guard pulls a joint—or possibly the worst hand-rolled cigarette I've ever seen—from his shirt pocket and walks my way. I can smell the skunk weed.

*Eight minutes.*

A whisper comes through my earpiece: "Too soon, brother. Let him go."

I'm so laden with armor, ammo, and weapons that I can't even turn to keep an eye on the guard as he strolls around the back of the truck.

He stops right in alignment with Tom and the SEALs.

Trust is key now; they're every bit as good as I am, and I have to trust they won't blow our cover before the meeting starts.

*Four minutes.*

Like it always does, waiting for guards to do their thing can seem to take forever.

The guard takes one last long toke, blows it out and sighs.

He's plodding his way back to the door when everything changes.

**82**

———

TransCargo Facility

I'm glancing at my watch. It shows 1305 when the explosion rocks the building all the way into our section.

A piece of cider block wall blows out in a cloud of dust.

I'm surprised but roll out from under the truck right into the guard, who's thrown himself to the floor.

The wide eyes of a not-so-tough-kid stare back at me, and I put him to sleep with the butt of the pistol versus two rounds to the head.

*I hope you survive, kid.*

I'm up and headed for the door.

The two roving guards run to the offices, their eyes wide, radios filled with screams for help.

I try the doorknob, but it's locked. "Ilena," I yell.

"We're here. The door is locked."

From the office side of the building, I hear what sounds like automatic gunfire.

"Step back," I say and put my ear to the door.

"Clear," she yells back. I put two rounds in the door latch area and two in the dead bolt, just in case.

When I kick it, the door is loose, but not giving way.

Just as I turn to donkey kick it, the door flies open, and I fall to my knees and spin pistol up.

"It's us Wolf. It's us," Ilena says, hands held high.

She puts herself between me and the pistol I have pointed at Leto.

His eyes are wide, and his mouth is open. He's shaking when I lower my weapon.

"We need to go."

Ilena grabs him, and I take them to the line of pallets.

The sound of gunfire from outside is continuous, and there's another explosion. I cover Ilena's body with mine. When the roof doesn't cave in, I point to the water.

"Swim under the door to safety. Go. I've got business with El Chapo."

"Did you kill Ochoa?" Leto asks, a scowl on his face.

"Yes, but that was not the plan. Now go, or I'll add you both to my list," I say with a wink to Ilena.

As she drags Leto toward the water, all hell breaks loose.

I slide on my knees beside Tom just as twenty-some goons swarm out of the office and into our view.

I want to scream. *Where is El Chapo?*

Tom doesn't hesitate to put hate on the cartel soldiers. S5 and S6 do the same.

I can't see, so I jump into the cab to get some height and fire three rounds.

Then I eat the floor as the cartel soldiers figure out where I am. I snake out backwards and race around the truck to dive into the room where Ilena and Leto were.

"Tom. I headed to the crane. I can't find El Chapo."

"Frag out," one of the SEALs radios, referring to the grenade he's throwing.

"Go Wolf. I'll give you covering fire." Tom fires on full auto, and I sprint for the base of the crane.

I'm happy when I get there; the base is concrete and steel. I peer over the top and see soldiers topple forward—they are being shot in the back.

*That means someone is outside with a long gun.*

As another guy falls over, I identify El Chapo, just before he is pushed down. He's not going anywhere held down by all those unmoving bodies.

I'm up shooting at the last of the soldiers when the Tom and SEALs drop them.

As I run to the pile, there is an eerie lull in the shooting.

I get target lock as El Chapo tries to wiggle out from under the pile of dead soldiers that were supposed to protect him. I scream a war cry and drop on him with the full weight of my right elbow, spotting it such that it knocks him out but doesn't break his jaw.

I'm like a Viking berserker throwing dead bodies off him so I can flex cuff him and *di di mao,* as my mentors would say: bug out.

There is a surge of gunfire from the office side, and I throw my body over El Chapo's then slide off.

*What are you thinking, Wolf?*

I return fire then add stack a couple of bodies for cover, and I pull El Chapo close.

*Like I really care if he dies.*

"Let him go, Wolf, and we won't kill you," Resendiz says.

"He's not able to walk right now. Send a couple of guys to get him. I promise not to shoot."

There's a whisper in my ear. "We're moving to a position to cover your withdrawal. Smoke first then CS. Copy Wolf?" Tom says.

"Much appreciated, brother."

Resendiz steps into my line of sight and orders two tough looking guys in Levis and T-shirts to get El Chapo.

They get thirty feet from me when one of them crumples to the floor.

What remains of his head is a red mist and a splatter of brain and bones on his comrade.

It's followed a split second later by the report of the rifle that just took his life.

The second guy turns and runs.

The guy's fear has killed him as he runs directly back into the path of the death dealer, whoever and wherever he is.

The soldier's blood paints the floor between Resendiz and me. El Chapo's lieutenant for transportation is cursing up a blue storm.

An AK mag dump keeps me in my place.

"Smoke in three... two... one..." Tom says over the team channel.

I hear the pop from dual smoke grenades, and they billow out a thick purple smoke.

I'm waiting for the clang of the spoons from the CS grenades when I hear Tom shout. "Gren—."

My vision whites out and the multiple bangs from several flash bang grenade disorients me.

I struggle until the darkness overtakes me.

# 83

———

Cement Products, Santiago De Cuba

"Wolf, noooo!"

*Where did they come from?*

Men surrounded an SUV; just as a heavier man was pushed inside, the security team pointed their weapons her way. Elle ducked as the mostly ineffective incoming gunfire sprayed her sniper hide.

She crab walked backwards and slid off the platform, landing on her feet. She grabbed the extra mag and slung the Russian sniper rifle over her shoulder and ran downstairs.

Elle had not gone to the airport with Morgan—and it had been a good choice. Once again, Wolf had not told everything that he had planned.

As she headed to their hasty ops center, there was another large explosion.

*Too late now.*

At the monitors, she stopped and scanned the video feeds.

There were vehicles headed her way, but TransCargo appeared empty.

She put her finger on the screen where there was brick debris on the north side of the building. What was odd was how it appeared to be blown out. She zoomed out and saw a similar look to the fence.

*It's their escape route.*

*Do they have El Chapo?*

*Did the SEALs stop them?*

The perimeter alarm sounded, and Elle executed the crash and burn command on both laptops.

In less than a minute, there would be nothing left to recover—except for the not-too-conspicuous hard drive that contained meeting audio and pictures with GPS data for the poppy fields and labs.

And the footage taken from the camera Morgan had deployed inside TransCargo that included the submarine.

She pounded down the back stairs. Whoever was coming did not know the facility; it would slow their advance as a natural part of the clearing process.

That was her time to run, hidden by the large stacks of concrete products in the yard.

A grenade detonated somewhere in the building behind her, and she knew they were not the Black Wasps.

At the car, she tossed the sniper rifle behind the front seats and drove out the back gate. Heading north, she took a right towards TransCargo.

Driving through the hole in the fence, she saw Tom with his arm around Wolf's waist. Wolf's shoulder was brownish red, and he looked dazed.

She slammed on the brakes and jumped out, sprinting toward them. "What happened?"

"I had him. Had my hands on him," Wolf said in a groan.

Elle grabbed his belt and led them to the SUV.

"Why are you here?" Wolf asked.

She ignored Wolf, and Tom got the hint: "Wolf got to El Chapo, but he was pinned down. We popped smoke—"

"Purple smoke, right?"

"Yeah, but before we could add CS to the party, the bad guys tossed some serious flash bangs. They landed at Wolf's feet."

"It was super bright, and I was 400 meters away." Elle said.

"The SEALs kept firing," Tom said. "When the smoke cleared, it was just Wolf. El Chapo was gone. According to the SEALs on the perimeter, they engaged an armored vehicle."

They sat Wolf in the passenger seat. Elle handed him a bottle of water.

"My eyes feel like I stared at the sun then face planted in the sand," Wolf said. How long since he escaped?"

Elle looked at her watch. "Seven minutes."

"Tom, take your SEALs and get outta here. We're going to the airport," Wolf said.

Tom looked at Elle for confirmation. She nodded.

Wolf held out his hand, thumb up. Tom took it and gripped hard.

"See you in Tampa, brother," Wolf said.

"*Fasioti o ia mo a'u, uso,*" Tom said in Samoan.

Elle executed a power-reverse U-turn and sped out through the gate.

At the first intersection she heeled the car over, the tires squealed, and she headed south toward the airport.

Wolf was pouring water in his eyes.

"What did Tom say?" she asked.

"Kill him for me."

"I like that idea. How's your shoulder?"

"Hurts but feels like a pass through. Arm still works," Wolf said, grunting. "Tom patched me up."

Elle blew through an intersection, taking left to intersect the highway to the airport. The horns and angry yells dissipated quickly.

"What are the chances we'll get to the airport before El Chapo jets out of here?"

"Low. But if there's any chance at all, it will be Morgan's doing."

*I hope there's something left for us to steal,* she thought, weaving around slow-moving cars.

**84**

———

Armored Convoy Racing to Santiago De Cuba Airport

"Drive faster. Our lives depend on it!" Aguila said.

"Any faster and we'll slide to a stop on our side. We're fully armored—no one can stop us," Resendiz said, focused on driving.

"How much longer?" El Chapo asked with a groan. He was leaning back in the seat with a wet towel over his face.

"Six minutes, El Jefe."

Resendiz and the Black Wasp captain had saved El Chapo, while Delgado had been whisked away in an armored vehicle of his own.

The captain's bravery would not be rewarded. Aguila knew Delgado would think the captain should have focused on him first.

*I will lure him to Mexico to replace Ochoa.*

Aguila understood he would be the fall guy, blamed by both El Chapo and General Delgado for the unraveling of the opium business.

But if he could convince the boss that in the end it had proved successful? *Weak but worth a try.*

"Delgado will ensure TransCargo appears to be a manufacturing mishap," Aguila said to his boss. "He'll make sure that is the message president receives and the press delivers. We will be back in business in three months... if not sooner. Good news is that we have a billion dollars in product off the coast of Louisiana, and a submarine in route to Mexico to pick up more for delivery to the Texas platforms. It will all work out with the timing of the next harvest."

El Chapo's hand reached over the seat. "Give me your pistol."

Resendiz did as ordered and El Chapo popped Aguila in the temple with the barrel.

"You shut up!" El Chapo said, pushing Aguila's head against the armored door.

"He knocked me out, tied me up, and was about to take me to America, and you want to put a bow on the operation and call it all good? No, I said shut up! This is your fault, you arrogant—"

"Boss We're here. Let's get on the plane," Resendiz said as he screeched to a halt in front of hangar seven.

As soon as El Chapo turned to open his door, Aguila was out and running for the jet.

Resendiz opened the door and used the frame to steady himself before aiming at the fast-moving Aguila.

He got off one shot when the ground around him danced with rifle fire.

Aguila glanced back in time to see Resendiz retreating around the vehicle and yelling.

El Chapo rolled under the armored vehicle and Aguila lost sight of him.

He took the stairs two at a time as the jet took rounds. "Take off! Take off, now!"

The pilot accelerated onto the north-south runway and pushed the throttles to emergency power.

Aguila buckled his seat belt and held his trembling hands in front of his face.

He decided to wait a few minutes before telling the pilot the coordinates for the airport in Costa Rica.

Blowing air out between pursed lips, he inhaled just in time to scream as the explosion ripped through the jet and it tumbled into the Straits of Yucatan.

## 85

Racing to Santiago De Cuba Airport

Elle's satellite phone buzzes and she passes it to me.

"Where you at?" Morgan asks, out of breath.

"How much longer?" I ask Elle.

"Four minutes to hangar seven," she says.

I relay the time to Morgan.

"Roger that. I held them as long as I could. Aguila is KIA. Resendiz and El Chapo headed south, bypassing secondary. There's a Chinese military helicopter waiting at general aviation," Morgan says.

"Chinese?" I ask.

"Yes. One of Resendiz's goons told me the plan. And I'm looking at it from a mile away. I swear it looks like one of the Sikorsky's that China bought back in the mid-eighties. Resendiz is three minutes ahead of me and five ahead of you. Pick it up, I'll do what I can. Leave the call open."

I put the call on the speaker.

"This junker is about to fall apart," Elle says, the steering wheel shaking. "Can you see now?"

"Yeah, it's better. I had my hands on him Elle."

I pound the dash like a little kid who didn't get the ice cream he wanted. When I stop, Elle says, "You done, Lance?"

One last thirteen-year-old smile and I'm good. "Yeah," I say, and stick my head out the window.

In the distance I hear sirens. Lots of sirens. I don't care—there's only one thing crowding everything else out of my mind, El Chapo.

Elle whips the car around the airport circle, taking us off Carriage del Morro to a straight shot to the airport and general aviation. Red lights are converging on hangar seven, but it's clear to our front.

Until it's not. There's a spray of tracer rounds up ahead. It reminds me of putting your thumb over the open end of the garden hose.

"Morgan's trying to buy us some time," I say.

"I'm getting us as close as possible so we can put maximum fire on that helicopter," Elle says, her calm face belies her grit.

"Deal," I say as a load a fresh mag into my TX4.

Sticking my head out the window, I let the tears lubricate the sand feeling in my eyes.

"Wolf, can you hear me? I see you guys. Follow the tracers and you'll find El Chapo."

"Roger that! See them now. Disengage and get out of here."

I hang out the window and dump a mag in the direction of the vehicle stopped 25 meters from the helicopter.

We're 100 meters away when I tell Elle to stop. She controls the slide, turning her side to the helicopter, then she's over the back seat before I'm out.

We both crouch behind the engine block. I reload and control my bursts with my built-in four round count.

Suddenly, our vehicle shakes from the violence of the incoming automatic weapons rounds.

I take a quick peek; the Chinese door gunner is returning fire.

While I'm focused on not letting El Chapo get on the helo, I sense Elle moving away

I sit up, back to the front tire. Elle settles in with the sniper rifle.

Boom. The door gunner disappears. Boom.

A round skips off a turbine housing. Boom.

The next round causes a puff of flame, then black smoke from the nearest engine.

"Good shooting, Elle," I say, then realize the armored vehicle is taking off.

"They're running!" I jump in the driver's seat. Elle hops in the back.

Resendiz is headed to the north-south runway, and I follow.

He turns south and I stay locked on.

Elle climbs over the seat and puts on her seatbelt.

"Seatbelt, Wolf."

She's right; I hate trips through the windshield. With my injured arm, I struggle to lock the belt and hold the car steady. Elle reaches across and clicks it in for me.

"They have nowhere to go," Elle said.

"Yeah, they do. The protection of a company-plus of soldiers with three armored cars, heavy machine guns, and Black Wasps."

"Party pooper! Can they really hide now? Or will Delgado bail them out? I think we've made such a mess that he cuts bait and makes himself the hero," she says.

"I like the last idea, but I'm not betting on it when we are this close."

"They had this planned too," Elle says as Resendiz punches through the fence. It parts like it has been unzipped.

The rear-view mirror is filled with lights of all kinds. "We're sure good at drawing attention," I say, pointing a thumb behind us.

"Forward's cool," my wife says.

I blast across the east-west runway and slow as we reach the edge of the apron. "Here we go, four wheeling."

We bounce off the apron and into the scrub. Grinding to a stop 30 meters in, we bail from the SUV. "Switch rifles," Elle says.

I hand her the TX4 and two mags. She hands me the Dragunov and one mag.

We sprint after the vehicle. It finds the road, then turns left to stop at a ramshackle, tin-roof house.

I kneel and take a shot that creases the front hood of the vehicle.

Elle has dropped behind me. "The cops and everyone else stopped on the other side of the runway, Wolf."

"They don't want to get caught in no man's land. Let's go."

We get about five steps when one of the KPV machine guns fire and we eat dirt.

I crawl into a depression, pulling Elle behind me. "If the gunner is out of the hatch, I'll get one shot."

"Take it or we're done," Elle says.

Squirming like a worm, I maneuver the rifle into position and get set into the stock.

I'm not looking up or through the telescopic sight. The gunner doesn't know where we are—yet.

When I do look, my head will be exposed, and I'll be a juicy target.

I grip the rifle, pulling it hard into my left shoulder. I grunt, exhale, inhale, and raise up as I exhale again.

There he is searching. Boom.

The pain takes my eyes off the target, but I hear the hatch clang shut.

I'm about to celebrate when Elle tugs and points to the water. "Seaplane!"

Cover me," I say as I lay the sniper rifle across a bush to get elevation.

I'm sitting behind it as the seaplane heads out into the rollers. Boom.

*More lead, Wolf.* Boom.

*More lead,* Boom, boom.

I pull the trigger again, but the mag is empty. It's outside the range of the weapon system anyhow, so I drop it and watch.

The seaplane turns left to reveal a broken canopy. It turns back right and accelerates, hopping the rollers before gaining altitude.

I scream a war cry at the top of my lungs and sit back.

There are voices on our left.

Elle fires as I draw my pistol. She takes out two and I drop the third.

"Time to go."

"Go where? They're surrounding us, Wolf."

"To catch a flight," I say, pointing to a Miami Vice plane sitting on the runway.

It's Morgan. He fires an RPG that strikes the nearest APC and waves.

"My brother from another mother is waiting."

Elle turns to the smoking APC. "That'll do," she says. "We could use some time off"

# 86

Morgan's Miami Estate

After two showers and a doctor's checkup, I'm feeling better. It could be the early evening combined with the drugs and lightweight Beam and Coke Elle made me.

I'm in an air-conditioned cabana; my wife is soaking out the kinks in the hot tub.

Morgan is dancing with one of his girls—who he says is a kickboxer that can beat our butts. She's pretty, but my eyes are locked on my wife.

Not for nothing; she's my everything. Elle has a huge hematoma on her right shoulder where the Dragunov bit back every time she took a shot.

"I should have you whipped for not following orders, woman." I joke.

Morgan stops dancing, his mouth drops open.

"Shut up old man, I'm relaxing here," Elle says. "This isn't the Foreign Legion. And you can't even whip up your own drink."

"See the disrespect I get, Morgan?"

"Well... I see you let stupid out of the box again, Wolf."

I'm belly laughing, then stop as I realize the voice was not Morgan. It came from behind me.

I sense movement from the darkness of the house, and I can't believe my eyes; it's General Davidson and his wife Samatha.

He's wearing beach clothes and carrying a drink. Samatha has a full glass of white wine.

"Yes, sir," I say. "You know me too well. What brings you and your lovely wife to Miami?"

"I won't be in the office when you get back, so I thought I'd say my goodbyes in person before we head to the Keys for a much-needed vacation.

I wobble to my feet and shake hands with the man instrumental in the creation of Shadow Tier—and me not going to prison.

The same man who told me I have no choice; I need to move into his position.

*One thing at a time, Wolf.*

"Can you stay for dinner?"

"Of course we can. The cartel's paying, right Morgan?"

Morgan has that smile—he knew Davidson was on the way.

Without needing to be asked, Samatha walks over to Morgan's date.

"The crazy gringos need to talk. Let's go look for steaks and lobster," she says in Spanish, leading the lady inside to the kitchen.

Morgan nods and heads into his study, which I know is protected like a Top Secret facility.

I grab a towel for Elle and drape it around her as she exits the hot tub, drink in hand.

We follow Davidson into the study; Elle is last and locks the door behind us.

The dark leather couches and mahogany wood give the room a rich feel. Morgan flips a toggle under the desk and nods. "We're good."

"Anyone watch the news?" Davidson asks.

We shake our heads no. "It is what it is," I say, expecting the worst.

"It's not what you think. It's all positive press on both sides of the Caribbean."

Morgan barks a laugh. "Sorry, sir," he says, looking at his feet.

"That's okay. Surprised the heck out of me too. I watched the whole thing from Tampa."

"How did you do that sir? We've been getting denied asset after asset. Heard backchannel that Miss Irwin was involved. Kennedy even had to devise a workaround using a NASA satellite," Elle says.

Davidson suppresses a smile. "Someone at the Agency reported the potential loss of an extremely sensitive asset that was transiting Cuba. Turns out it was just lost comms that were restored when the failover system finally detected the problem. Thank goodness Kennedy, Harding and Q worked the problem to resolution."

That brought a well-needed laugh from my teammates.

"I—I mean we—thought we had a pretty good plan to contain the principals."

"But El Chapo had several contingency plans of his own," Morgan says.

"What happened inside TransCargo?" Davidson asks.

"I entered the facility with Tom Kakoa and two of the SEALs. We were able to set up with no issues. I expect it was the same for the squad on the perimeter."

"Local activity kept them from moving past the northeast corner," Elle says.

"We had no comms."

"Yes, I was briefed by Kid on the shielding of the building."

"When our control element triggered, I dispatched a guard then immediately worked to free two assets we had placed in the facility."

"Kennedy said her name is Ilena—and that she devised the plan to get inside?"

"Yes, sir. Her actions presented Kid the ability to manipulate the security system and cameras. Both her and Lisa are amazing. We couldn't have done even half of what we accomplished without them and their cell leader, George."

"They are smart and very brave," Morgan says. "George has built an extensive network of underground-like support."

"Continue," Davidson says.

"Once they were free, I turned my attention to the door we expected the principals to be forced to move through. We engaged a contingent of twenty some soldiers and with Elle's help, took them out of the fight."

"You had line of sight into the building?" Davidson asks Elle.

"Yes, sir. I opted to not go to the airport with Morgan. I thought there was a hole in the plan. How would the principals be forced to enter the ship repair section of the facility? I was unaware that Lisa would bring an RPG. They didn't mention it when they supplied me with the Dragunov."

"Wolf, you failed to communicate an important element of your plan to the team?"

"Yes, sir. On purpose. At the time, George was not sure he could procure the weapon."

"And if they didn't, how were you going to get them to enter the ship repair area?"

"Surrender."

"Lance!" Elle said, a portion of her drink slurping out of the glass to the thick carpet.

"Didn't need to. When Elle dropped the last soldier, I saw El Chapo struggling to get out from under the men who'd covered him with their bodies. I rushed over, knocked him out and flex cuffed him. Seconds later, Resendiz called out telling me to give him El Chapo and they wouldn't kill me. Tom popped smoke and was about to pop CS when the flash bangs appeared. The next thing I remember is coming to, sitting in a vehicle outside the facility."

"Elle, what did you see and do?" Davidson asks.

"Prior to the flash bangs, I engaged some of the cartel soldiers through the hole left by the RPG. I also took shots at Delgado as the Black Wasps escorted him to an armored vehicle. I tried to disable the vehicle, but with no luck. Then the flash bangs went off and I could tell Wolf was in trouble. My position was engaged, so I withdrew and drove to TransCargo—where I found Tom with Wolf."

"I was disoriented," I say. "I ordered Tom and the SEALs to depart. Elle and I headed to the airport. When we arrived, Morgan was doing his best to stop El Chapo's escape."

"They stopped at hangar seven first," Morgan says. "I engaged El Chapo, Resendiz and Aguila as they tried to cross the tarmac to the jet."

"We were able to watch your actions live. The next issue was a Chinese helicopter, right?"

"Yes," Morgan says. "At first, I thought it might be Venezuelan, but the door gunner was definitely not South American."

"So, you catch up and fire at the helicopter, and it leaves, and so does Resendiz with Shorty," Davidson says.

*Davidson's chill: that's the first time I ever remember him calling El Chapo by the English translation of his nickname: Shorty.*

"They head to the beach house," Davidson says. "Wolf and Elle follow. Gunfight with APC. Shots at the seaplane. Morgan RPG's the APC. You fly here to maintain your cover... right Morgan?"

"That about sums it up sir, with the exception that Alpha squadron is now emulating Charlie by selling the drugs they captured on the platform. It's all tagged, and Kennedy says we are already seeing hits from the distribution network."

"Excellent news, Davidson says. "As for the submarine, they surfaced without a fight once the USS Hudner made its presence known. And that's a good thing. It had two live torpedoes on board."

"Holy cow! That's an unexpected escalation," Elle says.

"Agreed, but not out of the realm of possibilities given all the military hardware we've seen the cartels procure. At noon, Irwin gave the Cuban Ambassador the package of evidence—as I thought she would, in spite of my request for more time. I'm sure there was significant delay before it reached the President of Cuba."

"We left a thumb drive with additional evidence and some of Kid's advanced threat malware in our ops center. The goons that stormed the place should have found it," Elle says.

"No comebacks to us?"

"No, sir," she says.

"During your fight, it was chaos at the White House. Irwin went ballistic and President Fairbanks put her on a paid time out."

"I like him better already," I say.

"I thought you would," Davidson says.

"So, what's the positive news from the Cuba side, sir?" I ask. "I'm sure the Cuban president is taking full advantage of their breaking up a major cartel operation. Was Delgado arrested?"

"Not yet, but you've experienced what kind of politician he is. He's a professional so don't count him out. The positive news is the Cuban president thanking our president for intelligence leading to the uncovering of the operation. Trust and cooperation are what's required to keep the Caribbean and it's sovereign nations free from the drug cartels."

"Nice. They must be wondering if we were there and they didn't know it.," Morgan says.

"I'm sure they are. Next topic... Wolf, you have four days before you report as my replacement. Hold on," Davidson says, holding up his non drink hand.

"It's been approved by the SOCOM Commander up through Secretary of Defense to the President of the United States. Don't be insolent and show up late."

"Yes, sir," I say, throwing on as much Ranger crispness as I can muster.

"I know you like leading from the front Wolf. And believe me, you'll get to do that in several new ways. But your ability to produce results has a downside, and that will manifest itself in more requests to expand the Shadow Tier charter beyond the counter-drug mission," Davidson says pausing to sip his drink.

"I have a feeling that you'll see an acceleration of cartel and terrorist partnership that may force your hand. Regardless of the external factors, never give up your connection to the men and women that make Shadow Tier great." Davidson says holding up his glass. "Here's to them."

We hold our drinks aloft and clink.
"To Them"

## 87

4 DAYS Later

Special Operations Command Headquarters MacDill AFB

The change of command takes place in my new office. One that was once filled with a man to whom I owe so much that it's hard to quantify.

It is a quiet, quick, and solemn affair. Congress has approved my promotion to Brigadier General. The SOCOM Commander and his J2 attend. Morgan reads the orders and Elle pins the star on each of my shoulders.

My first order of business is to leave the tower of power, as SOCOM HQ is known, for the relative safety of Shadow Tier. Elle and I change out of our dress greens and into our utilities.

In the SCIF where I spent most of my time planning operations, I'm now sitting at the head of the table, about to receive a complete overview of the unit's readiness and budget requests.

It will be followed by an operations and intelligence briefing. A long day for sure, but I need a reset to include all the items I did not concern myself with as head of just operations.

I look at the video teleconference screen and smile at the familiar faces. "Let's start with Colonel Morgan. Congratulations on your promotion, Gus. Proceed."

My moving up as pushed Morgan into the Deputy for Operations position. We need to introduce someone else to take his place working for Resendiz.

Poor Morgan, he's not sure what to think about his promotion, he's never liked Colonels and now he is one. Elle and I laugh about it in private.

Elle is promoted to Colonel and I'm able to promote all three squadron leaders to Lieutenant Colonel due to the increases in squadron size and their achievements.

During the next three hours I take notes to check on why certain items have not reached the teams and why there is a slowdown in our contracts shop responsiveness at SOCOM.

The squadrons have continued to grow and are experiencing lower than normal levels of personnel attrition—which I consider positive as compared to the active duty.

I'm talking with Elle and Kennedy between sessions when Kid passes me an 8x10 sealed envelope. "It just got here via courier."

On the outside is the presidential seal and a notice: EYES ONLY Commander Shadow Tier.

The three of them step away and I use my SOG folding knife to open the package. I read the contents twice and remind myself to breathe.

The president's former drug policy advisor and her oldest daughter died last night from a fentanyl overdose.

I sigh and my stomach churns.

The President of the United States has just ordered Shadow Tier to stop the poisoning of America.

His exact words—Make the Chinese pay, Wolf.

# EPILOGUE

Puerto Peñasco, Sonora Mexico

Luis Arca dropped off his tired family at the resort letting his wife know he'd be back in an hour. "There's a shop nearby that can check the transmission, I'll be back," he said.

The two plus day drive from Montana to the resort in Mexico stretched his patience. The kid's hadn't been cooped up for that long ever and his wife was angry at driving in the first place.

When he joined them at the beach, his wife was on her third drink and feeling no pain.

"I'm beginning to like this place. Can we stay a few days longer?" she asked squeezing his thigh.

"Yes, my love, we can. The minivan won't be ready for at least two days, they have to order parts. There is no rush to get home. The kids don't like school away."

She kissed her husband and laid back closing her eyes, not a worry in the world. Initially suspect of the money he'd "put away" for the trip, Luis had convinced his wife that it was meant to be a surprise.

The half-now, half-on delivery payment had made the trip possible and he was already planning for more.

This trip and others like it would fund his growing fentanyl business in Montana and on the Indian reservations.

#

Five kilometers inland at the Dodge dealership their van sat in a garage at the back of the facility. Two young men took apart the dash. floorboards and overhead lights.

Experienced in the art of preparing packages and hiding drugs they began by creating spaces where the rubberized ropes of fentanyl pills were installed along side of components meant to deaden sound and protect wiring from the engine management system to the taillights.

$250,000.00 in fentanyl would head north to the cartel's reemerging business in Montana.

# AFTERWORD

Thank you!

I greatly value your support and look forward to your honest rating and review of Shadow Tier - 4 Caribbean Harvest.

Everyone who posts a picture of Caribbean Harvest will be entered in the Wolf Pack swag like coins, patches, mugs, etc. giveaway.

Best Steve

# ACKNOWLEDGMENTS

This novel, as with the other books in the Shadow Tier Series, would not have been written but for the inspiration to read instilled by my mother, and with the support of my wife.

Add to that the lessons I've learned, and insights gained in courses with Jerry Jenkins, Career Authors, The Outliers University, and at conferences like International Thriller Writer's ThrillerFest, Bouchercon, and Killer Nashville.

I keep learning through reading this rich genre and I pick up something to make my craft better every time I read a Brad Taylor, Mark Greaney, Jack Carr, Don Bentley, or Tim Hendricks novel, to name just a few.

To my amazing cover artist Momir Borocki, you keep knocking out of the park and I'm honored to know you.

To my crack team of beta readers: Mark Elliott, David Quigley, Colonel (R) Michael Carlson, Colonel (R) William Stevenson, and Elle Pope I owe much.

To my ITW critique partners: Millie Hast, Traci Abramson, Jack Stewart, Brian Gooden, Ann Feinstein, Alan Spire, Dave Elliott.

To my writing family that continues to provide insight, advice, and support: Jeff Wilson, Ama Adair, Eric Bishop, Mark Sibley, and a host of others. You know who you are, and you are appreciated.

To the hosts of the podcasts and radio shows who graciously allow me to join their shows, many thanks.

And to the past and present men and women of the US Army Special Forces Regiment, De Opresso Liber - To Free the Oppressed!

# ABOUT THE AUTHOR

Steve Stratton started his US Army career at the White House Communications Agency, where his work took him around the world. The jump from WHCA to the US Secret Service meant switching from supporting role to that protective operations. The mission, the protection of the President of the United States, the Vice President, and others as assigned.

Several years later, Steve left for the defense sector and joined the 11th then 20th Special Forces Group. Where he deployed on counter-drug and training missions in the SOUTHCOM region.

During this time his defense work included supporting USCENTCOM, USSOCOM, and three letter agencies. Today he consults to cyber security companies that support the DOD and Intelligence Community.

When not writing or working, Steve splits his time between Aurora, Colorado and his cabin in the Tarryall mountain range west of Denver for fishing, mountain biking, hiking, and hunting.